SPIRIT SHATTERED

THE GUARDIANS BOOK FOUR

TESSA MCFIONN

PRAISE FOR TESSA MCFIONN

"An up and coming talent, her books are full of snark, wit, and beautiful romance. Tessa McFionn is one to watch."

#1 NYT BEST SELLING AUTHOR SHERRILYN
KENYON

"In a paranormal genre ruled by vampires and shifters, Tessa McFionn brings to life a new kind of alpha. Fall into a world where magic is real and love truly conquers all."

STEAMY ROMANCE STORIES

Creativity does not happen in a vacuum. To my friends and family, who never cease to support my special brand of insanity. To my beta readers, who willingly answer my messages at 2am to read a short scene. To my tribe, never stop being awesome. To my husband, who will always be my hero. Thank you for believing in magic and in me.

THE CALL OF THE GUARDIAN WARRIOR

You have been chosen to take up the mantle of the Guardian
Warriors.
It is an ancient honor, given to those who have sworn to protect the
lives of others.
You were chosen for your skills and for your valor.

The world is a dangerous place, with many mysteries veiled from the
eyes of man. Creatures of evil, bent of turmoil and destruction, hide
within the souls of the Rogue Warriors. You have been called to do
battle with your sword, your wits, and your soul.
To this arsenal, we give you an extended life in your current form and
the ability to move with the wind.
You can hear the thoughts of any mortal and can heal with a touch.

Many miles will you travel and many lands will you discover.
No place will you call home for more than two score and ten years.
You will be drawn to your enemy across time and space.
Your enemy will hide within the heart of men and within the realm

of the In-Between, the void betwixt the land of the living and the
land of the dead.
They will influence dreams and move in shadows.
You will vanquish your foes, sending them back into oblivion.

You will fight until you find your spiritmate.
She will bring you balance and quiet your restless soul.
Once you have made her your own, you will choose to find another to
take up the battle in your stead or to bring her into the service of the
Guardians.

Do you accept?

THE CLAIMING RITUAL

I claim you, body and spirit.
I claim you, heart and soul.
Your life I tie to mine, your joy and your sorrow.
I give you all that I am, and all that I will be.
I take only what you offer freely.
I will be with you today,
And tomorrow and after,
Until the end of days.

PROLOGUE

KIEV, Ukraine
1039

THE GOLDEN DOMES of Saint Sophia's Cathedral glittered in the waning sunlight, its needle-like spires reaching toward the heavens. Antonius Mykola Yurchenko, boyar-warrior under Prince Yaroslav the Wise, gazed upward in rapt admiration. He lifted his hand to shield his eyes from the brilliant glow, his fringed, heavy woolen cloak keeping the cold winter at bay. For three years he'd watched the monument to honor the defeat of nomadic Pechenegs, as well as to honor God, take shape.

In truth, their enemy posed no more of a threat to his people than had their leader's siblings. He recalled hearing of the savage brutality of his prince's ascension to power, but court politics were of little consequence to him. The handful of men and women who looked to him for guidance and protection would now be forever safe.

Anton fought for peace, as ironic as it sounded to all the high-ranking nobles. He dreamed of a time when war would be a distant memory. His father told him battle would make a man of him, so he was sent to train in every manner of combat while he was still a child. Yet, he preferred to reason his way out of conflicts. Negotiations came easy to him. His empathy in any situation made him the ideal voice to soothe differences. No matter the cause of dissension, he saw conflicts from all sides and instinctively knew the path to the best solution.

This omniscient talent also gave him a distinct advantage in any hand-to-hand fight. As if studying a chess board, he mapped out any and all moves, anticipating possible courses of retaliation. To him, strategies and tactics came as naturally as breathing. Even when his heart was not invested in the outcome, his mind was assured victory.

"Do you think God wants all this grandeur?"

The oddly timbred voice off to his right only echoed his own curious thoughts. He did not hear the man approach with the construction noise drowning out all but the loudest sounds. He blinked rapidly, turning his gaze from cathedral, and met an unfamiliar pair of smiling blue eyes. They held his perplexed stare for a moment before looking away, admiring the massive structure. Anton used his companion's distraction to study him more closely.

Radiant copper hair captured the sun, and pale skin marked him as a traveler from far away. If his strange accent and unique features had not given him away, his eclectic attire definitely would have. White fur trimmed the dark hide cloak draping across his shoulders with an ornate circular brooch holding the sides together at his throat. Pale saffron covered his broad chest, and the square neck opening was embellished with an intricately twisted braid of blue and silver ribbon. Tubes of woven cloth wrapped tight around his legs, adding more of an illusion to his staggering height. His feet were encased in more thick leather, the black hide covering his legs to the knees and held in place by straps and bizarre metal fasteners.

He casually rested his forearm on the rounded pommel of the battle-tested sword hanging at his waist as he studied the gilded domes. The man carried himself like a true warrior, yet Anton did not read any risk of attack from him. Even if the man did stand shoulder to shoulder with him.

The stranger gave a curious smile. "Personally, I'd like to think the Almighty isn't looking to be remembered with all the pomp. Piety and devotion are better served through direct actions." The man shifted his gaze and leveled his eyes. His youthful face sat in contrast with his wise words.

Anton opened his mouth to respond when boisterous voices caught his attention. He sighed as he recognized the owner of the loudest shouts. *Damn you, Borys.*

"*Pereproshuyu, ser.*"

He ducked his head, hastily excusing himself from an interesting conversation, and stalked toward the source of the commotion. Peace was not greeted with equal enthusiasm from all his men. In truth, many were disappointed by the ease at which the marauders had been defeated. The need to fight still ran hot in their blood, so some opted to battle each other.

Grumbling under his breath, he approached the growing cluster of onlookers. The gathered audience cheered and egged on the two opponents. Anton shouldered his way through the throng, angrily shoving aside the foot soldiers.

Sure enough, his second-in-command, Borysko Krishenko, stood above the cowering body of some unlucky squire. Using his riding crop as a weapon, he struck the young boy over and over, his shouts reverting to nothing more than grunts of rage. The sight of a tortured innocent spurned Anton through the muddy muck.

He grabbed Borys' arm before the next blow fell.

"What is the meaning of this?" His voice cut the din with surgical precision as he held his lieutenant at bay. He shifted his gaze around to the sheepish crowd, many of whom now seemed more interested in the ground beneath their feet.

"If battle is what you so desire, then find a worthy foe." He tensed his arm, holding back his sanguine comrade's urge to finish his attack. To his men, he would not show any weakness, but he would remind them of who was the rightful leader. "Train and spar to your hearts' content. The exercise will do you good. Another campaign will come along before you know it. Men will always find a reason to fight." His gaze continued to scan the surrounding faces, finishing his circuit.

He fixed his attention on his snarling underling. "What I will not tolerate is cruelty toward those weaker for the thrill of an easy victory."

Borys, true to his name, was one of his best warriors, but the man was unbalanced. His penchant for violence served him well on the battlefields, but Anton did not like the crazed anger simmering just beneath the surface. Something dark gave the man power, and though Anton was reluctant to call it evil, the chills that crept along his arm told a different story.

Anton held the man's wild stare as the seconds ticked by. Hatred swirled in the air around them as the unspoken venomous barbs from his lieutenant hung like frozen daggers. He narrowed his gaze, growling in a rough whisper as his fingers bit hard into the trembling arm of his countryman still poised to strike.

"Do not test me, *zemylak*. I am in no mood."

The fire dimmed in the man's ice-blue eyes and the tension vanished, sucked away like air through an opened door.

Borys curled his lips into a paltry excuse for a smile and stepped back. "Anton, you are never in a mood. Perhaps you should find a woman."

"I believe you are in more need of a release than I, Borys." Still on guard, Anton reached down to help the young stable boy to his feet. Shifting his gaze, he nodded to the youth and sent the terrified boy on his way with a guiding pat on the back. Fear lingered in the air as he watched the scrawny boy dash back to the safety of the corral.

"The boy needed to be taught a lesson," Borys said. "You should see what he did to my saddle. And if that is how..."

Anton chose to ignore the rest of his second's long list of supposed atrocities he believed justified his actions. On the battle-field, Borys was a force to be reckoned with, strong, quick, and steady with his aim. Anton had trusted his back to the man through many campaigns. Yet, as of late, Borys had changed. Anger had replaced his tempered control and the man yearned for a fight. Any opponent would suffice, but it was his current disposition toward pummeling those weaker than him that truly worried Anton.

"...if the boy cannot bother to see to the proper care—"

With a weary wave of his hand, Anton silenced him. "The child simply needs guidance. Tell him what needs to be done; do not beat it into him."

"Were we not beat for smaller infractions?" The sneer on the man's hawkish features called forth an answering frown from Anton.

Ah, this argument again. Borys delighted in referring to the "Old Days" whenever they had a disagreement.

Anton offered a tired smile and clasped him on the shoulder. "It is true, *tovarysh*. But we lived during a time of war. Peace will bring its own punishments, my friend."

A strange light danced in Borys' ice-blue eyes for a moment. Anton hesitated, his eyebrows drawing together, and then he shook his head at the glimpsed trick of the light. Fatigue must be giving rise to his imagination.

Borys thumped his fist across his heart and with a low bow, he turned and stalked in the direction of the barracks.

Anton sighed heavily, dropping his shoulders as he stood in silent thought.

"Not a fan of fighting, are ya?"

Once again, that odd voice crept along his back. He shook his head, yet his focus did not stray from his lieutenant until the building swallowed him whole. Curious, he turned around. His strange companion wore an inquisitive mask as they looked at each other.

Anton pondered the question for only a moment.

"Fighting for what is worth protecting is understandable. Fighting for the thrill of an easy victory is not honorable."

A lightning-fast smile split the man's face, washing away the earlier scrutinizing gleam in the peacock-blue eyes. Anton arched a brow, cautious at the man's sudden change of heart. He folded his arms across his chest as the other man stepped beside him, beaming from ear to ear. The loud thump on his back knocked him a step forward, and his mysterious companion led him toward the awaiting cathedral.

"Is it, now? Would you be interested in pursuing this conversation a little longer?"

ONE

Boston, MA
Present Day

"WELL? WHAT DO YOU THINK?"

Danika's jaw hit the floor as her eyes drank in the sparkling gem held out before her. The two and a half carat multi-faceted diamond stood tall and proud, surrounded by a bevy of deep blue sapphires, all nestled comfortably in the platinum setting.

Her gaze lifted up to the smiling face of Patrick, her oldest, best, and only friend.

"Do you think she'll like it?" His bright green eyes were wide in anticipation.

And just like that, a blast of frigid water iced over her veins. Two blinks later, her mouth remembered how to form word-like sounds.

"Huh?"

"Do you think Alice will like it?"

Reality reared its ugly head, sticking out its forked tongue and flipping her off with a wicked grin as it flitted out. In one of those "life flashing before your eyes" moments, she remembered the exact day Patrick Reilly had moved in with his family, complete with three older brothers and two younger ones as well. They'd taken the house across the street from her building in South Boston when she was five.

After twenty years of riding bikes, ditching school, bumming cigarettes and beers off his older brother, and dreaming of getting the hell out, she actually thought he finally realized she was more than a tomboy after all. In all truth, she had been in love with him since that first day.

Choking past the harsh burn of disappointment that coated her throat, she managed to fake a somewhat convincing smile as she nodded and handed him back the gorgeous ring.

"Yeah, Paddy-boy. She'll love it." She hoped her voice didn't mirror the rejection she truly felt.

Apparently, she should move out to Hollywood and take up a career in acting. Patrick flung his arms around her shoulders, hugging her tightly.

"Thanks, Nika. You're the best."

As quick as his arms found her, they vanished, leaving her to mutely watch as he dashed off, weaving his way through the normal weeknight crowd of regulars at Donovan's Pub. If she stood on her tiptoes, she could spy his dark red curls bouncing between the ball caps until they came to a halt at the bar in front of a head of perfectly coifed blonde hair. The encroaching patrons swallowed up the deep copper locks for an instant before a squeal of girlish delight and congratulatory cheers rang throughout the whole place.

She lowered her heels as a heavy sigh dragged her spirit through the cold flagstones beneath the worn-out soles of her black Converse. Of course, she'd say yes. Who wouldn't? Patrick Finnigan Aquinas Reilly was every Southie girl's dream. The classic Celtic Viking complete with strong jaw, pure green eyes and the wavy, coppery hair that was perfectly squeezed between the obnoxious carrot and soulless ginger.

Tossing back the dregs of her Black and Tan, she elbowed her way toward the front door. The second blast of cold in the past five minutes slammed into her chest, but she was prepared and semi-shielded herself from this one. She yanked the sides of her battered brown bomber jacket closer together before venturing into the foggy, early spring night. Dingy snow still littered the gutters, and several gray pockets were scattered on the sidewalks, searching for solace near the red brick buildings.

She had to get out of there. Everyone would be passing around the champagne and toasting to the happy couple. And she was in no mood to keep forcing the dumbass grin she'd painted on her face for her best friend.

Oh, who the fuck was she kidding? Patrick had never seen her as anything more than a little sister. None of them ever did. If she fancied a guy, he never returned the sentiment. Some were out of her league, but most wanted a girl who didn't sport a shiner on a regular basis. She tapped an unfiltered Pall Mall out of the red box, grumbling to herself. Clamping down on the end angrily with her teeth, she fished the crappy blue Bic out of her jacket pocket. The tip flared to life as she continued to wander, her worn rubber soles slapping out a determined pace against the ice-slick asphalt.

She inhaled deeply. The burning tobacco and cold air stung her lungs as the familiar stench of the Reserve Channel tickled her nose. Tendrils of coiling smoke swirled around her head as she put the Boston Athletic Club in her rearview, the blue tiles gleaming nearly black in the night. Alone with her thoughts, Danika barked out a bitter laugh as she swiped at her blurred vision. *Yeah. Like you ever stood a chance with Paddy. What the hell were you thinking?*

Danika was so lost in her own musing, she missed the approaching footsteps slapping in the pothole puddles. But there was no mistaking the gun barrel shoved into her back or the meaty hand wrapped around her throat.

"Gimme your wa—"

Any other words of wisdom about to fall from the perp's lips dried up as her arm snapped back and her fingers clenched around his most prized body part. "You seriously wanna be moving that piece, fucker. Ain't in no mood to play."

She gasped as the pressure built on her windpipe, but it did nothing to diminish the squeezing of her own hand. The muzzle of the snub-nose pistol wobbled as a pained groan rumbled at her back.

"Shit, girlie. You that dumb?" Tiny pinpoints of light sparked along the edges of her vision, creating a pretty halo around the fading streetlight. She gritted her teeth and tightened her grip one more time.

"Do you want to find out? That gun moves from my back, or I will hand you your best friend." Another clench of her fist and her wannabe assailant yanked his hand away. As air burned into her starving lungs, she released her grip, glancing over her shoulder. Her once-bold assailant limped back into the shadows, cursing her and cupping his aching junk. Danika dragged in a painful breath. She flinched as she reached up and gingerly touched the tender skin across her throat.

"Fan-fucking-tastic," she croaked. A couple good coughs to re-engage her vocal cords and she blinked away the weak tears. Her cigarette had fared worse from her ordeal; the bright white paper was crushed into the puddle at her feet. Sighing heavily, she dropped her head back and cursed the lone star peeking innocently through the veil of gray.

"What else, huh? Anything else you wanna throw at me tonight?"

A siren's wail in the distance was the answer she got. Soft mist dampened her cheeks. The threat of impending rain thickened the night air. Rather than tempt fate, she shook her head and squared her shoulders before continuing on her walk back to her apartment.

Shoulda let that guy punch my ticket tonight. Save me the trouble of dealing with another day in this shithole.

Soon enough, the streetlights lining her street came into view. One dingy yellow bulb flickered in the growing downpour, and a second farther down the road had finally given up the ghost. She jogged the final distance to the stoop of her building and dug into her pocket for her keys. Her mind spun, frantic for a plausible explanation of the finger-shaped marks sure to be visible on her neck in the morning. She gripped the door handle when the familiar sounds of a scuffle caught her attention. Fists smashing into flesh rang out, as did the strange clang of thick steel against steel.

Danika paused, cocking her head to focus in on the exact source of the crashes. Maybe it was just a neighbor with the TV on some Hollywood blockbuster blaring loud. She eyed her watch with a frown. At half-past 2 a.m. on a Tuesday?

She stayed close to the structure as a cloud of thick red dust sailed out of the alley. Cautiously, she crept around the corner and peered into the dark. She blinked repeatedly to ensure her eyes were truly open and functional.

She stared in slack-jawed silence as two mammoth guys battered each other with...

Oh, yeah.

Those were friggin' *swords*. Big, wicked-looking blades that flashed in the amber glow of the overhead lamps. Giant bites had been taken out of surrounding buildings, and she wondered how come the entire block wasn't outside, betting on who'd win. Deciding to think on that later, she returned her attention to the fight. Judging from the deep, ugly cuts on both of them, they'd been at it a while. They were decked head-to-toe in black, one with a long trench that swung like a cape as he defended the vicious onslaught from the other guy.

She squinted, trying to ferret out more details. Both appeared to be about the same height, but the caped one was more built up, broader than his wiry counterpart. Strange shadows obscured their faces, as if the night itself was afraid to look at them. By all rights, she should be cowering in fear. This level of violence was out of the ordinary, even for this neighborhood. Yet she was glued to her place of relative safety, captivated by the brawl.

She continued to call the guy in the long trench Superman for sake of ease. And in truth, she was more interested in him. Maybe it was his size, or the fact he was refusing to give up, even as he was bloodied and battered. Peering into the dark, she wasn't able to pick out more of his features, but she swore his eyes sparkled with green fire. She gasped as Superman locked his paired short blades over his head, blocking a limb-cleaving strike but missed the kick to his gut. Her caped superhero faltered, stumbling back and barely dodged a powerful slash from the Hulk.

Another volley of driving blows and Superman fell to his knees, collapsing in a still heap. The immense sword arced high, one thrust away from ending this match for good. Her heart raced. Electricity ran through her veins, demanding action. She couldn't just sit by and let Superman be slaughtered.

A compelling need whispered to her soul, defying all reason and it beat out common sense and self-preservation. She rushed in, the unearthly silence of the narrow alley masking her rapid approach. Using the closest light post as a catalyst, she kicked off the pavement and grabbed the slick steel tightly. She whirled around the pole in practiced ease. As she returned from her quick spin, she kicked out hard and released her grip. Her feet connected with the shoulder of the asshole about to take a swipe at his opponent's exposed back.

Momentum gave her an additional boost of power, and the Hulk staggered off balance. Hoping to cement her surprise advantage, she made a grab for the behemoth's sword arm as she sailed out of range. She managed to wrap her fingers around his linen jacket but couldn't pull hard enough for him to release the weapon.

The ground raced up to meet her, and she tucked her chin to her chest. She slammed her shoulder blade hard into the unforgiving surface and rolled to her feet. Asphalt made for a shitty cushion, but at least nothing went snap. She spun to face the fight.

As she turned, her Spidey senses crawled up the back of her neck, and she flung herself backward as a massive piece of gleaming steel whizzed above her nose. The sword looked like something out of one of those crazy anime shows she had teased her nephew about watching.

It probably appeared so large because it was close enough to her face that she could count the microfine teeth on the razor-sharp edge.

No sooner had the blade flashed into her vision, it bit into the building at her side and chunks of red brick rained down. She ducked the jagged rubble, coughing to clear her lungs of the silty powder. Silence echoed in her ears before she was yanked unceremoniously to her feet. Instinct kicked her reflexes into high gear, and she drew back her balled-up fist.

Something deeper paused her follow through. A chill ran down her spine and buried itself in her gut. The eyes staring back at her were evil. Darkness swirled in the strange, pale orange depths. Within the span of a heartbeat, every prayer of benediction fired through her mind. Primal fear sprinkled with a healthy dose of Irish Catholic upbringing sent her knuckles pistoning straight into his perfect nose.

Bone cracked and blood sprayed in the amber pool of dingy light. The mountain howled and flung her away. Certain her feeble attack wasn't going to stave off the brute for long, she scrambled into a fighting crouch and prepared for another strike.

Nothing.

She swung her head from side to side, but nothing of her opponent remained. He had simply vanished into the night.

And that just notched up his level of evilness on her wicked shit scale from freaky to Satan incarnate. The absent sounds of South Boston crept back into the alley, free to be heard now that Beelzebub had left the building.

Her own breathing echoed in her ears as she continued to scan for any signs of the mysterious sword-wielding asshole. How did someone the size of a Mack truck disappear like that? Did she imagine all of it? Even the piles of rubble vanished, magically returning the alley to its normal filthy status.

A groan off to her left snapped her out of search mode and back into the reality of the night. With more sense than she'd showed earlier, she cautiously crept toward the figure on the ground. From the looks of his wounds, he probably wouldn't make it through the night.

Armed with a pair of curved short blades, he lay sprawled and unconscious. He had one arm wrapped around his stomach. A vicious slash went from shoulder to hip, peeking above and below his leather-bound forearm. She was surprised his insides weren't on the outside judging from the depth of the gash and from the size of the weapon the other guy was swinging. It was hard to tell his hair color. Between the garish streetlamps and the blood, his hair could be anywhere from blond to black to striped with polka dots. One eye was swollen purple, and the other was simply closed.

The closer she got, the bigger he got. Shit, he was the size of a friggin' battleship. His shoulders nearly stretched the width of the sidewalk, and his legs seemed to be as long as she was tall. She might be off in her measurements a little, but not by much. Barely topping 5'5", she was gonna have a bitch of a time trying to get him moved. Frowning, she stared down at the guy as weight ratio calculations danced around her head.

Did she really have to move him? If she even owned a phone, she should just call 9-1-1 and be done with things. She didn't even know who he was. Hell, for all she knew, she'd backed the wrong dog in that fight and the one she'd helped was even worse than the one she'd fought.

Why had she stepped in?

Why did she always step in?

Same reason.

Danika Mairead Callaghan loved to fight. It never mattered if the fight was wrong, or justified, or a random bar brawl. Something hardwired into her refused to let any battle happen without her throwing in a punch or ten. Ever since she was a kid, she had a knack for sniffing out any trouble and, if fists were flying, that's where she would be found. To all around her, she was never happier than when she was beating the ever-living crap out of someone.

Her father had blamed her mother and vice versa. Neither parent truly cared enough to ask her why she was so belligerent and violent. Both assumed it was just a phase she would outgrow. Even after her mother was called back to God when Danika was barely nine, she continued to find solace in physical confrontations. Twelve years of Catholic school, two stints in juvie, and some well-meaning neighbors with friends in the legal system keeping her out of serious jail time didn't seem like a phase to her.

Danika stared at the warrior passed out at her feet, her muscles trembling as adrenaline began to taper off. She gathered the discarded blades and searched for a way to carry them without slicing off her own arms. They were surprisingly light, the dark rust-stained sliver weighing next to nothing in her grip. She knew enough that leaving blood on blades seriously screwed them up, even if the shade was oddly blackish. With a shrug, she used the torn corner of his tattered shirt to wipe off the gore. After a quick pat down, she didn't find anything that resembled a sheath.

Fuck a duck. Just leave him for the cops. She could. Hell, she should. But some unexamined instinct in her refused to simply walk away. As carefully as she could, she slipped them behind his back, using the belt loops on his ass-hugging leather pants as makeshift homes. Unwilling to leave him out in the open, she grumbled and maneuvered behind his shoulders.

"This would be so much easier if you were awake, sweet cheeks."

Crouched and prepared, she levered him into a semi-seated position and quickly ducked under his armpit before he fell back to the ground. A pained hiss escaped him, and he tightened his grip on his split abdomen.

"No...authorities."

She craned her neck upward and scoffed at his slurred plea. "Yeah, like the cops would believe any of this." More wriggling and gasping, and she finally had her feet beneath her.

"Geez, hon. I'm really sorry about this, but I can't let you stay out here in the rain hurt like you are."

She had no idea why she was talking, but she hoped maybe he'd understand her intentions and not squish her on the spot. Struggling to get both of them vertical, she was rewarded with an assist from above. Her charge staggered to his feet, leaning heavily on her and shuffled forward.

"That's it, Superman."

She guided him the best she could toward the front of her place.

Fuck.

Her heart fell as she looked at the impossible task ahead of her.

Stairs.

Great. How the hell was she gonna maneuver this massive, semiconscious man up the half flight that led to the door, not to mention the five flights to her front door?

Shit shit shit shit shit.

She gnawed on her lower lip, deep in thought. A glance at the cracked face on her watch told her the bad news. 2:47 a.m. No one home would be conscious, and she definitely had no one to call.

With an exasperated sigh, she used muscles she didn't even know she had and hauled him up the red brick steps. Each foot gained seemed a hollow victory considering the vast distance still to go. At the wobbly entry screen, a brilliant idea struck.

Danika fumbled with her keys in one hand while keeping her charge semi-vertical. With skill that defied reason, she managed to get the heavy inner door open. A deep breath and a long stretch later, she held the door open while she hooked her foot around the flimsy outer screen. Both doors shut as she half-dragged him into the entryway. Huffing, she sent a silent prayer to anyone who was listening at this hour that the open apartment on the first floor was still vacant.

"Hang on." Calling on her delinquent-level skill set, she jimmied the lock open with the slender pick she kept on her key ring. She'd learned to always be prepared in case her uncle tried to lock her out...

or lock her in. The door swung inside silently. She breathed a sigh of relief as unoccupied dark met her.

"Okay, big guy. Just a little farther." She croaked the words out as she strained against the growing dead weight around her shoulder. His helping steps seemed less and less frequent after the journey up the stairs, and she really hoped she wasn't carting a corpse around.

She shuddered, shaking off that lovely image, and dug in, making it inside. As she trailed her questing fingers along the wall, the world tilted. She'd overestimated the distance from the entryway to the light switch. Her companion completely collapsed and attempted to take her down with him. He landed on his back with a serious thud and a pained growl. Completely off-balance, she windmilled her arms and spun on the ball of one foot before jumping over the unconscious hulk on the floor.

Again, the vision of a dead body flashed in her mind, and she dropped to her knees at his side. She forced her racing breathing to slow as she pressed her ear to his chest. A labored thumping and a rattled inhale assured her of his status of still among the living. Relief washed over her, and she lifted her head.

Or would have, if a strong arm hadn't fallen across her back, pinning her in place. Panic kicked in and she backpedaled, scuttling away until her ass hit the still-open door. One quick shove closed the door, and the room was again plunged into darkness. Her hand flew to her chest, hoping to stop her pounding heart from jumping out onto the faux wood floor. She squeaked out a weak laugh and ran a shaky hand through her hair.

"What the hell have you gotten yourself into this time, Nika?"

Leaning her head back, she opted to hang out long enough to catch her breath. The eerie silence worked better than a lullaby and soon, her heavy eyelids slipped closed.

TWO

THE THROBBING ache inside Anton's skull refused to go away. Pulses of piercing light illuminated the insides of his eyelids. He vaguely remembered the fight with Claude Fournier. Rather, he remembered the Rogue Warrior's ambush. He should have suspected something when a female companion suggested meeting after her workout. What woman wants a man to see her after she'd sweated at the gym? But it had been a while since he'd gotten his rocks off, and desperate times called for meeting a girl after her spin class.

Claude's attack was sloppy and sudden, but that didn't make it any less effective. He managed to shield the alley before things got too dicey. The last thing he wanted was an impromptu audience. Even though the Rogues and the Guardians battled on opposite sides, neither team wanted the truth of their existence made public. At least he only had to contend with one opponent. His slick foe had opted to leave his standard entourage of assholes at home. After three hundred years, Anton had almost forgotten what originally started the row. *Aside from the fact the bastard and all his cronies were bent on destroying the world.*

He wasn't exactly sure when the battle shifted. It might have been after the top floor of the building landed on his head. Things got fuzzy after that. He must have been dealt a couple more serious blows judging from the stinging pull of the freshly healed gash across his ribs. He winced as he rolled through his shoulders; the dull stiffness whispered of a forceful meet-up with asphalt. He had a dim memory of movement, maybe stairs or something like that.

Where the hell am I? The surface under him was solid, but not as cold or damp as the pavement. It had that musty aroma that spoke of disuse and an untended leaky faucet. An abandoned building, perhaps. He had passed battered tenements on his way to his rendezvous. Had he managed to stumbled and stagger inside on his own?

Another scent wafted through the stale air, faint yet unmistakable.

Female.

Somewhere in this vacant room was a woman. Wild jasmine and dark spices oozed off her skin, blending with the tang of stale smoke and stagnant water of the vacant room. He sniffed cautiously but caught no trace of fresh blood. She was uninjured, which returned him to the next part of his original question.

And how the hell did I get here?

He begrudgingly peeled open his eyes, squinting through the haze of exhaustion. Details sharpened, and he dragged in a slow, deep breath. Cracked ceiling tiles created a haphazard checkerboard pattern over his head, and the outlines of cabinets cast square shadows on the edges of his vision. Something poked him in the ass, and he slid his hand to his lower back. Fuck. His blades. Cleaning them would be a bitch, the blood crusted over by now. Gingerly, he rolled away from his tremendously bruised side and groaned as he levered his body off the floor.

"I was wondering if you were ever gonna wake up."

The relieved voice to his left tugged his eyebrows together. "Sorry if I kept you from a hot date. Next time, I'll try to die when it fits your schedule."

He coughed to clear the gunk from his lungs and pushed up into a less painful, seated position. His gaze remained on the shoddy flooring as he waited for things to settle back into place. Dragging his fingers through his blood-matted hair, he hissed as he discovered a still tender gash at the base of his skull.

"Geez, you're welcome." A chair screeched against the linoleum before tumbling over. Footfalls padded further away, and a door swung open in the distance. "I shoulda left your ass on the damned sidewalk."

The walls shook from the forceful slam, and he cringed, both for his aching head and his stupid actions. Swearing under his breath, he climbed to his feet as quickly as his beaten body would allow. He took one step before two razor-sharp knife points nearly perforated the top of his thigh. Continuing to swear, he retrieved the blades from his back and paused as he noticed the lack of dried gore across the silvery lengths. He snapped them quickly into their safe state, and then he tucked them into his jacket and staggered toward the room's only exit. He reached the hallway just as the building's main door swung closed.

"Crap."

He *moved*, covering the short distance in a blink, and caught the rusty barrier before it latched shut. He shielded his eyes from the mid-morning sun but not before he saw the shadow of a retreating figure nearing the bottom of the entry stairs.

"Wait, please."

The slender girl with her back to him paused. Long black hair with thick blue streaks was tied in a high and neat ponytail. Her fit legs, wrapped in faded denim, reached from the saggy hem of her weathered brown leather coat into a pair of equally battered Chuck Taylors. The jacket hid any trace of her feminine curves from the hip up, as did the broad shoulder seams reaching midway down her bicep. Tension radiated from her whole body, her arms hanging rigidly loose at her sides. He recognized her stance in a heartbeat. She was on guard, prepared in case he tried to attack her. By the itching dance of her fingers, she was hungry for it.

How could someone so young be this eager to fight? Not wanting to trigger a potentially volatile response, he opted for a simpler and less sarcastic tactic. Lowering his own defenses, he sighed and leaned against the door jam.

"I'm sorry, and thank you."

DANIKA WISHED the voice behind her didn't make her knees buckle. She also wished season tickets for Fenway Park would appear in her mailbox, but that wasn't happening either.

After waking from a quick catnap, she'd stayed and watched over her mysterious fighter while he'd slept. As the daylight grew and more of him came into focus, she'd seriously wondered why she thought he needed any help from her. She crawled closer to better take in all the details.

Her first analysis of his size was spot on. He was a big as a tank and twice as solid. She should have realized that since she'd dragged his carcass into its current surroundings. Even through the slashed and blood-soaked thermal shirt, she could count each defined cut in his washboard abs. His biceps rivaled her thighs, and she hadn't even started on anything below the beltline.

Black leather wrapped around his tree-trunk legs, the thick Harley Davidson biker gear a little out of place even in her blue-collar neighborhood. The worn duster and massive boots looked to be cut from the same cloth.

Damn, they sure didn't make guys like that anymore.

Funny, she thought he'd been more injured when she'd hauled him inside. She'd have sworn his guts were about to spill out when he lay on the asphalt. It must have been a trick of the crappy streetlights, because he didn't look to be knocking on death's door now. Only faint traces of bruises marred his strong square jaw, and a healing cut shadowed his cheek. His shiner had also faded, ringing his eye with a pale, greenish-yellow and offsetting the warm beige of his skin. Light brown hair fell in disarray, and dried blood stained his left temple. A brush of stubble dusted his face, adding to his sexy allure. His chest rose and fell in a smooth, hypnotic rhythm, loose and relaxed. When nothing more seemed to be happening, she returned to her post, sitting in the room's only remaining chair which she positioned near the wall. Spinning it around, she rested her forearms on the backrest

As she'd waited, her imagination spun stories of her sleeping guest. What was he doing in the alley, having an honest-to-God sword fight in the middle of the night? Maybe he was one of those LARPers. Some poor schmuck who took cosplay a little too serious and got in over his head.

Nah, that wasn't right. His opponent wasn't some scrawny gamer with a foam and duct-tape weapon. These guys had been hammering away at each other with deadly intent before she arrived, and chances were this was not their first meeting. Her blood turned cold as she remembered those eerie eyes of the one that got away. Rubbing her arms to chase away the unholy chill, she shifted her thoughts back to the man across the room from her. Who was he?

The sun had been about an hour old when he finally stirred. Grateful for an end to her guard duties, she stretched her arms over her head, yawning as she straightened her bowed spine. Her simple statement was meant to gently break the ice.

Although she didn't consider herself as much of a morning person, this grouch and his snarky response made her look like friggin' Pollyanna. Pissed beyond reason, she stormed out as fast as she could.

What an ass. This is what I get for trying to be nice. No good deed goes unpunished.

She made the stoop as his voice called out behind her. It had to be him. She thought she detected the hint of an accent when he first insulted her, but she was too mad to think longer on it. When he spoke again, she clearly heard the exotic rise and fall of his few words.

Willing to give him the benefit of the doubt, she dropped her rigid stance. She was prepared to give him a piece of her mind and a lesson in manners as she turned to face him.

She gaped, speechless as she stared at the damned near perfect specimen of manliness that lounged in the doorway of her building. Soft green eyes looked out under hooded lids and lit up his sun-kissed tawny skin. The black leather trench coat hung off his massive frame and he oozed sensuality. A smooth smile curved his full lips, and he raised an arm over his head, lazily holding the top of the entry.

Even as her imagination ran wild, spinning fantastical scenes of hot nights and steamed up car windows, a tiny and still rational part of her brain reminded her of just how she found him. He was walking and talking deadly danger. He might be a sex god in the flesh, but something in his practiced smile gave her pause.

Danika folded her arms across her chest and tried to hide her earlier schoolgirl reaction. Frowning, she glared at the obvious play-boy. By all rights, she should stay pissed at him. But he did just apologize. Hell, he even tossed in a thank you to boot. Maybe she could give him the benefit of the doubt.

"Gee, I hope you didn't hurt yourself with that admission there."

Her bitter remark did not have the effect she wanted. Instead of completely deflating the big guy's ego, he chuckled, ducking his head sheepishly.

"I guess I can be a real bastard before my first cup of coffee." He dropped his arm to his side and squared his shoulders. Shit, she couldn't even see light from the hall behind him.

"Please. Allow me to at least thank you with some breakfast." A boyish smile warmed his face and set fire to her blood. "Besides, it's not every day I get rescued."

Her eyebrows pulled together at the inflection of his last state-ment. She tilted her head and studied him carefully through slitted eyes. Maybe she was off in her earlier judgment of him. Sincerity resonated in his tone, a quality too often missing from the standard

Southie manwhore. No matter how she tried to spin it, he looked too damned good to be for real.

Her pause only spurned him on. Raising his hands, open and at shoulder height, he turned down the charm another notch and leveled his sage green eyes at her.

"Honest. Just breakfast."

Did she dare trust him?

THREE

Anton stayed perfectly still as his unlikely savior contemplated his offer. She had a touch of wildness in her, something deeper than the surface survival instinct he'd picked up on earlier. Keen intelligence reflected in her chestnut-brown eyes, her pale cheeks kissed with a smattering of freckles. Wispy bangs covered her forehead, their tips resting on her eyebrows. He guessed her to be at least half Irish, but the rest was a mystery. As was her name.

He dipped his chin and reached out his arm to cut the tension between them.

"My name is Anton Yurchenko, and I thank you for saving my life."

She frowned and held her self-protective stance. Seconds ticked by, and he had almost given up when she grasped his hand.

"I'm Danika."

Her grip was firm and was surely meant to dissuade him from taking an interest. On the contrary, it only intrigued him more. The old bomber jacket swallowed her whole, and he shivered at the threadbare state of her painted-on jeans and once-black high-top sneakers. She wore no make-up, but she needed none as far as he was concerned. Soft oval face, defined cheekbones, and a stubborn jaw with a pouty lower lip completed her natural beauty.

Perfect for nibbling on.

He bit his tongue to stop the stray thought from taking vocal form. Something in her stance told him she might not be open to any such advances. And again, that only added to his growing interest. She was far too somber for one so young. No laugh lines crinkled her eyes, and she carried herself with a feral grace. He caught the telltale pale shimmer of scars across the apples of her cheeks, and a fine line altered the shape of one eyebrow. Life had not given her a decent turn up until now. His special skills as a Guardian Conduit could have given him complete access to her innermost thoughts, and he could watch the events of her life in a single heartbeat. Yet never before had he pressed his advantage with a female, and he had no intention of breaking that rule now.

He would take his time and learn of her what she was willing to share. He lingered a moment longer than customary with the hand-shake, enjoying the feel of her skin against his. His mind spun images of her grip on another part of his body, and his leathers shrunk. A quiet voice in the back of his head whispered the word *spiritmate*, but it was far too early to make that call. He had heard of cases of love at first sight when a Guardian met his spiritmate, the one female to ground him back into the mortal realm, or in extremely rare instances, to take up arms and stand beside her lover. With the fire he glimpsed in her, he would be well matched if she were truly the one.

She tugged her eyebrows together and slid her hand from his, wiping her palm along her jeans with a quaint gesture. He fought to keep a straight face, and it took a good pinch of his cheek between his teeth to hold back his grin.

"Yeah. So, anyway, um. You seem to be alive enough." She turned and headed down the steps leading back to the street. "I know a place a block up that serves an okay meal."

"Shouldn't we lock your apartment?" He hesitated at the main door.

"That ain't my place. I live up on the fifth floor." She tossed the words over her shoulder, shrugging as she stuffed her hands into her pockets. His stunned expression encouraged her to continue. "What? You didn't really expect me to drag your happy ass up five flights, did ya?"

He let the door close behind him and raced to catch up to her. "Are you telling me we...we squatted?" He stammered at the incredulous possibility. During his long life as a Guardian, he had experienced times when money had been short and he'd stayed in less-than-favorable places. But that was a very long time ago, before he learned his skills in reading people fetched a pretty penny, and a soft bed, from the career politicians down to the bored widows.

She scoffed and lifted her shoulders again. "It was open, and I needed a place to stash you. Didn't hurt anyone, so it's all good. Besides, it's not like I broke into the place. Okay, so the door ain't busted up. That make you feel any better?"

She was so open with her delinquency it took him aback. He knew life was hard, had experienced it firsthand. But to see a young girl who should be full of life and joy so jaded and harsh hurt his heart.

He caught up to her and gently pulled her to a halt. "It does not. Why did you put yourself in jeopardy for me? I am a complete stranger to you."

She jerked her arm out of his grip, her mental message zinging through the air. *"Don't touch me."* So powerful and unexpected was the sentiment, he stepped back and gave her some space.

"Ain't in no kind of jeopardy." Her tone was calm and matter-of-fact, at odds with her frantic reaction. "The place'd been open since Rudy moved out two months ago, and I knew Mr. Arcelloni hadn't rented it out yet."

Her soft brown eyes peered up at him, the unexpected play of emotions swirling across the surface. He sensed a modicum of fear centering more on self-preservation, a dash of curiosity, and a healthy dose of stark honesty. But hiding behind all those walls, he saw a faint glimmer of attraction.

Soon enough, the shutters slammed down and he nodded, forcing his gifts back into their box. A dark bruise in a very familiar shape across her throat caught his attention and a wave a panic churned his gut.

"How did that happen?" He gestured to the handprint on her neck and prayed he hadn't hurt her in her attempts to be kind to him.

With a frown, she reached up, rubbing at the five-fingered contusion and flinching slightly. "Oh, that. Yeah, well. Let's say I wasn't making friends last night." She seemed to dismiss the rest of the thought and continued walking toward the other side of the street.

He kept pace and wished to push, but something in her body language said the matter was closed. For now, at least.

"You did make one friend, if that helps." He tucked his hands in the pockets of his leather duster, keeping his eyes on the horizon as he offered her a crooked smile. He shifted his gaze to his side, watching the multi-colored ponytail bob up and down with each step. The top of her head hit his shoulder. She was a little shorter than his usual fare, but in her case, he would definitely make an exception.

Danika fished out a pack of cigarettes from her inner jacket pocket and barked out a short laugh as she slipped the coffin nail between her lips. "Bully for me. One less person who wants a piece of my ass."

A deep furrow creased his forehead at her fatalistic comment. He glared as she fired up the lighter and took a long drag. Did she truly believe the world was out to get her? Her hand trembled slightly as she reached up for the smoke and a question poised on the tip of his tongue.

"We're here."

The sudden appearance of their destination pushed a pause button on his inquiry. He looked over to the small restaurant on the opposite corner. The sign read "The Kozy Kitchen" and by the looks of the cracked blue paint on the outside, cozy wasn't quite the word he would have chosen.

A chuckle to his left drew his eyes down. His companion took one final pull on her cigarette and bumped him with her shoulder. "Hey. Don't judge a book by its cover."

She blew out the last of the smoke and crushed the red cherry on the bottom of her Converse before tossing it in the trashcan by the light post. After a quick glance up and down the block, she jogged across the street.

Anton smirked, considering her comment a moment before following her lead. Maybe her book was more than the cover first led him to believe.

FOUR

WHAT THE HELL was she doing?

The little voice in the back of Danika's mind was wondering the same thing her heart was. It pounded faster than if she had run a marathon, but all she'd done was cross the damned street. She tried to tell herself it had nothing to do with the six-and-a-half feet of drop-dead gorgeousness next to her, but that simply wasn't ringing true.

He definitely wasn't from around here, judging by the simple fact no Southie boy she had ever seen was named Anton. His accent was faint, but it hinted at something Russian. At least Eastern European, of that much she was certain. Just as she was certain that each time he spoke, all the liquid in her body shot at light speed to between her legs. Shit, no guy had ever gotten her this hot without touching her.

Not even Patrick. She mused about her childish infatuation with him, but that didn't hold a candle to what she was feeling now. Maybe that was why she freaked when he touched her arm. Even through the thick jacket and her black thermal underneath, it felt like she'd stuck her finger in a light socket. Her own experience with sex had much to be desired, mainly due to the fact that only a scant number of them were consensual. And he oozed sex. Of course, he would. He was a friggin' god among men, especially in this crappy neighborhood. His type dated fashion models, not broken trouble-makers like her.

Her hands were still shaking when she reached for the door handle at Mary's place. She'd hoped the cigarette would calm her nerves, but the short smoke was about as helpful as pissing on a forest fire.

Before she touched the knob, a large shadow dwarfed her and a different set of fingers opened the door.

"Allow me."

She tried to skirt away as the door swung toward them, but not quick enough. She backed right into his rock-solid chest, and his close proximity kicked her instincts into high gear. Unsure if it was a residual fight response from the attempted mugging last night or old memories, she rushed forward, banging her knees on the wobbly door as she sought sanctuary inside.

"Geez. I'm not a cripple. I can open my own friggin' door," she grumbled under her breath as she headed for the nearly deserted counter. Most of the patrons had left a while ago to claw their way to their cubicle zoos, so they had the place to themselves. The aromas of crisp bacon and warm toast lingered and mingled with the perme-ating fragrance of strong coffee and cheap cigarettes.

Maybe this wasn't such a great idea.

His deep chuckle over her shoulder sent chills down her spine that had little to do with the cold temperature outside.

"I am sure there is much you can handle, *koxána*."

Damn, but that sounded so hot, whatever it was he said. It reminded her of the phrase her kindly neighbor, Mr. Grishenko, used when he talked to his loving wife. She kept her eyes facing front, but the smile on his face rang through his voice. She shook her head, forcing her blood to stay in her brain and not drop into her pants as she plopped down in her usual seat at the farthest edge of the chipped Formica counter. Gladys, the usual morning waitress, waved a tired hand toward her and disappeared behind the swinging door.

Only two other tables were occupied; one guy taking his last bite of a stack of pancakes and an older couple buried in their newspapers.

"Back to the wall, able to see all people entering or exiting."

His astute observation drew her gaze up to his. Admiration shone through his crooked grin, and he took the stool beside her. Jingling from the front door caught her attention and she glanced up in time to see the single guy depart. At this rate, it was going to be deserted before they opened their menus.

Maybe sitting in the corner wasn't the brightest thing she'd done today. He took up half the damned restaurant, and the bolted-in swiveling chairs were impossible to scoot. God knew she gave it her best try. His thigh brushed against her knees, and she shimmied on the unwieldy cushion.

"Okay, Goliath. How about you stay on your side?" Still squirming, she settled in as far from his magnetic presence as possible. The waitress brought two cups of black coffee and set both mugs in front of them before leaving again. Danika glanced around, half wishing for a busier shift. The bell above the door jingled, indicating the exit of the other remaining patrons and the ushering in of an uncomfortably intimate locale.

He laughed again and she almost slid off the seat and landed on her ass. Crap, no one had the right to have that sexy of a laugh.

"We could move to a booth, if that would make you feel more comfortable." He inclined his chin toward the vacant two-seater across from them. "You would still have the same vantage point from there."

She narrowed her gaze, peering into his hauntingly deep, sea-green eyes. There was no mocking tone in his words, nor did he seem to think she was some sort of freak. If anything, he took her paranoia in stride. But even as part of her welcomed the idea of not being so close to him, a hidden and silent piece enjoyed the calming presence at her side.

She swallowed hard before shaking her head. "Nah, it's cool." She grabbed the nearest mug and took a quick swallow, the black fire burning as it raced down her throat. The bitterness sharpened her mind, giving her something to think about besides the drool-worthy hunk next to her.

She had never thought of what her type was, if there even was such a thing. She'd had the hots for Patrick for as long as she could remember, and he was safe. He was safe because in her heart, she knew he would never return her affections. Captains of the football and lacrosse teams didn't go out with the freshman freak.

Her cousins would point out hot guys to her when they were at the mall or catching a Bruins game. Their tastes were definitely in their mouths. Scrawny, hipster douchebags with skinny jeans and perfectly shaped beards seemed to be their thing.

But not her. During those brutal games, her eyes stayed glued to the action on the ice. Big, beefy barbarians slamming into each other without mercy. That did it for her. There was something primal that called to her blood. Maybe it had to do with her own twisted thirst for battle. When the giggling girls around her would bat their eyes at some androgynous dweeb, it took everything in her not to gag.

She knew they would never be man enough to handle her. She would break them in round one.

I guess I do have a type after all. She needed a warrior, someone strong enough to drive away her demons.

Her gaze slid covertly to her silent companion, snapping back in a flash as he watched her, a faint smile on his lips. "What?" she remarked, covering her embarrassment with another swig.

He leaned in close, whispering softly. "Is it any better if you put sugar in it?"

She nearly sprayed her mouthful across the scratched Formica. He patted her lightly on the back, helping the coffee into the right tube as she coughed and gasped.

"I'm sorry. I didn't mean to drown you." A napkin appeared in her blurred vision, and she gratefully accepted it.

"Yeah. Thanks. Once a night is my limit on asphyxiations." A couple of painful swallows later and things were as right as rain.

Until she met his eyes. A strange combination of remorse and rage seethed in the beautiful green depths. Nervous, she frowned, easing back in case things got dicey.

"Is that what happened?" His eyes darted down to her neck as quick as a wink, his face an unreadable mask.

She slouched farther into the uncomfortable metal seat, rubbing her raw throat self-consciously as her defenses slammed into high gear. Panic spurred her reflexes, and she batted away his approaching caress.

"Why the hell do you care? Like I said, just a disagreement between me and some asshat." She suddenly wished she had opted to move to the booth. But in truth, she wasn't sure if there was anywhere in the whole restaurant that would be far enough not to feel his magnetic pull.

Her harsh words hit their mark with deadly accuracy, and the concern in his eyes vanished. Replacing it was a strange sadness. Anger rose in her, tempered by self-preservation. She had to get out and quick. Tender emotions were wasted on her, and she knew enough about life not to get tangled in the possibility of additional pain.

"You wanted to eat? So, eat," she snapped out. "Here's the menu. Have a nice day. Bye."

She yanked one of the white laminated papers out of the condiment caddy and tossed it in front of him as she jumped to her feet. Hoping to outmaneuver him, she sidled past his stool and made a fast break for the front door.

Was she that broken that she couldn't accept kindness from anyone?

Her nose bumped into something solid and male that wasn't there a heartbeat ago. And that something smelled delicious, the scent triggering something inside her deeper than physical hunger. Something about him called to her soul, to that withered part of her buried under so many layers of neglect, hate, and pain she almost forgot it existed. His mere presence whispered that some humans still had humanity and maybe not all hope was lost for a chance at peace in her life.

Torn between the urge to hold on to him tightly or flee for the hills, she split the difference and did nothing. Her mind screamed and swore at her to do something, but her body was on another call at the moment. She knew better than to trust a stranger, especially given the track record of disappointment wrought by her own blood.

Choices could prove deadly and she had already made such a mess of her own life. Could she afford to let someone else suffer so she experienced happiness?

ANTON FORCED his arms to remain at his sides as Danika struggled with her inner demons. Her turbulent thoughts and emotions battered at his mind, and the drive to pull her in close and banish the hateful foes that tormented her became a visceral force. Only experience and lessons pounded into his head by his teacher when he first became a Guardian stopped him from jumping in and fixing her.

"You must remember, boyo. It's all about choice." Éamon shook his head sadly as Anton knelt down and reached for the conquering horde's camp whore. It had only been a scant decade since he had accepted the mantle of Guardian and each day brought more and more information. Some, like today's lesson, made him question his new path. Hate and rage poured from her as she snarled defiantly at them, hissing and clawing in their general direction from the safety of an overturned wagon. Anton frowned and turned his confused gaze to his mysterious teacher. Grief coated his words and the man took to his feet.

Anton waited for a moment longer, his gaze swiveling back to watch as the girl scurried through the smoldering wreckage and dashed off to follow the men who had used her so violently.

"But we could have helped her. Taken away all the memories of those vile things and she could have—"

"Could have what?" Gone was the teasing and light tone he had come to associate with the friendly Celt. The dancing blue eyes had morphed into chiseled bits of sapphire, dark and stormy. He flung his arm toward the receding army. "Could have lived a normal and happy life? Why not replace those stolen events and make things perfect for her, huh? Maybe buy her a pony on top of it all."

He stared, slack-jawed. "Then what good are these powers if we cannot help others?"

Éamon sighed, his harsh demeanor dropping as he placed a comforting hand on Anton's shoulder. "There is helping and then there is interfering. In order to offer help, it must first be requested." He shook his head. "Yes, it can be confusing at times. But you must remember what it is we protect. We allow people to have free will and to make their own choices in life. It is not our calling to pass judgment; only to ensure the chances for people to do the right thing when the opportunity presents itself."

Anton's gaze drifted back to the horizon as the last of the wagons disappeared into the dusty orange sunset. "Does the plea have to be aloud?"

The missing smile must have returned to his teacher, his pleasant lilt back in full swing. "Nay, boyo. Sometimes it only takes a look." He quirked his head and eyed the Guardian at his side. Ever since he had accepted the dubious honor of fighting for all eternity for the sake of the human race, Éamon had steered him toward the path of the virtuous warrior. His earlier training as a boyar-warrior had steeled him for battle, but he learned soon after becoming what he was now, his natural mental skills were in need of honing as well.

"And her 'look' was not sufficient?" Yet as the words left his lips, he knew the truth. She did not ask to be what she was, but neither was she asking to be anything other than what she had become. His shoulders dropped at the heavy weight of his realization.

Éamon nodded sagely. "Now, you understand the meaning of free will, deartháir. She was not ready to be saved, and she might never reach that state either. As much as you want to save them all, *remember life isn't fair and not everyone is strong enough to bear the burden. You must learn to listen with more of yourself to truly hear the silent request for help."*

And the trembling female standing tall before him was screaming for aid.

"I am sorry, Danika." He lowered his voice, keeping his words private and for her ears alone. "I'm not very good around others."

She barked out a sharp laugh and relaxed a fraction, allowing the top of her head to rest against his chest. "And here I thought it was just my sparkling company that was pissing you off."

He released the breath he was holding. "No, *koxána*. You have been a very gracious companion." Testing his ongoing theory, he took a chance and carefully placed his hand on her shoulder. She flinched but did not flee. Not wanting to press his luck, he stepped back and shifted his gaze down. Her high ponytail of black and blue hair slid down her back, and her soft brown eyes captured his heart. Conflicting emotions poured off her, ranging from the timid to the terrifying. Seconds ticked by, allowing him more time to study the quiet female.

This was not someone who chose the life they led, but by stepping in to aide him had showed him the depth of her true character. Brutal events had shaped her, yet she still fought to retain her humanity. His heart ached at the atrocities she must have suffered that made this beautiful, vibrant woman into a suspicious shell, jaded and skittish.

"And I still owe you breakfast." He kept his face as neutral as his racing pulse would allow. A deep crease furrowed her forehead, and one corner of her lower lip disappeared, her white teeth gnawing on the idea as well as the plump skin. Blood thundered in his ears as it fled below the belt line. A hungry growl rumbled low in his chest, and he prayed that she would attribute it to his empty stomach.

She arched an eyebrow and smirked at him. "Sounds like you need food more than I do."

The mischievous glint in her eye encouraged him to give an

answering grin. He let his hand slide down the length of her arms, barely grazing the supple leather sleeves. "Then I suggest we hurry back before they give up our seats"

He winked playfully, earning a weak chuckle, and he followed her to the still-waiting coffee mugs. In his many centuries, he had sampled the best and the worst that crossed a table. But this brown sludge could unquestionably land in the top five of the inedibles.

Please tell me they don't pride themselves on their coffee.

FIVE

Rage fueled Claude Fournier's steps as he stormed through his palatial estate on Nantucket Island. The exclusive zip code allowed him more freedoms than his city-dwelling opponent, including the ability to house a large number of his Rogue brethren. He couldn't shake a stick without finding a portal to the In-Between, the deep void that fed his powers.

Too bad he couldn't rattle the same sabre and rid himself of that fucking Ruskie.

"He's Ukrainian, not Russian."

He growled and pinned his second, Boris Chrystian, with an unamused gaze. "I don't fucking care what he is, unless it's dead."

His lieutenant shrugged in bored reply. He'd chosen the man because of his skills as a Conduit and a fighter, not his witty repartee. The fact he had immense history with the current thorn in his side was an added bonus. The man was slender to the point of malnour-ished. Claude stared at his hawkish features, complete with beady blue eyes and a harsh voice. His naturally perturbed expression had Claude scanning their surroundings to see if anyone had tracked in dog shit.

The Armani suit hung off his wiry frame, hiding the arsenal the man strapped on every morning. Thin blades and palmed Derringers littered the table whenever he was required to disarm. Shoulders hunched forward as he thrust his hands into the pockets of his slacks. Jet black hair cropped stylishly short and tawny hued skin completed his lethal assistant.

With a growl, Claude halted, shifting his gaze to pin Boris' wandering eyes.

"You said this time, it would be foolproof." He jabbed his twitching fingers in the man's general direction, eager to fulfill his need of violence. "The trap was baited and perfect."

Perfect. He scoffed at the poor descriptor. For the past three centuries, Anton had eluded every one of his well-thought out snares. Across continents and through time, he pursued his foe. Even if they were not warriors on opposite sides of the human spectrum, he would still despise the man. The bastard lacked ambition, content to help and guide instead of rule and dominate. Too concerned with all that free will shit and raising humanity to great heights to see the perks of having phenomenal cosmic powers.

Pausing in his laundry list of Anton's wearisome qualities, Claude shifted his attention back to his right-hand man. "So, who was that female who ruined the whole thing? Is he mated and you neglected to tell me of this?"

Boris remained silent a moment before his expression melted, his blue eyes now vacant. Claude shuddered involuntarily. He knew that some Conduits could see either past events or future glimpses by forcing their minds to wander through the Void. This did tend to make them psychotic and mentally unstable, but what was a little madness between friends?

Seconds slipped by. Boris blinked slowly, refocusing his attention and glancing up.

"She is no one, sir," he said. "A child who likes to fight and wandered into the wrong alley. Nothing more."

Claude tugged his eyebrows together as a chill dripped down his spine like ice water. His Rogue Conduit had never openly lied to him, but the man wore deceit as easily as he wore his suit. His instinct warned him to tread lightly, so he filed it away to use later.

"I seriously doubt she is nothing," Claude remarked. Boris smirked, one eyebrow lifting in silent contradiction. "But no matter. She only postponed the inevitable, whoever she is."

The pair strode through the courtyard, barely acknowledging the sparring Rogues surrounding them. Arms froze mid-strike and the young recruits dropped to their knees to pay homage. Some of the newer lieutenants did not adhere to the archaic notions of bowing, but Claude still relished the sight of men groveling at his feet. Power to make others quake at his mere passing was a drug of which he would never grow tired.

His lips curled into a devious grin as ghostly images of long departed females danced in the dark corners of his mind. Beautiful, shapely women spending their final hours in exquisite agony, and their only crime was the catching the eye of his adversary. At least, Anton had good tastes when it came to nightly companions. Not too bright, but that suited his needs fine. They had been so easy to manipulate, especially given the unique twist of his second-in-command. While any Conduit could influence the thoughts of others, when he stumbled upon Boris, he discovered a rare gem indeed. Boris was a Latent, one of a scant few with the ability to mask their thoughts as well as the thoughts of any they chose. It was like having his own personal cloak of mental invisibility, one he used with devilish enjoyment.

"Perhaps, she can add fuel to the fire, if he is given time to get close to her. The others were momentary playthings. I believe her death might shatter the man's mind."

"Death?" Boris yanked Claude to a halt, his eyes wide with dangerous inspiration. "I have a better idea. I say we turn her." A wicked smile split his second's face. "You said she fought you and handled herself quite well. Bring her into our ranks. Think about it. Seeing the woman he loves serving us will destroy him."

Claude responded with an answering smirk. "Remind me to stay on your good side." Or at least stay armed at all times. By the twinkle in the soulless blue eyes in front of him, his personal musing was intercepted and undoubtedly filed away for future use.

He sighed and shook his head. Nothing was truly private with a Conduit nearby. But lucky for him, the man was on his side. He almost pitied Anton once he learned of the trail of bodies following him through the centuries, slaughtered after they served their usefulness as bait for each attack. Anton was a powerful Guardian, his mental skills keen before he joined the preternatural Boy Scouts. But he lacked vision. He naïvely believed the women had been spared the consequential violence.

He shifted his gaze to his ace in the hole. When he first met Boris in the last days of the Battle of Mazikert, it was plain to see the man was Rogue material. His fair skin screamed mercenary, standing out among the swarthy bearded Selijuk Turks. He mowed through the crowds of Byzantine soldiers like a thresher through winter wheat. Neither pity nor remorse held his hand from its deadly swift strokes. Offering Boris an endless lifetime to cause havoc and destruction was all of the temptation he needed to harness the man's proclivity for brutality.

Discovering centuries later he was once friends with a powerful enemy only added to his usefulness. For the past two hundred years, he had been patient, moving pieces across the board with calm diligence. Time would be on his side and soon, the trap would snap shut.

"You are certain he has no idea of your allegiance?"

Boris leveled a bland stare at Claude. "He thinks I died on a battlefield ages ago. He doesn't have a clue."

Claude slapped his second on the back, a delighted smile warming his dark heart. "My friend, I do believe this is turning into a most interesting day."

SIX

ANTON WASHED down the last bite of his surprisingly good omelet with the final swallow of fresh orange juice. Nothing could salvage the coffee, but at least the food made up for it. Throughout the meal, he attempted to engage his companion in light banter and after each of his leading questions, he received a short, monosyllabic response.

He wondered what it would take to see her smile.

He caught her on several occasions glancing at the front door before her brown eyes snapped back to her concoction of scrambled eggs, bacon, and cheese slathered on dry white toast. She downed two mugs of the dark sludge, offering him the occasional shrug until she dropped her fork onto the empty plate.

She intrigued him with her overly cautious mannerisms. He had only seen convicts or victims of abuse behave in that way before. Coughing to hold down his disgust at either prospect for his innocent beauty, he wiped the corner of his mouth and leaned back as far as the swiveling counter stool would allow. He glanced sidelong at her, intrigued by the unapologetically strong woman at his side. He recalled her flippant attitude about carrying him into the apartment building.

Her body was still a mystery, most of her engulfed in the weathered leather bomber jacket. Lean, athletic legs poked out of voluminous coat, the faded denim clinging to the shapely limbs. Battered Chuck Taylors held on for dear life around her feet, the shoelaces and a couple small strips of canvas keeping the cold air at bay. As much as he wanted to unwrap the offending clothes, loosening the painfully tight ponytail was first on his list of priorities. The fluorescent light muted the high shine in her glossy black hair, and thick blue streaks danced with each move. Pale skin spoke of many cold winters spent indoors and summers hiding from the sun.

His fingers tingled, eager to feel the touch of her cheek. He imagined her skin, soft and warm as her silky hair trailed across his chest. The corners of his lips tilted up, lost in a delicious fantasy. Would she allow him to take control? Or would she dominate in the bedroom?

"What the hell are you smiling at?"

Her terse tone only deepened his grin. With a light chuckle, he drew his focus from her hair back to her chocolate brown eyes. He thought he spied a glimmer of mirth in those eyes, but it vanished just as quick.

"Can't a gentleman smile in the presence of a beautiful woman?" he replied.

She barked out a sharp laugh, shaking her head as she fished out a pack of cigarettes from an inside jacket pocket. "Hon, you ain't gotta be trying to pay me a compliment."

His eyebrows pulled together and he rotated his seat toward her. "You don't believe you are deserving of kindness?" Tension vibrated the air between them and he forced his arm to remain relaxed on the back of the counter stool. "You risked your life to save the life of a stranger. Not many would have done the same."

She shrugged carelessly, but the hint of pink growing on her porcelain face told a different story. "All I did was bring you in out of the cold. Besides, you don't really look like you needed any help from me after all."

As she dug around, searching for a lighter, he took a chance and clasped her fingers gently. Her face remained downcast, but her eyes snapped up to catch his. Her mental cry battered him and it only fueled his need to pull her into his embrace. Simple joys and loving warmth had been stolen from her, yet she still offered aide to a stranger.

"No, *koxána*. You did much more than that."

He relaxed his light hold, but continued to rest his hand on hers. Her body thrummed, the fight or flight urges firing through her veins and clouding her thoughts. He smiled, infusing every ounce of understanding into the simple expression. The anxiety in her soft brown eyes screamed for his immediate attention, but her word would be the final say.

DANIKA'S GAZE darted in every direction, scattered and seeing nothing. Her heart pounded so loud and the blood raced through her body drowning out anything else her ridiculously sexy breakfast partner was saying. If he was talking at all.

Damnit all. No one this fucking hot had the right to be this...nice. During their meal, she swore she could hear his voice resonating inside her head as it tickled her skin. He did his best to start polite conversations yet all she did was grunt answers as she shoveled in the food. In her twisted mind, if her mouth was full, she wouldn't be able to make more of an idiot of herself by speaking.

The guy must have been a reverse waiter in a former life, since his timing was impeccable. The instant she swallowed one mouthful, prepping the next, he would chime in with a simple question. She mulled over his inquiries as she scarfed down her meal. How long had she lived here? Did she have a pet? Did she have any siblings?

Were those any different?

If he wanted to know how to break into a Lincoln without tripping the alarms or how long to wait before the local restaurants would ditch their day-old bread, she had that info on the tip of her tongue.

The personal stuff? Hell, she didn't know the answers to some of his questions, and it made her feel like she was back in high school.

She struggled to breathe as his hand covered hers. His mitts were huge, but more than that, they were warm and comforting. The heat zinged from her fingertips to her toes in a blink. Did he have some kind of magic power? She imagined this was what a rabbit must feel like looking into the hypnotic gaze of the wolf.

Geez, Nika. What are you doing?

She dared to test her lungs, inhaling slowly and forcing her body back under her control. He was an unknown, and at the end of the day, unknown meant dangerous. Even the cologne that tickled her nose and drove her feminine side into a frenzy screamed predator.

Predator.

Shit.

With a quick glance at the clock on the wall, she bounded to her feet.

"Uh, sorry. I gotta jet." She dismissed him and stepped toward the door. Freedom was a couple yards away when a tug on her sleeve froze her in her tracks.

"Wait. When can I see you again?"

She screwed up her face at his ridiculous question and spun around to stare perplexed at the runaway fashion model by her side. Instinct kicked in and she twisted out of his tempting hold. "Why the hell would you want to do that? Look, you wanted to buy me breakfast. You did. We're even. Now, I have to go."

His voice brushed against her back as she darted out, the screen clattering in place. An unfamiliar stirring in her chest whispered for her to turn around, and an unbelievable corner of her mind nearly followed the command. Only the image of the toothy grin of a certain scrawny four-year-old boy kept her feet on its intended path.

Anton was a mammoth mountain of male power. He could take care of himself. Liam, on the other hand, was just a kid who deserved to grow up better than she did. Cursing her weak cousin for dumping her unwanted son while he was still so young, she turned the key once again in the rickety door of her ramshackle building. She dashed up the five flights, waving to Mrs. McIvney on the third landing as the old lady shooed two of her escaping cats back inside.

Her palms slid on the banister's finials and panic pushed her to take the last leg of the journey two steps at a time. She wasn't sure if she was running faster toward her destination or away from those intoxicating green eyes. She mulled over his final words to her. He wanted to see her again. Why? What could someone that gorgeous want with someone like her?

She barely registered turning the key before the barrier was flung open. A massive mitt yanked her into the crappy apartment she was forced to call home. Fighting would only make things worse, so she allowed herself to be dragged down the cluttered hallway. It would be so easy to slip the leash-like grip. The drunken asshole had only managed to get a hold of her sleeve and God knew she'd escaped from better men.

She slogged along behind her uncle's muttering back, and her thoughts strayed to the hulking hero she had stupidly left. Anton could have made mincemeat out of her Uncle Cian and probably not blinked an eye. From out of nowhere, his voice crept along her skin and she shook her head, angry at her stubbornness. No, family would always be her burden. And she would bear whatever punishment that bastard could dole out to keep her innocent nephew as safe as possible.

Her uncle spun on his heels, and bloodshot blue eyes glared at her from the blotchy and bloated weathered face. She gave the man Brownie points for not falling on his ass with that Bolshoi-worthy pirouette, but the good vibe only lasted until the back of his hand connected with her cheek. Blood coated her tongue as her teeth clamped together. Her stomach lurched at the prospect of the coppery liquid chaser to her tasty breakfast. Lucky for her, the asshole dragged her into the tiled kitchen. God knew blood came off easy from these floors. She'd done it enough times. She masked the purge with a well-timed cough, red drips dotting the marbled beige tiles.

"Look what the cat dragged in. Where were you all fucking night? Sucking cock down at the docks?" Day-old whiskey breath singed her cheeks and flecks of spittle did little to cool her disgust. Her gaze burned a hole through the floor, but she would not give him the courtesy of seeing the anger in her eyes.

"A poet and didn't even know it," she muttered, hoping her whispered sarcasm would go unnoticed. A second cuff, this one to the back of her head, told her that her prayers were denied.

"You watch your mouth, bitch. You're only here by my good graces."

She locked her jaw, holding back the vicious slur on the tip of her tongue. So many beatings had been heaped upon her predicated by those exact words. If Cian owned a dictionary, he would learn how far off his treatment was from the true meaning of the phrase.

It had been thirteen years since they had been forced to move in with her sleazy uncle after her dad got laid off and they lost their own place. Her father never really got over the loss of his wife, slipping away from his remaining family and away from the daily drudgery of life. She did her best to find a job. Too bad there aren't many places willing to employ a scrawny, ill-tempered twelve-year-old.

After the beatings started with fervor under her uncle's drunken lash, the hunt for gainful employment moved into desperation. She didn't care about child labor laws, but she still had enough common sense to stay above the legal line. Yet, fate seemed determined to keep her firmly locked into the painful shit hole, giving her only snippets of part-time work. There were times when she believed she truly was in Hell. The over-glorified, two-bedroom apartment was way too small for three adults, and it shrank into nothing when Liam arrived.

But as much as she wanted to escape, she worried about her nephew. Who was she kidding? She worried about him while she was at home, and God only knew what torments the poor kid had to deal with while she was trying to make a better life for herself.

She kept her gaze aimed at the crappy linoleum at her feet, searching for images in the spray of fresh crimson polka dots. Taking the time she needed to rein in her temper, she dragged her jacket sleeve against her mouth before she squared her shoulders and stood .tall. Years spent living at the bottom of a bottle of scotch had morphed the quiet, kind uncle who had taken them in during difficult times into the hateful shell glaring at her with malicious intent.

She held her ground, suppressing a shudder as his gaze lingered too long for comfort on her covered assets. He dragged his thick tongue across his cracked lips and her breakfast threatened to make an encore appearance. She managed a couple of shuffles backward before her ass hit the fridge. Panic set in. Swearing at her piss-poor planning, she did a quick weapon inventory and came up sadly short.

Her uncle must have smelled her fear. His typical condescending sneer shifted, a sickening gleam burning in his pitiful blue eyes. He reached out, shaking fingers clawing at her hair. The stench of stale cigar smoke and cheap bourbon fouled the air as he stepped into her personal space. The safe distance between them dwindled, her heart racing as she prepared to fend off this coming attack.

"Auntie Nika!"

Grateful for the timely cry of joy from her nephew, she slipped out of her uncle's sloppy cage and managed to control her shudders as she painted on a smile for Liam's sake.

"Hey, scrawny. Whatcha you doing up this early?" She ruffled his mop of tow-headed bed head and led him to the kitchen table. Ignoring the unwelcomed and unwanted heat from her uncle's stare, she grabbed a bowl and the half-full box of Cheerios from the rickety cabinet over the stove. She prayed she poured more of the crunchy o's in the bowl rather than on the floor. Nerves rattled, she nodded in all the right places as Liam rambled on with kid enthusiasm, swinging his stick legs under the table.

The presence of her nephew did its job and her uncle grumbled and staggered out of the kitchen.

"Better clean up this shithole once you're done," he barked, tossing the spiteful words in his wake before leaving her in relative peace. Danika heaved a relieved sigh and shrugged out of her thick coat. The room was no sauna, but the added bulk would only slow her down if her uncle decided to start round two. Besides, her washed-out, black Henley kept her warm enough.

Shoving her paranoia back into its box, she fetched the milk. Normally, she would have had a bowl alongside him. But the run-in with her uncle soured her stomach and she had no appetite for food. Oblivious, Liam invented happy tunes with nonsense lyrics and his playful antics filled the cold space with much-needed lightness. An empty smile tugged at her lips as she returned the container to the fridge. She wished she could bottle her nephew's innocence, if only to take sips when the world took more than it gave.

She slipped wearily into the chair next to him, getting lost in the cracked table top. Her uncle was right about one thing: this place was a shithole. It was a seething, gaping maw of hate and violence that sucked the joy out of everything. It had long since broken her beyond the point of no return. No one would ever want someone like her. Paddy had long since been lost to her, the same with all the other boys she dared to fall for.

Just as assuredly as would this new crush. Better if she completely put him out of her mind. With those model-quality looks, he'd probably already forgotten her name.

And she would never forget his.

Anton.

He said his name was Anton.

"Auntie Nika, are you okay?"

She shook her head, hoping to jostle her wandering brain back to reality. Bright green eyes blinked up at her from beneath an unruly mop of stick-straight blond hair. Freckles dotted his sun-kissed cheeks and his mouth hung open, the spoon frozen mid-shovel.

She offered him half a smile and nodded. "Yeah, squirt. It's all good."

His furtive gaze proved that he was no dummy. He pointed toward her neck, his little eyebrows tugging together.

"But that looks like it hurts." He leaned closer and kid-whispered over the table. "Did Papa Kee-kee do that?"

Danika chuckled. Her nephew had a tough time pronouncing her uncle's name, Cian, right, so he made his own version of it. She shook her head and rested her elbows on the table, edging closer to him.

"Nah. I'm too quick for him." She winked and wrinkled her nose. Her reward was soul-lifting laughter and the world didn't seem so bleak. To be a child and to be innocent.

That was a luxury she was not afforded and she swore to give Liam more of a chance at a normal life than she ever got.

Liam's giggles turned into more silly singing as he tucked back into breakfast. She wished someone cared enough about her to be sure she had a decent meal and a safe place to sleep. So much shit had happened in her life since her mother last held her, leaving only vague recollections of maternal warmth. Soft lullabies tickled the back of her mind and she remembered light laughter. During times like these, she wasn't sure if the memories were her own, or wistful dreams and scenes from television.

Liam's happy bobbling head blurred for a moment, the edges growing hazy, and she quickly blinked back the pitiful tears.

Stop feeling sorry for yourself, Nika. Life's a bitch and then you die.

She recalled writing that phrase over and over in her high school notebooks. The harsh words ground her down and still she fought against the promised dark. Even now, she wondered how long she would have to suffer before meeting her inevitable demise.

A powerful cuff on the back of her head yanked her out of her thoughts. Her reflexes sprang into action and she braced her arms in front of her face, saving her forehead from bouncing off the table. She saw stars from the staggering blow but instinct and experience kicked her body into gear. Pivoting her chair on one leg, she ducked under the expected follow-through and jumped to her feet. Her ass bumped against the table as she placed herself between her newly enraged uncle and her terrified nephew. Liam's fearful cries drove her need to protect.

"What the fuck did you do?" Malicious frenzy swirled in her uncle's rheumy blue eyes. His flailing arms rained down open-handed slaps in all directions, a couple connecting with painful accuracy. Cowering behind one arm as best as she could, she searched the room, her fingers skimming on every surface hoping to find some weapon suitable to defend herself. She grabbed a spoon. The dull metal edges cut into her palm.

"What the hell are you talking about?" She shuffled back, keeping both eyes on the psychotic in front of her while trying to calm her panicking nephew.

Cian advanced, his sloppy steps forcing her to retreat again. "Why are their fucking cops combing the place?" He gestured wildly toward the window. The wail of approaching sirens bled through the thin walls, seeping between the cracks in the cinder blocks protecting them from the cold outside. Momentary relief gave her a second to exhale, but she did not drop her guard.

"Why does it have to be something I did? The cops raid this craphole every other friggin' day."

That was true. Gang members and drug dealers found her building a choice spot, not to mention the occasional petty thieves and low-brow prostitutes. There were always vacant spaces for the junkies and pimps to ply their trades and every cop in Boston worth their stripes knew to hit here first.

Round up the usual suspects. She remembered hearing the line somewhere, but she would dwell on that later. Like when she wasn't fending off the latest attack. Liam hugged her back, his tiny fingers gripping tight to her shirt as he buried his head in fear.

Cian panted, glaring at her as they stood in the growing silence. Voices carried through the flimsy walls and floors, shouts in every language under the sun echoing through the cinder blocks as the officers continued to pour in. The pounding footfalls stopped somewhere beneath their feet. Muffled orders were barked out and a door splintered in the distance.

Current crisis averted, but she knew this game of chicken all too well. If she blinked first, she would have another smack on the mouth. She snaked her arm behind her and clutched Liam close. She waited, keeping her face passive but her body coiled like a spring. Her cheek stung and blood trickled from a new gash on her bottom lip.

"What's goin' on here?"

Her father's sleepy voice from down the hall diffused the tension in a snap. Her uncle shifted his demeanor, an oily smile sliding across his lips as he stared at her with malicious intent.

"Just taking bets on who got popped this time, right?" Even as she expected the sycophantic cordiality, she still flinched as the bastard slung an arm around her shoulder as he turned to face her father. Liam scurried to the opposite side of her body, snuffing back his fearful tears. Her heart thundered, but she stood tall.

"Yeah, sure." She shrugged out of the uncomfortable embrace, steering her nephew away from clinging hands. Using the cuff of her sleeve as a rag, she wiped away the fresh red evidence and raised her gaze.

By the vacant cast in her father's eyes, job hunting today was a no go. She didn't know his drug of choice this week, but judging by his pie-pan pupils and languid pace, he was still soaring. A drowsy grin tugged his pallid lips and brought a hint of life to his sallow complexion.

"Hey, pumpkin. I didn't hear you come in. Did you eat already?"

Danika swallowed her rage at life, hatred building in her gut as she took in the man who once held the world in the palm of his hand. Tough times had robbed him of his power, and now he was nothing more than the walking shell of her childhood idol. Between the death of her mother and her older brother disowning the family in favor of a Martha's Vineyard socialite, her father had fallen into a deep melancholy. He turned first to whiskey, then a more pharmaceutical bent soon followed. She couldn't remember the last time she'd seen a real spark in his kelly green eyes.

"Yeah, Da. I grabbed a bite earlier." She wanted to shake him hard enough to knock the monkey off his back, but nothing short of the manifestation of God himself could perform that miracle. With Liam glued to her thigh, she stumbled over to her father and guided him toward his seat at the table. A couple pats on the head later and her leg-leech let go, making her current job much easier.

As she prepared her father's standard fare of black coffee and toast, she froze, listening to the typical sounds of her neighborhood. Yet, whispering in the air was a sensual voice, breathing hot against her neck as she stood alone by the sink. Her eyelids fluttered down, and she dared to dream. The breath became a touch, gliding along her skin. As the imaginary fingers reached the column of her throat, her eyes flew open and panic-laced reality crashed in around her.

How she managed not to scald herself as she swatted away the phantom caress was miraculous. Instead, she shuddered until the tingling sensation passed and returned to her task at hand. A strange sadness filled her heart as she filled the chipped white mug. She gritted her teeth, banishing such sappy sentiment and she set down the meager meal.

"Nika, are you fightin' again?"

She lifted a shoulder lazily. "Just a mugger. No biggie."

So many hits had come since leaving the bar, she'd almost forgotten how everything started. But she was sure how it would end.

The same as every day before this one and every day that will follow: stuck in this hell.

Resigned to her fate, she plopped down into Liam's vacated chair before three knocks on the front door echoed in the strange quiet.

She blinked, frowning at the polite tapping.

A similarly perplexed expression painted her father's face as he looked up from his coffee. "Who could that be?"

SEVEN

ANTON STOOD in front of the faded blue door. Paint flecks sprinkled the worn and threadbare carpet beneath his feet. He hit the rewind button in his mind, reviewing the morning's events while he waited for an answer to his knock.

Her words slammed into his chest, their emptiness like a vise on his heart. As she disappeared behind the rickety screen, he could only stare at the vacant doorway. She was fire and beauty rolled into one delectable package. Judging by the faint scars barely visible as they peeked out from under the ribbed sleeves of the oversize leather bomber jacket, life had taken much more than it had ever given her. The way she flinched at his light touch turned his stomach. No one became that skittish without dangerous reasons. She guarded her back, never smiled, and scanned the room with lethal skill.

All signs pointed to one sickening outcome: abuse. The degree, as well as the exact nature, was a mystery, but he would not rest until he uncovered it. As a Guardian, he was sworn to protect humanity and allow them the chances to make life choices based on free will. He could not force a pathway to the unwilling, but in the short time he'd spent with Danika, he saw the pain in her heart. The destruction of innocence screamed out for him to rectify.

Reality took form as the annoying buzz in his pocket. He frowned, glaring at the innocent exit and fished inside his jacket. Could his timing be any worse?

He headed back to their deserted plates and tossed down more than enough to cover their meal. After a quick wave to the solitary waitress, he thumbed the green button as he stepped out into the cold.

"Éamon? Are you sure you're not a Conduit?" He flipped up the collar on his leather trench coat and strolled down the bustling street. With the day in full swing, traffic had picked up, the bright sun and frigid air blending into a standard late February, New England Wednesday. Taxis and buses whizzed by on their appointed routes while fitness-conscious moms jogged behind bundled strollers. He nodded politely as they passed, ignoring their wide-eyed stares and sheet-scorching fantasies in his wake.

"Why? Is there something I should be knowing, boyo?"

Unwilling to move too far, he headed toward his parked car a couple blocks away as he pondered his response. "Uh, no?"

A knowing chuckle bled through on the other end of the line. "Anton, y'ain't been able to hide anything' from me for going on a thousand years. What made you think you could start now?"

Anton triggered the after-market remote and the driver's side door on his cardinal red 1969 Pontiac GTO popped open. With a heavy sigh, he plopped down into the cream, leather bucket seat and closed the door, shutting out the growing street noise.

"Too many blows to the head, I guess." He rubbed his temple, banishing the painful remnants of his little white lie. In his early trainings, Éamon warned him that Guardians must only speak the truth. *"In order to choose freely, people must be told the whole story."*

Éamon scoffed. "Now that, I will agree with. Hold on." Music blared through the phone line before slipping away. Anton turned the key and cranked up the heat as he waited in the forced silence.

His eyes slipped closed and an image of his feisty savior coalesced in the darkness. She was so stern and stoic, he wondered how she would look draped in a smile.

Would her deep brown eyes sparkle with light? Was her laugh husky and intoxicating like her voice?

The longer he pondered the possibility, the tighter his leather pants became. He painfully shrugged out of his trench, ditching his blades in the backseat, and peeled off the tattered shirt. Grumbling, he rummaged through the stash of spare clothes he kept on hand. Long ago, he'd discovered his wardrobe would inevitably be sacrificed to his calling. Also, most people frowned at the sight of slashed and bloodied attire.

The still-healing evidence from last night's melee twinged as he raised his arms and slipped into the thick, sky-blue woolen sweater. He studied the interplay of his black coat and the muted shade of his new shirt and his mind snapped back to Danika's shimmering ponytail. It shone like silk at midnight. He inhaled deeply, savoring the faint traces of her scent. She kept her distance, but her uniquely individual perfume clung to his shredded thermal. He buried his face in the ripped material, imaging his nose tucked into the hollow of her throat. His mouth watered, eager to sample her wildness.

Blood fled from his over-active brain to his rock-hard cock. A painful groan slipped between his clenched teeth and he tossed the ragged fabric into the back.

"So." Éamon's voice jolted him out of his reverie and refocused his wandering mind on the ongoing conversation. "Tell me."

Anton dragged his hand through his hair, searching for the best opening line.

"Boyo, I can hear you thinking from here. Just out with it."

He laughed at his friend's no-nonsense command. "Never one to mince words, were you, *tovarysh?*"

"Oh, I've been known the chew the fat at times." The calming lilt on the end of the line conjured pictures of smoke-filled pubs and flowing pints of dark ales. "But you've got something on your mind, Anton. Wouldn't've heard you calling out if you didn't."

"Yeah." Anton drew the word out in a long sigh. "Hard to know which to hit you with first. The fight with that damned frog or the girl..." He hesitated, choosing his next words carefully. "Or the fact that she saw us fight."

With a cringe, he prepared for the inevitable backlash.

"I'm sorry. I must have a bad connection. I thought you said that *she* saw you and Claude in a fight." Gone was the playful cadence, and Anton amped the heater another notch.

"Before you say it, yes, I did shield the site. And I didn't pick the spot. That was His Royal Fuckness."

"Then how do you know—"

"Because when I woke up, I was in an empty apartment being watched by a..." He faltered, tongue-tied.

"Tell me more about the girl."

Danika, his mind whispered. Her name swirled through his soul. Everything about her flashed into his mind, from her multicolored ponytail to her soulful brown eyes. Her slender legs and battered clothes screamed of difficult times, and his heart skipped a beat.

"Oy! Earth to Anton!"

Anton groaned as he readjusted his straining leathers. "Yeah, I'm here. She must have seen something, but how much, I don't really know."

The silence encouraged him to spill the rest of the story. "When I woke up, my blades had been cleaned, and she did, uh, kinda mentioned she should've left my ass out on the street."

"So, let me see if I've got this right."

Shit. Here it comes. Anton squirmed in the cozy confines. If he had left right after she vanished, he could have taken the call in the spaciousness of his two-story Cape Cod in Woodbourne. There, he would be able to pace around and expend some of his pent-up energy. Instead, he fidgeted, bouncing his leg and knocking his knee against the bottom of the dashboard.

"Claude managed to push your buttons. Again. As he has since Christ was a child."

Anton gritted his teeth but held his tongue. He did have a point. The damned Frenchman did know how to get under his skin. No matter how many places he lived or how often he relocated, that bastard knew just where to show up and what to do to ruin his life.

Éamon continued his reprimand. "You get caught with your pants down–"

"That's not–" Anton sputtered before Éamon tsked him into submission.

"Now, let me finish." Anton groused under his breath and settled back into his seat as much as his tense muscles would allow, his mouth pulling closed in a tight line. "You let a mortal see you and Claude battle, and from the sounds of things, you fancy her for a shag, so you didn't wipe her mind."

"You leave her alone." Anton hardly recognized his own voice, the sharp venom taking him aback. "Oh God. Éamon, I am so sorry. I didn't mean—"

A knowing chuckle bled through the phone. "There it is. Sorry, boyo. I had to be sure. Do you think she's the one?"

The one. His spiritmate, the only woman fated to hold his heart and to return him to a single lifetime. Could he dream it?

"Honestly, I don't really know for sure." He leaned his head back and stared at the ivory headliner covering the roof. "We haven't had much time for conversation. And not that way." He paused before continuing. "Perv."

"What's the hold up?"

Anton pulled his brows together at the tactless query. "What ever happened to romance?"

Another laugh. "Always the fairytale hero, *pàirtí*. All right, all right. So, tell me this: what do you know of her?"

He heaved a sigh, opting not to extol her wild beauty. "She's strong but very damaged. I sense a great deal of rage. I would love to have seen the look on the smug asshole's face when he realized a tiny slip of a girl beat him."

"Wait. She joined the fight? Are you sure?"

"Hell, after half a ton of bricks land on your head, we'll see just how sure you are of details." His eyes slipped shut for a brief reprise, and he sifted through his vague memories of the previous night. "I remember being guided up a couple stairs, but things are pretty fuzzy."

Blinking in the disquieting silence, he turned off the engine and prepared to face the cold once again.

"Éamon, I..." *I what?* He had more questions than answers, and that was not helping either of them. "Shit, *tovarysh*. What do I do?"

"You listen to your heart, *deartháir*, as you have always done." He imagined his mentor's hand on his shoulder, giving him a needed bit of comfort. "But first things first. You need to find her and discover what she knows. If she's your other half, then she'll be protected. If not, then you know what needs to happen."

Yeah. He knew. He prayed that she was his match, because he didn't want to think of how she would react to him wandering through her mind.

"That might take some time," he muttered under his breath as he climbed out of the warm interior. Slipping back into his trench, he dropped his keys into his pocket.

"Did ya have something else to be doing there, boyo?" With the return of Éamon's lyrical lilt, Anton stepped out into the chilly day. A trio of police cars whizzed by, sirens blaring, and he flattened his ass against his door to avoid becoming a speed bump. He shook his head and chuckled.

"Okay, so you got me there. I'll let you know how things go." His gaze followed after the flashing red and blue lights, a little voice telling him to investigate. He was aware of Éamon biding him farewell, but his mind was already around the corner. Soon enough, he mumbled his responding goodbye and headed off after the boys in blue.

His heart dropped as the officers piled into Danika's building. Had they discovered the apartment they had broken in to for the night? Was she in danger?

From his safe distance, he expanded his mind and trailed behind Boston's Finest. As they hit the stairs, he relaxed a fraction. Up they climbed, and to his relief, stopped on the third floor. His warrior princess was safe, for the moment. Certain the law was occupied, he returned to his body and kicked off the wall, intent to search for the specific apartment of his lovely savior.

A sloppy and strung-out denizen kicked and shouted unintelligible slurs as he was escorted into a waiting police car. Anton halted, giving the officers a wide berth and ensuring he didn't catch a jab in the nuts on accident. He arched an eyebrow as the protestations of innocence, racial profiling, and claims of police brutality were shouted from the extremely Caucasian suspect. Heaving an unimpressed sigh, he shook his head and headed up the stairs.

"Hey, mister? You see who they took out?"

Anton swiveled his gaze toward the apprehensive pair of dark eyes. More curious faces poked out of open doors, eager for the same news. He had gleaned the name of the culprit, as well as the laundry list of charges.

"I believe they said his name was Hanson."

Groans, jeers, and cries of *told-ya-so* echoed in his wake, and he continued his trek up the steps. He paused on the landing midway between the fourth and fifth floors and searched for the right stop. Closing his eyes, he pictured her, her black hair silky smooth, the sapphire blue streaks shining through the thick curtain of night. The jacket hung haphazardly on a nearby chair, and a flimsy faded charcoal thermal shirt wrapped her body. She busied herself with something in the sink, and he sensed violent and turbulent emotions swirling around her.

With tender and hesitant care, he brushed against her shoulder. She tensed and froze. Could she sense his presence? He trailed his touch along the collar of the worn shirt, delighting in her soft skin when he was forcibly thrown out.

What the hell?

He shook his head, confused and stunned. Never before had he been ousted in such a decisive manner. After a couple blinks, he completed the trek up the remaining steps and arrived at her door. What he was going to say, he didn't have a clue. All he knew was he needed to speak to her. He needed to be close enough to find out how she shrugged him off so easily. His thoughts strayed to the previous night's dustup. Somehow, she managed to discover the cloaked skirmish between him and Claude. Was it possible she was a Conduit, her skills untrained but powerful?

One deep breath and he knocked.

Voices spoke in hushed whispers, and a light pair of feet padded close. A feminine call to stop bled through the door as it swung open. Anton dropped his chin, meeting the wide green eyes of a curious young boy. Shortish blond hair stuck out in unruly spikes. His sun-kissed freckled cheeks warmed as his little mouth hung agape. A faded blue T-shirt swallowed him from neck to knees, adding to his diminutive stature.

Anton smiled. "Does Danika live here?"

"Auntie Nika! There's a giant man here."

Anton blinked, slow and deliberate. More voices chimed in, all of them male and vying for supremacy.

"What man?"

"Who's here?"

"What did you do this time?"

"Auntie Nika, he's really big. Do I let him in?"

His gaze swung in a frantic effort to keep up with the rapid fire of questions. Peering farther into the apartment, he glimpsed his beautiful warrior, and judging from her agitated and angry expression, he should prepare for battle.

EIGHT

"It's okay, Da. I got this. No, Liam. Hang on."

This so is not happening.

Danika shot to her feet, hoping to defuse this unbelievable turn of events. The sheer fact that he'd sought her out after she had so rudely deserted him stirred the dormant butterflies in her stomach. A giddy blush warmed her cheeks, excitement and embarrassment running neck and neck for the leading cause. She sidled past her father, placing a hand on his shoulder to keep him seated.

Dammit. Friggin' kid was like a rocket and he'd grabbed the door handle before she could sneak around the table. Her heart hammered in panic and disbelief at the sensual voice emanating from the hallway. Her uncle poked his nose out, glaring at her as he chimed into the cacophony of inquiries.

"It's the cops, isn't it?"

"No, I–"

"I'll start some coffee."

"No, it's—" She shouted over her shoulder to her dad, her eyes flaring wide.

"Can he come in?"

"NO!" she squeaked, swiveling her head back to Liam as the door swung open in slow motion.

"Who's this?"

"Nobody." She snapped her gaze to her sneering uncle. "He's just a guy I met last night." Her feet refused to budge, glued to the worn floor panels as her world exploded. She blinked, checking the working order of her eyes. Deliberate focus and wishing for the appearance of a sudden black hole beneath her feet did not shift the surreal scene.

Anton took up most of the entryway as he waited. Heat touched her cheeks as she gawked. His smoldering sea-green eyes bored into her soul, and a strange weakness stole her staunch resolve. He had changed out of the ripped shirt and now sported a pale blue sweater. Black leather still hugged his legs and dripped off his massive shoulders. No one that gorgeous had the right to be standing so relaxed in this shithole.

"Wow! Is he a giant?" Liam asked. "Mister, are you a giant?"

Cringing, she dropped her face into her open hand, regretting reading Liam all those Celtic tales. "No, squirt. He's—"

"Am I interrupting something?"

That sexy voice cut through the static with surgical accuracy. She locked her jaw, holding in an embarrassingly hungry growl, as her closed lids fluttered against her palm. Grateful to have something to use as a hiding place, she forced her rampaging libido back into its shattered cage. Unexpected thoughts of happily-ever-afters raced through her heart and quickened her blood. She lifted her head and struggled to remember how to speak.

"You a cop or a john?" Her uncle slurred as he stumbled toward the door, his vile words poisoning the mood. Anger and panic fused in her gut, combining into a volatile rage that finally got her legs back into working order.

The room temperature dropped as Anton leveled a frigid glare toward her drunken uncle. Fragments of last night's fight drifted into her memory. Here was the man wielding two wicked-looking blades, her Superman taking on Satan himself, and hope dared to tap her on the shoulder.

"I am neither, sir. My business is with Danika alone."

She had to give her uncle credit since the man actually had the good sense to back down, a healthy dose of fearful respect reflecting in his eyes. Liam, on the other hand, glommed onto Anton like a leech. Maybe it was because the little kid never knew his real father, and God knew his current male role models weren't the best. Whichever, her nephew wrapped both hands around Anton's arm and beamed as he dragged him inside, bouncing with each step.

"Can he stay, Auntie Nika? Can he? Can he? Please?"

Her heart screamed the same questions, wishing for the strength to voice a response. Yes hung on her lips, but the word refused to take form. Instead, she only stared, wide-eyed and mute, at the man who dwarfed her uncle and stood tall. A conquering hero of old made flesh and real in her hallway.

How could she really say no?

MANY OF ANTON'S concerns about Danika were solved in the short minutes and strange interchange between her and the three others inside. As sharp as her words might have sounded to an untrained listener, he caught the truth and depth of each relationship.

The young one latched onto his arm brought out her protective side. The boy brimmed with life and innocence. He called her auntie and with no other female presence in the place, the child's mother must be an absent force in his life. Bright green eyes sparkled and danced as he grinned happily up at him.

The gentle man in the kitchen drew forth her kindness, his lethargic pace the result of illness or some other ailment. A faint and off-key tune filled the uncomfortable silence, the humming punctuated by the clinks of porcelain mugs landing on a solid countertop. True to his offer, Anton caught a whiff of fresh coffee.

The sneering male off to his left was the source of her unease. Dark and lecherous vibes oozed off the walking devil, carried on alcohol-born wings. Close-set blue eyes glared at him from a brutish face. Mottled cheeks and a bulbous nose stood testament to years spent at the bottom of a bottle. Only Anton's current role as guest stopped him from ending the man where he stood.

Yet none of the men were the reason for his visit. That honor was reserved for the lovely statue only a few feet from him. He gazed at Danika, soaking in the sight of her. A faded and thinning Henley hung on her slender shoulders, nearly concealing her plump assets as the lower edge rested mid-thigh. However, as interested as he was in her blanketed curves, he was more bothered by the fresh bruises and purplish ring encircling her right eye.

Deeply ingrained self-control and patience learned over the centuries held him in place. Hers would be the final word and if she said no, he would honor her wish.

Silence became a physical entity, dragging its empty gaze from Anton to Danika.

"Pleeeeeeeeeease?"

Danika rolled her eyes with a sigh and relaxed her stance. "All right, all right. Just give me a sec."

Anton had a moment to recover before he was nearly yanked off his feet by the excited boy. He managed two steps forward when his path was diverted by Danika's tug on his free arm. Disentangling his hand, he patted the young man on the head and willingly followed where his beautiful warrior led. He cast his gaze in all directions, taking in every minute detail. Drab walls covered in smoke-stained beige flowed from room to room. A lone spark of bright blue winked from a closet of a space where trucks and dinosaurs littered the dingy rug.

She bypassed all open spaces, a muttered string of strangely familiar expletives falling from her lips. He recognized a couple of the phrases, but this was the first time he heard them coming from a female. Seemed that she and Éamon had the same Gaelic teacher.

A wall loomed close and she halted at the end of the hall, staring out the window to the street below. In such close quarters, the driving urge to gather her into his arms was nearly overpowering. Her wild scent swirled in the space between them and his leathers shrunk several painful inches. He waited as she took a couple deep breaths and turned to face him.

"What the hell do you think you're doing here?" She narrowed her dark chocolate eyes, her voice a harsh whisper. Her bottom lip puffed out, a painful slit still damp and raw. He dared a step closer as he reached out to touch her chin. A confused frown creased her brow, and her gaze dipped to his approaching hand before darting back up to meet his eyes.

"You disappeared without answering my question."

Danika swatted his fingers and leaned against the window frame. "Oh, so you decide to stalk me. Awesome. How did you find me anyway?"

Anton arched an eyebrow and one corner of his lips tilted up. "Well, you did say you opted not to drag me up all five flights, if I recall correctly."

She squirmed and dropped her shoulders. "Yeah. Yeah, I guess I did." Exhaustion laced her words and this time, he covered the scant distance between them. He brushed his thumb against her swollen lip, encouraging healing and reveling at the warm softness.

"Is there a way I can help?"

Her body shuddered, but she did not flee. She lifted her gaze from the floor and pinned him with her soulful eyes.

"I fight my own battles," she whispered. Strength and conviction bled through her simple words. He trailed his fingertips along her jaw, holding her gaze as her bruises began to fade.

"But you don't have to fight alone, *koxána*."

Standing close enough to feel her breath on his skin, he peered into her eyes, losing himself in their intoxicating depths. Heat flushed her pale cheeks. Her lips parted. He leaned in closer.

"Nika! Coffee's ready!"

The spell broken, she stepped away, and Anton sighed and dropped his hand to his side. This moment may have been disrupted, but it was real. For an instant, she allowed him near. As frustrated as his body might be, his heart was overjoyed by the minor step forward.

"*Togha, Da,*" she called out to her father, knowing her voice would carry to the kitchen.

Danika wiped her hands on her jeans, her gaze darting around the cramped space before she quickly sidestepped him. He watched, entranced by the sight of her swaying hips as she moved away, shapely and strong legs wrapped in threadbare denim moving confidently down the hall. Sadly, the exact curve of her ass was still a mystery, hidden by the hem of the overly large man's shirt.

She spun to face him, and he shifted his gaze up, hoping she hadn't caught him drooling.

"Look. It's not that I don't appreciate you looking in on me, but you ain't gotta be doing me any favors. I can handle this." Nervous, she folded her arms, shoving her hands under her armpits and tipped her head toward the kitchen. "So, do you want some coffee or what?"

Anton chuckled and nodded politely. In his mind, "or what" was definitely on the menu. He reined in his rebellious desires and flashed her a wicked smile.

"How could I refuse such a gracious offer?"

Her eyes sparkled for an instant before she shook her head, grumbling low. "Yeah, well. Don't expect too much. I think my dad learned his coffee making skills from Mary down at the diner."

NINE

Boris stared out at the gray building from the safety of the shadowed alley. From Claude's description, it was easy enough to find the exact location of last night's failed ambush. Normally, his "do-gooder" counterpart would have completely erased any residual energies afterward. A metaphysical handi-wipe in human form. Instead, lingering traces of the battle still clung to the stones. They may have been returned to their original places, but the sloppy seams could only be the work of his commander. Apparently, Anton's injuries must have been as grave as Claude indicated for the bastard not to have handled this important task.

Too bad too much time had passed. Since there was no disturbance in the Force, he knew his old friend continued to draw breath. Even though they fought on opposite sides of the war, he would have felt his passing. As a Conduit, he could tap into the cosmic consciousness and link with the mental pathways of all, comrades and enemies alike. He sucked in a slow, deep breath and opened his mind's eye. The solid building faded out, leaving its inhabitants visible and hovering in gravity-defying ease. People slept, fucked, argued, and stole while he scanned the scene from his own personal window on the world.

His once commander would never deem to use his powers in such a manner. Boris scoffed. The man was an idealistic fool. Always was, always will be.

When Claude Fournier approached him with the promise of eternal youth and power, and a rather clandestine mission, he did not hesitate to accept. People were cattle and needed to be controlled. It wasn't until later that he discovered Anton had also been recruited, but not on the same side. Honestly, it did not surprise Boris in the slightest. Anton never had the stomach to make the hard choices. Instead, the man insisted on finding the path of peace.

The path of cowards, more like it.

A shape, brighter and larger than the others, caught his attention. Smiling, he shifted all his focus to the cramped two-bedroom apartment. His long-standing opinion of his foe did not change as he watched the chivalrous sap dance around the obvious object of his attraction. If their places had been reversed, she would have been bent over the nearest table, her wants or feelings of no consequence.

He sneered, shaking his head as the pathetic interplay ensued. He took a moment to study the girl. She was pretty enough, nothing remarkable about her common looks. Only the wide swaths of blue in her long black ponytail coupled with a smattering of visible scars set her apart from every other female in this derelict neighborhood.

But her tumultuous spirit caught his immediate attention. A slow grin curled his lips. Oh yeah. She was prime material for the Rogues. No maternal figure, so her softer side was never fostered to grow and bloom. The males in her life were either weak and useless, or abusive and destructive. A small glimmer of care flickered when her thoughts strayed to the young child currently fascinated by his nemesis.

He shrugged to himself; this could be easily dismissed. Kids died every day, and no one batted an eye. Something else stirred in the depths of her being, something undiscovered and untapped. It was as if he were strolling past a sleeping lion. Dormant for the moment, the beast was safe, but things could change in a heartbeat.

This might be very interesting indeed.

With this new intel, he shifted back into the darkness and vanished.

DANIKA HALF LISTENED as Liam interrogated her surprise guest with embarrassing voracity. Just as before, she tried to lose herself in the bottom of her coffee mug but was about as successful as a virgin in a whorehouse. Between Liam tugging on her sleeve, repeating every friggin' thing Anton said, and the burning stares boring into her brain from the other men at the table, she was tempted to run screaming from the damned apartment.

Each set of eyes sent a different tingle down her skin. Her dad was hopeful that she'd nabbed some rich sugar daddy to keep him soaring for the rest of his days. Her uncle's lecherous and possessive vibe made her want to vomit right here and now on the table, in front of everyone. Only the continued swigs from her cooling coffee forced the rising bile to stay down.

Anton.

That was a story all on its own. His voice scrambled her thoughts, and she yearned to scoot her chair closer, if only to feel the sultry air sizzle across her skin as he spoke. Never had she experienced such a powerfully magnetic pull from a guy.

No. He wasn't a guy.

Anton was a *man*, pure masculinity wrought by fire and forged in battle. The more she listened, images of ancient knights popped into her head. Silver-clad warriors atop brutish black steeds riding fast and furious toward their enemies. Swords and other medieval weapons swung down, hacking and annihilating any and all in their paths.

And didn't that just turn her on six ways to Sunday. In the rare moments she mustered enough courage to glance up from her mug, his hypnotic gaze was focused on her, a devilish hint of a smile tilting one corner of his kissable lips. She dove back into her coffee, praying she hid fast enough so he missed the blush warming her cheeks.

Add to that the unnerving sense of being watched by something dark, just outside the nearby window, and she wondered how this day could get any better.

"Auntie Nika? Did ya hear that?" She blinked out of her mental wanderings and looked at Liam. She took a long drag from the cigarette held loosely in her fingers. "Ant'n says he's been to Europe and been in a castle before! Isn't that neat?"

Of course, he has. Probably owns a few as well.

Her mouth knew better than to repeat her thought this time. Instead, she offered a weak and patient smile to her nephew, crushing the dying cherry into the overflowing ashtray beside her.

"Yeah, squirt. I heard." Normally, she avoided indulging in her bad habit around the kid. Today, she smashed the rule, glued the pieces back together and broke it again until nearly an entire pack had been destroyed. She blew out the lingering smoke, aiming the fumes toward the ceiling before taking to her feet. "All right, kiddo. Go on. Play time's over."

She fully expected the impending whine and silenced Liam's petulant pout with a stern look as she rose to her feet. "No buts, mister. Go on." She headed over to the grumbling kid, lifting him out of his chair and setting his feet on the floor. "Get your books and I'll be there in a minute."

She barely registered the screech of another set of spindly legs across the linoleum. Her eyebrow arched up as she found Anton standing beside her. He stood up when she did? Recollections of fairy tales rang in her head. Details of chivalrous men who would rise when a lady entered a room or got up from the table or did practically anything at all.

No way was this guy for real.

Yet here he was. Living, breathing, and far too fucking sexy to be seen in this crappy hovel. She shoved her feminine side back into its locked box deep in her soul and squared her shoulders. He was just doing what he would have done for any other woman. Nothing special. She was nothing special.

The longer those hateful words swirled through her mind, the angrier she grew.

"Can he come back tomorrow, Auntie Nika?"

Liam's green eyes were filled with such happiness that her stomach churned. In her heart, she knew the answer. Of course, he wasn't coming back tomorrow. Why would he? It didn't matter that his gaze warmed her skin or that she imagined his fingers brushing along her cheek the whole time he sat across from her. He'd done his good deed and when the sun rose tomorrow, he would have forgotten about her.

Words failed her as she stared down at Liam's eager little face. "Uh, I'm sure he's got important things to be doing..."

"I would be delighted to return, Liam," Anton said, and her entire body quivered at the sound of his deep and rumbling voice. "But that completely depends on Danika."

The top of her head tingled, and she fought the urge to look up. Too bad it was a losing battle. She wanted to look into his eyes, wanted nothing more than to fall into those ridiculously gorgeous pools of sea green. Following a primal desire, she lifted her gaze.

Grateful she hadn't stepped too far from the table, she reached for the back of the nearest chair to avoid landing on her ass. Her elbow locked just as her knees buckled. She swept her wobbling leg out, casually crossing her ankles as she rested into her cocked hip.

"We'll see," she finally managed to reply. "I gotta check up on some job leads."

Cian scoffed behind her back. "'Bout damned time you brought in some money, lazy bi..."

She tugged her eyebrows together as her uncle's voice petered out. Maybe it had to do with the dangerously intent stare aimed over her shoulder by the walking god in her kitchen. In a flash, she saw the warrior hammering away at an evil opponent. The image vanished in the blink of an eye, but the powerful presence still lingered.

When Anton swung his gaze back to her, the predator shifted into the protector. Sharp flecks of green ice softened and fired her blood lightning fast. "I could help."

She arched an eyebrow, butterflies swarming in her stomach. The man reeked of cultured power as he stood so gallantly beside her. What kind of work would he find for her? Every part of her psyche debated with the other, no clear voice pointing in one single direction. "Fuck you" and "Hell, yeah" were currently tied for the lead, with "What kind of work?" and "Thank you" trailing by a nose.

His gaze did not falter as thoughts zinged through her brain. Patience reflected in those hypnotic green eyes, but nothing really screamed for her to run for the hills. Except for the little hairs standing at attention along her neck as if invisible fingers traced tiny swirls against her skin.

This sensation was something new and created its own brand of terror.

The brief quiet crept on. She was lost, transfixed by his silent power. Certain this standoff would continue until Hell froze over, she opted to make the first move. She managed to tip her chin a fraction of an inch before Liam surprised the shit out of her. With innocent exuberance, he flung his arms around Anton's legs.

"Are you gonna come back? I wanna hear more about the castles and stuff." His contented and toothy grin stole her breath. She wished nothing more than to see that expression on his little face for the rest of his life.

But if she had learned anything in her twenty-five years, it was that life was never fair and pain and disappointment were the only commodities you could count on.

Just when her lungs remembered how to function, Anton smiled.

Sweet baby Jesus in the manger. Heat blossomed on her cheeks and flooded her veins.

If only she believed in miracles.

TEN

Anton rested his hand on top of the mop of blond hair latched onto his leg and waited for his beautiful warrior to answer. She telegraphed her conflicted thoughts with her actions as well as her silence. Fear hung thick in the air, tainting the momentary peace.

True to her warning, the coffee was on par with his earlier cup. However, to be in her company, he would willingly suffer the occasionally nasty beverage. Her enthusiastic nephew dominated the conversation, firing question after question as only children did. With each new inquiry, he patiently replied, one eye trained on his pensive host. She smoked like a chimney, lighting the next cigarette on the dying embers of the previous one. The quickness of her actions belied a frantic nervousness rather than an enjoyed habit.

Even now, she fidgeted and twitched, the lack of distraction becoming a physical manifestation. Under normal circumstances, his first response would have been to gather her into his arms, stroking his fingers along her back. He longed to feel her pressed against him, her soft curves molding into his hard body, one part in particular getting harder by the moment. Her hair would feel like silk on his cheek, as well as draped across his chest.

A hungry growl rumbled deep in his bones, and he dug his nails into his palm to keep his cool. Given the current company and her strict "hands off" vibe, he was sure any advance would not meet with success. Instead, he stayed firm and watched from a painful distance.

Her gaze darted around the room, never lingering on one place for longer than a heartbeat. In her own home, she feared for her safety. His mind shot back to her hasty retreat from their meal. She was racing back to something, and that reason was clinging to him for dear life. His warrior woman was returning to protect the only male of worth in her house, her young nephew.

Spiritmate.

The single word rang through his head and fired his blood. Hope filled his heart. He would be fortunate indeed to be honored with such a match. Now, to prove to her that she was meant to be with him. His earlier conversation with Éamon crept into the forefront of his thoughts. This definitely would take some more time.

For the promise of peace, he accepted the mantle of Guardian.

For the promise of love, he would learn patience.

He sighed and tipped his head toward Danika. His continued presence only caused her additional tension. With delicate care, he pried his thigh out of the surprisingly strong grip of two spindly arms. A warm smile stayed on his lips while Liam grumbled in petulant whimpers. His height was a disadvantage when trying to console the child, so he opted to take a knee. The bright green eyes before him radiated pure optimism and joy, and he was helpless.

"If your aunt agrees, I will come back."

"Pinkie swear?"

Anton smirked as tears welled up in Liam's eyes, hanging unshed against the bright green backdrop. Their appearance timed in perfect synchronicity with his quivering bottom lip. He extended the requested digit happily.

"Pinkie swear."

Liam hooked his finger and gave his hand a firm shake. Unable to remain serious, Anton chuckled and rose to his feet, smiling warmly as he captured a stunned pair of chocolate eyes. He slipped his hands into his pockets, shrugging casually at her slack-jawed expression. Her shock vanished in the wake of a cautious frown.

"All right, all right." Anton detected a hint of amusement in her blasé tone, even if the grin was absent from her lips. "Just go get your books. This ain't over, pipsqueak. We'll talk later."

However, judging by the happy squeals bouncing down the drab hall, Liam was already sure of the final outcome. A crushing thought rushed through his mind. What if she said no? In his world, the female had the last word. If she was indeed his spiritmate and refused him, he would be cursed to roam the earth as the very enemy he fought. He remembered the Éamon's cautionary tales regarding Guardians who lost the other half of their souls and succumbed to the darkness of the In-Between and the depravity of the Rogues.

Unwilling to let the negativity blemish the moment, he tipped his head toward the two remaining males. He shifted his attention to the powerful female, his warrior, holding her unwavering gaze and searched for a glimmer of hope.

Deep within the chocolate pools, he saw a spark. It flared brightly before vanishing like a candle in a rainstorm. But it was there. His heart leaped and only his battle-tested skills prevented him from racing across the room and kissing her senseless. That would be for another day. For now, this flickering light would buoy his spirit.

His intent stare must have spooked his beautiful host. She fidgeted nervously and swiftly crossed the small space between them, tugging his sleeve in passing as she marched toward the door.

"I take it this ends our visit for today?"

He kept pace with her hurried steps and nearly bowled her over when she froze a few feet from the front door. Her firm ass bumped against his zipper, and he clenched his jaw to hold in his primal growl. Recalling her earlier "hands off" response, he scooted backward, giving her breathing space. His body ached for more than the accidental contact, but this was neither the time nor the place.

She released his jacket, her arm limp, and he picked up a

dangerous swirl of confused emotions. Risking her wrath, he placed his hand lightly on her shoulder.

DANIKA FLINCHED and slipped out of arm's reach.

"Danika? Are you all right?"

The touch was gentle, a caress meant to comfort. Whether his tenderness was fear of her response or respect for her psychotic idiosyncrasies, she didn't know. Neither did she truly care. He was there, he was real, and he scared the crap out of her.

She stared at the back of the door, unable to move, speak, or think. For the whole of her life, she had stood up against meatheads twice her size and dealt with self-entitled bimbos on a daily basis. She'd been mugged, beat down, brutalized, even stabbed a time or two. But here, in her own home, she was powerless to resist the thoughtful words of a gorgeous stranger.

Her natural response to his kindness was violence. She shook as she half-dragged him toward the apartment's primary exit. Tossing him down the fire escape momentarily crossed her mind, if only to get him out safely. She truly feared what would happen if he stayed any longer. Her uncle glared venomous daggers at her as well as her unplanned guest. Her father stared and smiled at nothing, too far lost down some rabbit hole, but time was rapidly fading on his latest trip. And Liam was completely enamored. Things were about to go nuclear, and she didn't want any witnesses.

At the soft words at her back, she stopped. She recalled a similar journey in reverse order not more than a few hours ago. All too well, she knew how it felt to be yanked around like a dog.

Was she no better than they?

Trembling in unchecked and chaotic rage, she frantically searched for a truthful answer to his question. Was she all right? Fuck, she was so far from all right, she'd need a map, a compass, and a friggin' bloodhound to get pointed in the right direction. No one had ever cared enough to ask her, and she struggled to give a response.

"What the hell is up with all the questions?"

Anger. Her go-to in any and all situations.

"How else can I learn about you if I don't ask?" His voice dripped down her back like warm honey, its deliberate and intoxicating tone sending shivers across her skin. She dropped her head, the weight heavy as it dragged her shoulders forward.

"Why would you want to know about me?" Her defeated words pooled at her feet, cementing her permanently into her hellish world. A wall of heat tickled her neck but she remained firm. Her senses were assaulted by his purely masculine scent and powerful presence. Her mouth watered, hungry for something it had never known.

Would kindness fill her with hope, or would it leave her famished and yearning for more?

"You saved my life, *koxána*. I can do no less in return."

His breath fanned a dying ember in her heart and sparked a dangerous fire of hope. But she knew the truth. She knew the sick power of this place. It sucked in dreams and spit out despair. She fought to keep her nephew innocent and safe. She was lost long ago.

"My life ain't worth saving." Resigned to her fate, she turned around and lifted her gaze. Piercing eyes of the purest pale green bored straight into her soul. His broad shoulders blocked out the rest of the room and she could almost believe in fairy tales.

Almost.

She reached for the knob behind her and swung the door open, careful not to smack herself in the ass. His lips opened, but he said nothing. Fire burned in his tempting gaze even as he acquiesced to her dismissal.

"I hope to see you again, Danika." He inclined his head in a most regal and chivalrous fashion. She shoved her hands into her pockets in case he tried to kiss her knuckles or some shit like that. A devilish hint of a smile tugged up one corner of his sexy mouth, and her cheeks tingled with embarrassed heat. "If only to convince you of your own worth."

"Yeah, well. Maybe. Never can tell what's gonna happen in this shithole."

Almost seven feet of gorgeous and ripped warrior loomed large as he leaned closer. Caught like a hare in the hypnotic stare of the wolf, she fixed her gaze on his face. Her heartbeat quickened. She swallowed hard past the lump in her throat as he brushed his lips across her cheek.

"I promise I will not let you fall in this place." He breathed the words against her skin and in her ear. Panic set in and she wedged her arms between them. Prepared for a fight, she only managed a twitch, nothing more than a tightening of her muscles.

As if he anticipated her reaction, Anton stepped out of her personal space apologetically, the hungry spark missing from his eyes. She immediately regretted her action. No one, aside from her four-year-old nephew, had ever made her second-guess her decisions. Who was this man? Why did she want to forget her fucked-up past just to bask in the light of his smile?

"Don't you trust me?"

Frowning, Danika gazed into his soft green eyes. "I don't know you."

He swallowed, and she watched, entranced by the undulating muscles close enough to touch. Was this what love felt like?

What was wrong with her? She tucked her trembling hands under her armpits if only to resist the urge to act on this strange connection between them. Her gaze dropped to the floor in an act of self-preservation. The foreign sensation melting her jaded heart terrified her.

Love. Who was she kidding?

"Would you allow me to prove myself worthy of your trust?" His soft voice trailed along her arms like mink.

"Dammit. Why can't you be a douche like every other guy?" The words fell out of her mouth as they spun in her mind. She shifted her weight back and forth, then settled on resting her shoulder against the open door. Mustering her failing courage, she flicked her gaze up from the ratty rug under her feet and met his eyes.

A wistful smile touched his full lips, and she was torn between shoving him out the door or shoving him against the wall.

"Because that is neither who I am, nor who you need."

He backed up, dipped his chin and simply left. She stared, his footfalls disappearing down the hall until the top of his head vanished down the stairs. Her eyes burned, and she remembered how to blink. With a confused sigh, she closed the door, shaking her head. A hero, just like in the stories she read Liam, had stood in her house. And if she wasn't completely off her meds, he actually seemed to hit on her to boot.

Could this day get any weirder?

"Auntie Nika? We gonna read today?"

She glanced at the silent barrier, contemplating chasing after the big guy for a full heartbeat. Defeated, she squared her shoulders, ready to carry the weight of the world for another day, and turned toward the eager face of her nephew. She offered him the best smile in her arsenal, ruffling his spiky hair.

"Yeah, peanut. C'mon."

She followed the bouncing tow-head and tried her damnedest to banish the heat beginning to simmer under her skin. This was her life and nothing short of divine intervention was going to make things any better.

She only prayed that her personal angel didn't just walk out the front door.

ELEVEN

Scenery blurred past the windows, and the V8 under the hood purred in pleasure as Anton drove at breakneck speeds. The conflicting urges to get the hell out of Dodge and to charge back into the pit of despair to rescue his beautiful warrior beat at him relentlessly. He clutched the leather-wrapped steering wheel as the beast hugged the winding roads leading to his home. His thoughts spun in sync with the tires gripping the asphalt for dear life.

Who was she? Never before had he seen such fierce determination to survive surrounded by so much hatred and violence. He understood why she'd fled from their meal. At first, he'd believed it was something he had done to scare her away. The truth, however, was more disturbing. She had dashed off to protect her young nephew. He pondered how many luxuries she had gone without to keep him safe. He dare not think on the pain she had surely suffered for the same reason. He had glimpsed faint scars across her pale cheeks and he shook, enraged, to imagine more covering her naked skin.

A primal growl slipped between his clamped teeth. He abhorred those who preyed on the innocence of others. There was no peace hiding in her soulful brown eyes, no joy coursing through the one he left unguarded. Even as his ire rose, a hint of a proud grin touched his lips. He might not be present, but his female was anything but weak.

His smile grew as fantasies whirled in his brain. In his wild dreams, she stood tall, a fierce gleam in her eye as she wielded an ancient Celtic leaf-bladed sword. Painted spirals of bright blue woad decorated her porcelain skin, complementing her jet-black hair and the supple ebony hides covering her mouthwatering assets. She lifted the weapon over her head, roaring in challenge to any and all foolish enough to cross her.

The wail in his mind spilled out of his head and filled the air. It grew in volume and pierced his eardrums. Jarred back to reality, he jerked the wheel, narrowly avoiding becoming a hood ornament for a passing semi. He cursed under his breath and readjusted the strangling strap around his waist.

Talk about distracted driving.

Blood thundered in his ears and a few deep breaths later, he pointed the GTO's nose toward the blue and white two-story that had served as home for the past ten years. Rules dictated that Guardians could not live in one place for more than fifty years. Apparently, the whole not dying or looking any older did tend to freak out the general population. For the past nine centuries, he had upheld his end of the deal. Yet, as the world shrank with the advent of new technologies, keeping secrets safe became trickier.

Deep in thought, he pulled into the narrow drive and cut the engine. It was still during work hours, so most of his neighbors were locked in their cubicle farms. He slid out, grabbing the bloodied shreds of his sweater from the backseat and secured his ride. The keys clinked in the wintery silence as he climbed the back steps to the door which dumped into his kitchen. Safely in from the cold, he dropped his keys onto the change tray on the counter and shrugged out of his leather trench. His fingers slipped inside, gripping the handle of his hidden weapon. Not a trace of gore remained on the blades. She found a secure refuge for him, watched over him, cleaned his swords and...

And vanished at the first possible opportunity. Chasing down the whys and hows in his mind made him thirsty. He continued to muse on his beautiful mystery as he reached for the handle on the fridge.

"S'bout time you showed up, boyo."

Anton jolted, swearing as he realized he was not alone. In retrospect, he should have paid more attention to the cherry red sports car parked directly in front of his house.

"Bloody hell, Éamon," he grumbled, fishing out two beers instead of one. "Remind me why I gave you a key." Snapping off the tops, he crossed into the living room and joined his surprise guest.

"Been meaning to ask you 'bout that." Éamon grinned as he lounged on the charcoal couch, one arm resting lazily against the padded back. His lilting laugh eased some of Anton's earlier shock, but the proof that his former mentor was sitting in his house did not bode well. He steeled his spine and passed the bottle to Éamon.

"Call it a moment of weakness," Anton muttered under his breath. After a toasting clink, he sank down into the matching loveseat, keeping a comfortable distance from his guest. The mere fact that Éamon's talent as a Channeler was second to none encouraged Anton to stay out of physical range. He studied the ceiling for a moment, but when no answer appeared from on high, he shifted his gaze back to his friend.

Éamon eyed him curiously, his peacock-blue eyes boring a hole through his rigid barriers. Groaning, Anton took to his feet and paced the blonde wood floors.

"What is it you want me to say? Because I'm feeling like I screwed up."

He took a long drink from the deep green bottle, letting the light lager cool his frantic mind. Had he made the wrong choice in not forcing his hand with her?

"You could say, 'Éamon, the best friend a schmuck like me could ever have, please tell a poor bastard how to solve this muck I've gotten myself into?'"

He pinned Éamon with a humorless stare. "Gee. Does someone need an ego boost today?"

Lilting laughter pinged off the ceiling. "Then don't ask right stupid questions, boyo." He paused long enough to finish off his beer. "So, let's get to the brass tacks of it. You didn't erase her memory, you haven't spoken to her about it. Have you at least gotten a kiss from all your troubles?"

Anton heaved a lovesick sigh. "Almost." Twice, in fact. On two separate occasions, she'd let her armor slide down, creating enough space for him to stand close. The memory of her wild and tempting scent swirling in the scant distance between them encouraged more of his blood to march below his beltline.

"Jesus, Mother Mary, and Joseph. Are ya gonna be mooning about like a teenager all day?"

He cringed, embarrassed by his wandering thoughts. The man did have a point. This would definitely need more direct action and less daydreaming. Halting his current circuit, he turned to face his mentor.

The standard smile on Éamon's face was strangely absent. He leaned forward, resting his elbows on his knees. "Tell me what you found out about her in your almost-kissing time."

Anton pondered his answer as he reclaimed his place on the dark gray two-seater. "When I said things about her were complicated earlier, I didn't realize how true that was." He sorted through his thoughts, reordering the information cards in his head. "She's surrounded by males who control her life. There is no mother or other female force, and neither has there been any for a long time. She's had to fight to survive, sometimes against her own family, and it's left her...jaded, to say the least."

He stared into nothing as images of the ramshackle apartment leaped into his memories. Dreary gloom coated the walls, dripping off the ceiling, and only the joyful laughter of an innocent four-year-old boy broke the dismal spell. To have lived as long as she had in such a hateful place, her spirit must be stronger than steel. His lids grew heavy and slipped down, allowing him a solitary moment, and his mind tripped down the path leading to her.

<Careful you don't spook her, deartháir.>

Éamon's distant voice echoed much-needed reason. Groaning, Anton hung his head and aimed his confused gaze at his mentor.

"You said that help must be given to those who seek it. I know she's asking. I can feel it in my blood. But how do I offer it to someone so poorly treated by every male figure in her past?"

The answering grin said more than words could convey.

Anton chuckled softly as they spoke simultaneously. "Very carefully."

Éamon took to his feet, stretching his long arms toward the rafters. Pops and creaks from his shoulders and spine bounced around the quiet space. He laughed, dragging his hands through his stylishly spiked blond and copper locks.

"Nothing like a bit of Scylla and Charybdis after an eighteen-hour drive."

Anton frowned, glancing up. "How the hell did it only take you less than a day to drive from San Diego?" The man had an iron foot and a car quick enough to oblige, but at some point, the laws of physics needed to be obeyed.

"Wasn't there, boyo," he yawned out. "Decided for a bite of gumbo, and wanted to see how Gabriel was faring back in the Big Easy."

Anton whistled low. He had done that drive for the past nine years before Gabriel de la Vega returned to his station in New Orleans. When things got busy, it was standard for his brethren to go where they were most needed. Territorial lines were always in flux, but he was grateful to have his boundaries shrink. He preferred the frigid winters similar to those of his homeland rather than the humid hurricanes along the Gulf Coast.

The thump on his back snapped him out of his reminiscence.

"Come on. I haven't eaten in well over a thousand miles and you know how much I hate to eat alone."

Anton rolled his eyes and dragged his body out of the comfortable seat. "Fine. But you're buying." He ambled toward the side door and scooped up his keys. "And real food. No drive through."

Éamon grinned impishly, shrugging as he followed him outside. "What? You can order a beer at Tasty Burger. That constitutes a real restaurant in my book."

His mentor continued to joke and tease as they headed to his car. Somewhere on the other side of the city, his beautiful warrior sat in a dingy room. Would she have dinner tonight? Would she have a warm place to sleep?

Stay safe, koxána. I made a promise and I plan on keeping it.

THE COLD DAY heaved its last dying breath, coughing out a trickle of freezing rain in parting. Danika huddled under the narrow eaves, her knees tucked under her chin as she sat on the entry steps. She shielded the flickering flame and struggled to light up the soggy cigarette. Yet puffing as hard as possible, she failed to kickstart the too damp paper and her jaw ached from the pointless effort. She tossed the lost cause into her butt can and dragged her tongue across her teeth. When she came up with the correct number still attached, she spat out the gathered blood at her feet and stared off into the distant inky sky.

She knew her uncle would retaliate after Anton left. To be honest, she was surprised he waited as long as he did. *I guess food is enough of a deterrent.* The bastard held his drunken rage until his dinner was on the table. Maybe he was afraid she would somehow conjure Anton out of thin air and beat the ever-living shit out of him. Whatever the reason, she barely managed one bite before the fists started to fly. Liam was already in bed, her father lost in another drug-induced fog, so her goal was to keep the beating quiet. After the coward grew too tired to keep pummeling her, she left. She had been so pissed off, she only managed to grab her keys and her smokes.

The once-white tank offered little warmth, but she would freeze to death before stepping back inside. Not until the fucker had passed out.

A white handkerchief fluttered in front of her nose. Remembering her current location, she blinked and glanced upward beyond the extended hand. The street light dug hollow shadows into the slender figure before her. She frowned and leaned away from the innocent scrap of fabric. Sharp features cut into his somewhat attractive face, but the strange glow in the eerie blue eyes gave her the heebie-jeebies.

"You look like you could use a friend."

The voice had a familiar cadence. A tiny part of her brain whispered that maybe Anton sent a buddy to check up on her. However, her gut had a much different opinion, and she knew to trust that instinct. This guy oozed arrogance, the kind players and pimps wore like a cheap suit. Hair blacker than the night sky, a predator's eyes, and one of those hipster Van Dyke rings of facial hair around a stern mouth finished out the visage.

It would be so easy to grab the offered cloth. It was clean, even if it was a little wet. Except she couldn't shake the feeling it had some dangerous strings attached to it.

She dragged her thumb across her bottom lip, wiping away the tacky drops. Out of habit, she used the leg of her jeans to clean off her hand.

"Thanks, I'm good."

"I'm sure you are," he murmured and tucked the fabric into his inner jacket pocket.

A chilling smile curled his thin lips, and she took to her feet. She suppressed the drive to cross herself by tucking her hands under her armpits. Even on the stoop, he had her by a few inches. Where Anton was solid, this guy was lean. Far too skinny in her eyes. His hair was too perfect, the black suit looking really expensive, and none of it sat right with her.

"Yeah, well. I gotta—"

"I'm sorry," he interjected before her hand reached the doorknob. "But I was wondering if you could help me. I seem to be lost."

Yeah, right. She leaned against the cracked and rigid frame, one eyebrow arching up. Saying nothing, she waited for him to continue spinning his story.

"I'm supposed to meet my friend at Donovan's and I think I made a wrong turn somewhere." His practiced smile filled her with anything but comfort. The frigid damp and creepy company stole the heat from her blood and only her stubborn streak kept her on the porch.

She tipped her chin in the pub's general direction. "Head three blocks down and take a left at the BAC. You can't miss it."

"I hate to drink alone," he added hastily, stepping to the bottom step as she tried again to escape. She retreated deftly, keeping the status quo in the space department. The black eyebrows pulled together, the corners of his thin lips drooping a touch. His momentary surprise faded and the air crackled around her.

"Thought you said you were meeting a friend." She bumped into the wall, the cold bricks at her back bringing needed warmth to her. Unarmed, she could still do some damage, but she wasn't in the mood for any more hits today. Option two: hold her ground and hope he would leave.

"So, I did." The lights from a passing car bounced off his eyes, the amber glow firing the pale blue depths. "But he won't be arriving until later. Can I tempt you into a drink?"

Every fiber of her being screamed at her to run and hide. Nothing tempting was worth the price. The prospect of returning to the violence of the shithole five flights up or enjoying a pint with a stranger was a no-brainer for the Irish Catholic.

She shook her head. "Sorry. Not interested." Snaking her arm behind her, she wrapped her fingers around the knob on the rickety door. In order to open it, she would have to venture into creepy guy's space. Either that, or turn her back to him to go inside. Neither idea filled her with glee. Back to option two.

He held her gaze, the visual contact a battle of wills and one she was not prepared to lose. A tic started between his upper lip and the moustache on his well-trimmed Van Dyke. She continued her impression of a statue. Only the rain broke the strained silence. If this asshat thought she would change her mind, he was in for a long cold night.

Mr. Perfect must have finally gotten her unspoken signal and he backed off. "Ah. Perhaps another time then." He reached inside his jacket and presented a shiny black rectangle. "Here's my card. Please feel free to contact me should you change your mind."

It was only a business card. Her father tried to drill manners into her since birth and the least she could do was feign some polite courtesy. She snatched the offered note, mumbling a half-hearted thank you, and shoved it into her back pocket. Opting to make the first move, she swung the screen open and fumbled with the secure, inner door. The flimsy wooden frame smacked against her ass before she slid inside as quickly as possible. Safely protected by the twin barriers, she let out the breath she was holding and rubbed her arms.

He still remained on the porch. She could feel him there, and that just freaked her right out. This time, she didn't stop her hand as it flew through the Stations of the Cross, pressing the simple silver cross around her neck to her lips, the sacrosanct period on the end of her religious sentence. Not wanting to hang around with a stranger at the gates, she climbed the steps leading back to her personal hell.

As she trudged the beaten path, she argued with herself about her choice. She could have accepted the drink. Also, she could have invited Anton to stay for dinner. A sharp laugh pinged off the hall.

Yeah. Wouldn't that have gone over like a fart in church.

Her pace slowed as she mounted the last flight before hitting her floor. The entire place was silent, most people already in bed and preparing for another work day. She envied them, the regular guys with regular jobs. Not having to worry about what little part of their soul they would need to give up for the next meal.

Her head started to ache the closer she came to her front door. Whether it was because of her own thoughts or her tight ponytail, she couldn't say. With a heavy sigh, she yanked off the rubber band and shook out the kinks. Sliding the key into the lock as she slipped the hair tie around her wrist, she paused, listening intently. Only snores over the droning TV bled through the door. She cautiously turned the key and stepped into the darkened hall.

The apartment was sleeping, but she stayed in the shadows just in case. She leaned against the wall and toed off her damp Chuck Taylors. No drunken curses bellowed through the rooms, and she relaxed as she made her way to the third door on the right. The hinges groaned as she fought to gain entry. Inside, she found chaos, her mattress turned on its side, same with her squat dresser, and the few clothing items she owned were either scattered or shredded.

Most were both.

She stared at the tattered remnants of her life. Is this all she had to look forward to?

Lead coursed through her veins as she righted the flimsy bed and flopped down. She didn't bother changing out of her clothes. Why? It was the only thing still in one piece. She grabbed the thin blanket and wrapped it as tightly as it would allow. Her lids shuttered closed, and she fought to find the quickest path to sleep. Tears stopped working as a lullaby when she was twelve and nightly prayers proved useless not too long after.

Tonight was different. For the first time in far too many years, she prayed. As the dark started to swallow her, she spoke to whoever was listening in the universe.

"Please tell me this is all worth something and life actually has some meaning."

TWELVE

DARK MUSIC BLED *through the shadows as Danika stumbled around. She grazed her bare shoulder against a rough wall. Bare? She did a quick wardrobe tally and discovered she was still wearing the tank top and jeans she'd crashed out in. Blinking, confused, she frowned and searched for a light switch. She batted around aimlessly but found nothing. The air was thick and cloying, reminding her of St. Luke's Mortuary after a service in mid-July.*

"Hey! What gives?"

A spotlight, harsh and searing, snapped on above her head. She squinted, shielding her eyes. The music shifted, pulsing bass beats replacing the techno Goth mix. Footfalls shuffled in the surrounding black.

Her forehead ached as she tried to peer beyond the garish pool. "What the fuck is this? If it's a dream, I gotta make sure not to eat whatever I did before hitting the sack."

From out of the darkness, fingers grabbed at her arms and legs. Skeletal claws clamped and scratched at her skin. Her survival instinct snapped into overdrive, and she kicked and punched in every direction. Yet she met with nothing, her attackers vanishing like mist in the morning. She fell into a low crouch, her go-to fighting stance, her legs wide and her arms loose.

"It does seem we have a scrapper among us."

The disembodied voice echoed through the surrounding nothingness. She detected a strange accent, an unfamiliar coloring of each word. It was snobbish and cold, aristocratic and condescending. She imagined some pompous asshole with frilly lace dripping from his wrists as he sneered down his pointed nose at her. Her head on a swivel, she scanned for the source of the voice, praying for a ripple in the emptiness to hone in on.

"Show yourself, dickless, and I'll scrap the shit out of your smug ass."

Her harsh language must have struck a nerve. The temperature dropped a degree or ten and she grinned, pleased at her success.

"A proper lady would never speak so—"

"Oh, cry me a river, fuckwad." If this was her dream, she was not about to get a lecture about manners. "And didn't your mother ever tell you that talking at people, instead of to them, is rude?"

The giant dimmer switch on the world dialed back the dark and eerie silhouettes crept into view. She did a quick count and realized she was vastly outnumbered.

C'mon, Nika. Wake up.

Danika moved to pinch herself, hoping that old wives' tale had an ounce of validity, but her hand froze before applying the needed pressure. In fact, no part of her responded to her commands. Panic gripped her heart and she gulped in air as fast as possible. Her coiled muscles trembled, but her body was not budging. Second only to being touched, her greatest fear was being helpless.

One shape loomed larger as it approached. She fought against her anxiety and kept her gaze on the growing shadow. An eerie crimson glow flared in the spot where normal people had their eyes. Chills marched up her arms as the satanic asshole from the other night stepped into the light.

"Bloody fucking hell." She breathed out in disbelief.

She didn't get a chance to really get a good look at his face, but she would never forget those inhuman orange eyes. His wavy blond hair and tanned bare chest said slacker surfer while his loping gait screamed psycho killer. Harshly cut abs led her gaze to an expensive looking pair of black slacks hanging low on his hips, the top button undone. Well, she thought, guess that answers the whole commando question. Inky tendrils crept over his muscular shoulder and peeked around his ribs, hinting at a massive tat on his back. The guy was well built, she would give him that.

But whereas Anton's hidden strength made her feel safe, this asshole seemed only to terrify and dominate her with this egotistical show of power.

He must have missed the memo that she was a Southie girl.

And we don't scare that easily, she mused. Her frozen body might freak her out, but she would be damned if she was going to let this piece of shit control her. If this was her dream, things were about to turn in her favor.

A pompous sneer spread across his regal face as if her fearful recognition pleased him.

"How sweet. You remember me."

"I also remember kicking your sorry ass. How does that sit with you?"

This is my dream. She repeated the words again in her head and with nothing more than a thought, she relaxed and stood tall.

The smirk across from her slipped a notch or two, his eyes flashing with deadly intent.

"Impressive, ma petite. But can you be so sure of yourself in my world?"

His world? Damn, the ego on this guy.

She hesitated, glancing around at the forms in the surrounding gray. She never had a dream feel so real before, but she knew enough to realize this wasn't anywhere in Boston.

He stalked closer, circling around her like a shark. Fear would be blood in the water, so she buried it deep under layers of bravado and a touch of courage.

"Bring it on, fucker."

She didn't see him move but a powerful backhand connected with her cheek. She spun sideways, opting to use the forceful blow as a catalyst for her own attack. Pulling her arms into a tight guard, she swung her leg up. Her high arching roundhouse kick slammed into his head and he flew off his feet.

Elbows tucked in close, she bounced on the balls of her feet, her gaze never wavering from her opponent. Rage poured off him and set the hairs on her arms to stand at attention. Even though her jaw ached, she managed to tug one corner of her mouth up. She glared over the tops of her knuckles, ignoring the trickle of blood dribbling off her chin.

"I didn't piss you off, did I?"

He snapped his feral eyes up at her and she sailed across the room. Her body crashed into a wall that wasn't there a second ago and she crumbled to the ground. Pain fired through her entire being and still she didn't wake up.

Shit. Not good.

A pair of hands yanked her to her feet and she countered with a rapid right cross. His head jerked away on impact but the big bastard stayed grounded. Switching tactics, she led with a left jab, cocking back her right for another strike, but her opponent read her sloppy signals. Instead of connecting with that smirking puss, she hit nothing.

Quick as a wink, the asshole simply vanished. Thrown off balance, she staggered forward into the inky black. Before she could right herself, fingers threaded through her ponytail and shoved the side of her face against a new solid backdrop. She bucked and kicked out, hoping to connect with some dangly bits. When his bare chest pressed against her exposed shoulder blades, she slipped into full-on panic mode. Squeezing her eyes shut, she struggled to slide her arms between her and the wall. If she could get a couple decent inches, she might be able to strike.

His breath blew hot against her cheek as he leaned in terrifyingly close.

"You will soon learn, my pet, it's not wise to piss me off."

Gritting her teeth, she found her last ounce of self-preservation. "Ain't nobody's pet." Without warning, she snapped her head back. A sickening crunch met her ears and something warm and wet trailed down her back.

"Release her now, Fournier!"

A voice straight from heaven boomed into the space. She would have to thank her imagination for conjuring her Superman right in the nick of time.

"This is far from over."

The sinister words whispered in her mind as bony fingers gripped her hair and slammed her face through the wall...

Danika screamed and bolted upright, kicking at the tangled blanket cocooning her. Sweat dripped off her in the frigid dark, and her lungs burned as she forced the air in and out. She pressed her hand against her chest, hoping to keep her pounding heart inside her rib cage. Her body shivered and ached. The rough intake of her own breathing was the only sound that broke the predawn silence. A handful of cars rumbled by while sirens wailed in the distance. Nothing out of the ordinary.

She wiped her brow with a trembling hand and scoffed at herself. Never before could she remember so vivid a dream.

"Damn, Nika."

The fight-or-flight energy rushing through her veins only moments ago slowed to a trickle, and she flopped back onto the damp sheets. Hoping against hope, she closed her eyes and prayed sleep would return. Yet, in the darkness behind her lids, those unearthly orange eyes flared to life.

Grumbling and grousing, she rolled off the flimsy mattress and rose to her feet. As carefully as possible, she reached out, stretching through her aching limbs. Her joints popped and creaked, forcing the combined pain of her uncle's thrashing and her imaginary beatdown to a palatable level. Everything hurt, but she was used to that. Certain nothing was permanently damaged, she headed for the bathroom.

A glimpse of a dark shadow at her back stopped her feet. Granted the small and shattered mirror above her dresser was not the best judge of character, but there was no mistaking the brick red stain down her spine. Nor could she hide from the chill that followed it.

THIRTEEN

ANTON ROARED IN FURIOUS ANGER, throwing off the warm sheets as he vaulted out of bed. Vile curses and promises of retribution spilled from his lips as he stumbled into the closet and grabbed a pair of jeans. Slamming his legs into the rough denim, careful to protect his ramrod manhood as he buttoned up the fly, he glanced around the room, searching for appropriate footwear for a serious ass kicking.

His black River Roads would be the best. The steel toes would inflict the most damage and the dark leather would hide the gruesome evidence. A thousand questions fired through his mind as he took out his frustration on an innocent sock. How the hell did Claude find her? Had the bastard tracked her down? Did Anton lead them right to her in his haste to see her again?

Each new query only created more problems and amped up his frantic movements. Shrugging into a black woolen sweater and his trench, he stormed out. He was halfway down the hall in mid-contemplation when he bumped into Éamon. The normally cheerful Celt yawned and raked a hand through his disheveled blond and copper locks. He offered Anton a drowsy smirk.

"Who peed in your Wheaties, sunshine?"

"Not now," he growled and attempted to shoulder past his friend. How he managed to forget that Éamon's special talent kicked into gear with physical contact he couldn't say. However, there was no denying the iron grip on his bicep, locking his entire body in frozen paralysis.

"I think now is an excellent time." Anton clamped his teeth shut and struggled to hold on to his rage.

Éamon stepped in front of him, a concerned frown framing his peacock blue eyes. Anton was well aware of his out of character response, but he had much more pressing matters on his mind.

"Anton? What has happened?"

The air sparked with electricity, a silent battle of wills. Anton knew in his heart he would lose this fight. Éamon was the strongest Channeler alive and, more importantly, he was his friend. An unwelcomed calm tickled along his jangled nerves the longer Éamon held onto his shoulders.

"I have to go." He hissed out the curt warning even as the sharp edges of his anger dulled beneath the onslaught of Éamon's powers.

"No, *páirtí*." The lilt softened, adding to the soothing blanket enfolding his senses. "You *want* to go and I promise I will let you. Hell, I'll even drive you and buy you breakfast." He tightened his grip a fraction, the squeeze comforting and difficult to resist. "But first, tell me what happened."

Anton gaped, his jaw opening and closing silently. Words refused to fall from his lips and he sighed, his head hanging heavily off his tense neck.

"He found her, Éamon." He spoke to the floor before he found enough courage to raise his gaze. "Somehow Fournier found her. Dragged her into the Void."

Éamon's eyes sparked and Anton flashed back to his dream. It had started as a delicious fantasy. He pictured his beautiful warrior stripped bare, her long black hair shimmering in the moonlight as it

spilled across his burgundy sheets. She smiled up at him, her chocolate brown eyes dancing with sensual fire. Beneath his hard body, she
responded with fierce passion and tantalizing enthusiasm. In his
imagination, her skin tasted like heaven and slid against his like silk.

Without warning, her hungry sighs morphed into cries of pain.
Instantly, the dream shifted. The location melted into the fathomless
black of the In-Between and his heart sank. Only two figures were
visible, captured by an eerie pool of light. He recognized the large
tribal fleur-de-lis across the right shoulder blade, but the identity of
Claude's prey was still hidden. It only took a heartbeat and a flash of
black and blue hair to verify his enemy's latest plaything.

Danika.

Fury raced through Anton's veins and he howled in rage.

Claude glanced over his shoulder, blood pouring from a broken
nose. A vicious smile split his face as he leaned forward, whispering
something in her ear before releasing her from the Void.

Since the In-Between was safe harbor for the Rogues, Anton's
Guardian powers were useless and he was nothing more than an
unwanted guest at the party. A turd in the punchbowl, and he
planned on living up to that reputation. With careful and measured
strides, he stalked toward the smirking bastard.

From the looks of the purple shiner and crooked honker fading as
he approached, his beautiful warrior made him pay for his abduction.

"Ah, Anton, *mon ami*. So kind of you to drop by so unexpected-
ly." Claude wiped away the remaining evidence of his brawl.

If he struck a Rogue in his own territory, he would be on the bad
end of a monumental dustup. Not to mention, he was vastly outnumbered and his only weapons were his mouth, his fists, and a driving
need to slap the shit out of the smug fucker.

He folded his arms across his chest and glared at Claude.

"Touch her again and I swear not enough of you will be left to
bury in a matchbook."

Claude pursed his lips and patted Anton on the cheek. "You
forget your place, *salaud*. You do not command here." He strode past

and stopped, casting a sidelong glance over his shoulder. "Besides, she came of her own free will."

His eyes flared wide, shock and horror filling his heart.

Claude snapped his fingers and Anton awoke back in his bed.

Éamon whistled low. With a sympathetic shake of his head, he released Anton. "Did he say how she got there?"

A dangerous growl rumbled in his chest. "Bastard said she went there willingly. I call bullshit."

Éamon scowled. "If it's true, then—"

"It's a lie." He didn't know much about Danika, but her heart was pure. He never imagined in a million years she would join the opposition.

Éamon held up his hands in surrender. "Just hear me out, Anton. Think about it for a moment, will ya? She ended up there somehow. It's not likely for any human to pass into the Black without guidance, or a dark soul."

Anton raked a hand through his hair, desperate for a way to get through to his friend. "You don't understand. You don't know her."

"And from what you've told me, boyo, neither do you."

His opening rage returned with a vengeance and only a strong sense of self-preservation kept his arms at his sides.

One brow arched in quizzical response, curving over an orb of bright blue. "You have something to add?"

"Yes. Are you gonna get the hell out of my way so I can get some answers?"

Éamon barked out a sharp laugh and slapped him on the back. "Spoken like a man in love. All right. Just remember to listen with your head," he glared harshly at him before adding, "And I mean the one above the belt line."

Anton rolled his eyes and headed down the stairs. He mulled over his friend's advice as he contemplated the best method for travel. It would only take seconds to *move* to her building, eating up the distance with nothing more than a blink. If he arrived in his present, flustered state, he might scare her off. Resigned, he grumbled and grabbed his keys off the counter. An analytical mind would definitely be needed in this situation, but his heart was too close to the subject in question.

In the short amount of time he had known Danika, never once had there been any trace of evil in her. Wildness and the courage to survive, that she had in spades. She was fiercely driven to protect her young nephew. No way did chaos take root in her heart.

But was he willing to stake his soul on it?

The question and answer played chase in his brain as he drove through the scant early afternoon traffic. Needing to reassure himself, he reached out to her mind. Yet, just as before, after only the briefest contact, she banished him with ease. The throaty growl of his GTO had created a living and breathing soundtrack for his turbulent thoughts until he pulled to a stop in front of her building. She stood her ground before Claude and bloodied him in the process. If she truly had found her own way through the Black, she would not have fought him.

He held that one kernel of hope close as he stepped out and locked his car. The cold in the air was not enough to mask the telltale scent of brimstone, a sure sign of a Rogue visit, still lingering on the dingy red bricks. Beneath it all, he caught a hint of his wild warrior. The trail was hours old, but his female had sat on this porch and was confronted by his enemy.

Anger mixed with fear and the forceful concoction fueled him as he dashed up the stairs. She had to be safe. He repeated the simple phrase over and over with each footfall. Before knocking, he reached out, getting a fix on the number of inhabitants.

The testosterone-rich environment was shy one male, her uncle missing from the group. That bit of good news encouraged him and he approached the door. He managed one good rap and the barrier flew open.

"Unka Ant'n!"

A green clothed streak with wild blond hair jumped out and wrapped a pair of tiny arms around his waist. The young boy's innocent and exuberant greeting touched his heart but did little to ease his panic. He buried his own concerns and smiled at the bright kelly eyes staring up at him.

"Good morning, Liam. Is your aunt awake?"

He only asked to truly announce his presence. He was more than aware of her. His senses snapped into overdrive as he scanned the small apartment. Lingering violence dwelled in every corner, and it was difficult for him to sift through the painful scars to find the most recent wounds. A thick, viscous trail of bilious green pointed toward the last room on the right and his spirit sank as Danika emerged from the hateful miasma.

Anton clenched his jaw, holding back a frightful growl. Red tinged his vision, but the voice of his mentor whispered, diffusing his outrage. Taking in a slow and centering breath, he realized his beautiful warrior trudged heavily, the tendrils of dark intent forcing her to fight for every inch. Yesterday's threadbare Henley still covered her arms, and if his eyes did not betray him, the same jeans cocooned her legs. New bruises marred her face, a sickly purple ring surrounding her left eye. He snapped back to the present and moved purposefully to her side.

"Are you hurt?"

Danika dragged her hand tiredly through her unbound hair as she stumbled down the hall. Deep blue streaks peeked between the black silk as it flowed past the middle of her back.

His fingers itched for one touch of the beckoning waves. Was it as soft as it had been in his dreams?

She frowned, raking her nails against her scalp as she pinned him with sleepy smirk. "What are you, my mother?"

As she continued past him, the air sizzled and cracked. Shit. She reeked of her journey through the In-Between, her heady wild scent slathered by the stench of the deep nothingness. Yet her actions were too normal, too lax for someone who had just sold their soul to an agent of Hell itself. He trailed a step behind her, his hands tucked into his pockets for her sake.

"I should hope not. That would seriously put me into a category far worse than creepy uncle."

She paused, straightening up before glancing over her shoulder. He chuckled at the perplexed crease across her forehead. Her deep brown eyes held his gaze, a curious glint flickering in the beautiful chocolate hues. It read as humor and he filed the knowledge away for later contemplation.

He shrugged impishly, earning an exasperated sigh and a slow head shake. She said nothing, only resumed her original path to the kitchen. Liam sat at the small four-seater table, humming as his little legs swung far off the ground. The empty bowl in front of him tugged at Anton's heart. As did the pained groan from Danika as she reached up to retrieve a box of cereal from a high shelf above the stove.

He stepped in quickly, resting his hand lightly on her waist. "Please, let me help." Her thin wardrobe offered little interference and his body tightened in eager anticipation. Heat pooled in his groin and only the presence of a naïve audience stopped him from slipping his hand beneath her shirt. He recalled her unmistakable "no touching" aura from their previous encounters and kept a respectful distance.

She flinched, but to his amazement, did not resist his aid. Instead, she sighed heavily and stepped aside, accepting his offer. He wished to savor the fragile success but something was still setting off his inner radar. He thought he caught a mumbled thank you before she slunk out of his loose embrace and sat across from her nephew. Exhaustion dripped off her in eerie waves. He hurriedly retrieved the milk from inside the sparse fridge and poured a heaping bowl of tiny o's.

"You sound tired." Anton kept his tone light and his statement innocent, with a trace of open concern. Now to wait and see if it was enough to spark a response.

"Just had some weird ass dream last night, so I guess I didn't sleep too good."

Once the morning meal was properly prepared for Liam, Anton knelt in front of his weary warrior. He tipped her chin up, encouraging her gaze to lift from the floor. Traces from the Void threw sooty shadows in her nut-brown eyes. Came of her own free will, his ass. Something, or someone, dragged her into no man's land, and he intended to find out how.

She frowned but did not push him away. His mouth watered at the urge to sample her lush lips. He settled for brushing his thumb across a jagged slash at the edge of her mouth. This was not the time for romance. He had a lethal mystery and the life of a beautiful woman resting in his hands.

"Do you recall anything specific about it?"

The crease in her forehead deepened and she shook her head. "Nah. The usual weird dream shit. Things appearing and disappearing out of thin air." She shrugged and stood up gingerly. With her delicious curves at eye level, a volatile jolt of toxic force slapped him hard. He leaped to his feet.

"There's a card in your pocket."

Her eyebrows tugged in close and one corner of her lips tilted up. "Gee, thanks, Mr. Wizard. You gonna pull a rabbit out of your hat next?" She paused, pinning him with a questioning gaze. "How did you know?"

This conversation needed more privacy. Truth was required from every Guardian in all things. To speak false would hurt. Literally. The pain accompanying any lie worked in direct relation. The bigger the lie, the greater the headache.

He did not want to sugar coat things, but neither did he want to expose her innocent nephew to the darker parts of the world.

Anton hemmed for a moment and glanced toward the empty hallway, away from the happy singsong voice enjoying breakfast. Narrowing her eyes, she followed his indicated path, cocking her head in curious contemplation.

She sighed loudly, tossing her arms up and headed down to the end of the hall. As he trailed a step behind, the sway of her hips held his rapt attention. Almost as much as the dark wave pulsing out from her right back pocket.

Danika stopped on a dime and spun to face him. He was so entranced with her body, he missed the invisible brake lights. Without thinking, he wrapped his arms around her shoulders to steady her as she knocked into his chest. Her gaze traveled at a snail's pace upward until she captured his eyes.

Dear God in heaven.

She was power and beauty personified. Fierce and caring. Protective to a fault. Could he have wished for a better spiritmate?

As the simple thought rang through his heart, the words of the Claiming Ritual followed quickly on its heels. *I claim you, body and spirit.* He traced her jawline with his fingertips, savoring the soft skin. Big brown eyes blinked up at him, guarded but steadfast, and desire drained any sense from him.

"*Tak harno.*" He breathed. *So beautiful.* He would risk the pain of a kiss, but only once he knew she was out of harm's way. Swallowing hard, he stepped away from her magnetic pull. "I'm sorry. I did not mean to overstep my bounds."

She raised a trembling hand and scratched her scalp. "Nah, it's cool. But why are you so amped up over a stupid business card?"

The Calling Card. Her simple question yanked him back into the present and her current danger. Many of the recruiting tools employed by his enemy used trickery and manipulation to bring about an anticipated outcome. In truth, very rarely was a Calling Card actually a piece of paper.

When touched, the recipient would find themselves hurdled through the In-Between. If they were lucky enough to survive the trip, their place at the table of chaos was assured. Sadly, most lost their minds before relinquishing their souls. He shook his head, dismissing her question as well as the dread churning in his gut for the moment. "Who handed you this card?"

Her frown cut painfully deep furrows into her porcelain forehead. "I don't know. Some guy looking for directions last night. I didn't ask his name. I guess it would be on the card. I can–"

"STOP."

His surprised shout triggered the pause button on the universe. She froze, one hand inches away from slipping into her pocket and seconds away from slipping into hellish oblivion. When he had that bastard Fournier in his sights again, nothing would stop him from scattering his ashes to the four winds.

"Take off your pants. Now."

FOURTEEN

DANIKA SWUNG her stunned gaze to the gorgeous hunk of pure male in her hallway as her mind pried apart his bizarre request.

"Beg your pardon?"

He seemed fixated on her jeans, and didn't that just turn her into an embarrassing puddle. But it was the method and not the message that confused her. If his demand held the same erotic rumble as the mysterious phrase he uttered moments ago, she would have peeled off the things in a heartbeat. Yet, his voice was different, his words choppy and a bit on the nervous side. She thought she sensed a touch of anger as well, but the feeling wasn't directed at her.

She stared at the top of his head, waiting for him to shift his gaze. When he leveled those intoxicating green eyes toward her, she was lost. As harsh as his command sounded, she only read concern in his chiseled face.

"I know you have no reason to trust me, Danika, but please, do not touch that card."

Someone actually cared about her?

The idea was too much to fathom and she remained unmoved.

"But I already touched it." *How else do you think it got in my pocket, Einstein?* She kept the final jab to herself, yet something in his eyes said her mental quip was received loud and clear. A hint of a smirk touched his full lips and her knees trembled. Holy crap, he was beyond gorgeous.

"I am well aware of that, *koxána,* but the connection between the holder and the card itself was still tangible. Is there something else you can change into?"

Realizing he was not going to let this go, she moved her hand away from her ass and slowly straightened up. He mirrored her, breath for breath. The deliberate slowness of his movements screamed predator. She pictured him hammering away on some opponent, sparks flying as their swords met. Fused with the memory of their initial introduction, part of her wondered why he hadn't just thrown her down and ripped off her jeans if it was that much of a big deal.

Her jaw tensed and she forced the words out. "Not at the moment."

Well, it was the truth. After her uncle turned her room into a war zone while she was on the stoop, she didn't really know what kind of clothing he left undamaged. She did hide a pair of sweats the last time Hurricane Cian flew into a drunken frenzy. Yet somehow, the notion of parading in front of Mr. Sex in the Flesh in baggy black fleece didn't sound like a wonderful way to spend the morning.

"Is there anything I can do?" A strange sadness darkened his eyes while she pondered her wardrobe selection.

Stunned, she could only stare dumbfounded. A couple of blinks and she remembered how to speak. "Why do you care?"

His momentary grief disappeared beneath a look so smoldering, she felt heat singe her cheeks. "In case you had forgotten, I owe you."

All the liquid in her body melted, including the protective ice around her shattered heart. He was more hero than human, and he deserved some fairy tale princess, not the troll under the bridge with scars both inside and out.

"I think you're giving me way too much credit." She hardly recognized the breathy tone in her words. Embarrassed, she turned on her heel and made tracks for her chaotic bedroom. Without pausing to check if he followed or not, she stepped over the scattered remains of her dresser and picked her way to the closet.

Her sides ached as she stood on tiptoe to retrieve her hidden stash of clothes. Relief washed through her as she touched the tucked away items. Instinctively, she knew the moment he entered the room. It was not because every one of her nerve endings tingled. It was more due to the fact the temperature of the room dropped, chilled quicker than a winter wind off the Charles.

"Why will you not let me help you?" Sympathy poured from his words and she blinked away the bitter sting of tears.

"Don't need your pity." Wishing she had a working door didn't make one suddenly appear, and she was in no mood to delay him any longer. In truth, a growing part of her brain begged her to strip off all her clothes and pretend she was normal. Pretend she could love and was worthy of love.

A strange heat blossomed on her right butt cheek, sending annoying jolts up her spine. Her jaw clenched tight and held in hateful phrases poised on the tip of her tongue. The electricity lancing through her body made the simple act of getting out of her damned pants a nightmare. Frustration grew and the battle with her reflexes encouraged her inner demons to whisper loudly.

You know, he's probably laughing his ass off right now. What a failure. You can't even strip for the man. Just imagine what he's gonna say when he sees you half naked. We'll see how interested he is after that shocker.

She fumbled with the button on her jeans, her fingers refusing to work right. The voices gained power, shifting into blind anger stealing away her coordination.

Fuck, are you even trying? You're pathetic. The small metal disc flipped up and she yanked the zipper until the teeth cut into her hands before it split open. Pain, dull and lingering, chugged through her limbs and she fought against the mounting urge to grab the damned card out of her pocket.

Why bother? Nothing is ever going to change. You might as well just give up.

More cackling voices in her head, and her spasmic St. Vitas dance as she disrobed grew more frantic. Once her legs were finally free from the clinging confines, she threw them in the general direction of the blurry mountain as he stepped closer to her.

"There. You want them so fucking badly."

The sickening rage vanished as soon as the denim slipped from her hands, but she was pissed off and was stubbornly determined to stay that way. Wound up tight, she turned back into the half-empty closet, fully intending to step into the ratty sweats, only to find her actions halted by a gentle redirection. She shuffled around and glared at the thick ebony woolen wall in front of her.

"Don't. Don't steal my anger." She wanted her pain. Needed it. It was the armor protecting her in the hell that was her world. It sharpened the blades keeping Liam out of the clutches of her sinister uncle. The thought of peace and serenity terrified her. For her, life was not meant to be enjoyed. It was to be endured.

But the calming arms encircling her shoulders and the brisk, clean scent assaulting her senses told of another path. Promises of laughter and passion teased her mind as he combed his fingers through her hair. Later, she could blame her girlie response on a lack of sleep. Right now, she would give in to an impossible dream, if only for a moment.

"I won't steal it, but neither will I let you carry it alone." His warm breath fanned her cheek as well as the growing fire within her.

Tension seeped from her body and she gripped the soft fabric tight in her clenched fists to remain on her wobbly legs. She gulped down air in rapid gulps and trembled as foreign and weak emotions shook her to the core.

"I can't," she choked out as the deluge threatened to hit. No. She couldn't let herself be weak. Not in front of him.

Quaking like a leaf in a windstorm, she clung to her pride and her sanity with fierce determination. His powerful and tender embrace offered no judgment, only a safe harbor of peace and serenity. Within the shelter of his strength, the hateful voices of her past disappeared. The vile bitterness and sneering disappointments melted away, leaving her trembling in the wake of the deafening silence.

<Tears are never a sign of weakness, koxána. They only prove us to be human.>

His imagined voice in her head sounded so real and provided all the permission she needed. In the privacy of her closet and in the arms of an earthbound angel, Danika wept.

FIFTEEN

CLAUDE GLARED at the empty room. This space should have been filled with Rogue recruits, evil faces eagerly hanging on his every word and every whim. The air should be buzzing with murmured conversations surrounding the nature of chaos and the human desire to do bad things. Given the current state of the world and the high level of socially glorified hatred, their numbers were astronomical, but duties had his standard retinue scattered to the four winds.

Growling in despondent exasperation, he stalked out of the quiet ready room and headed toward the gardens. Spring had yet to place its life-giving kiss on the bulk of the grounds. Trees still spread skeletal branches to act as a weak shelter to the dingy earth beneath his feet. Tiny delicate shoots of green poked out tentatively, dotting the muddled brown in a haphazard checkerboard. The setting sun's rays through the spindly foliage cast ribbons of shadows, their questing tendrils of darkness nearly spanning the full length of the dead patch. The air was biting cold and whispered of another possible flurry.

He stared at the depressing scene for a moment longer, allowing the oppressive emptiness surrounding him to center his mind.

That female was the key to his adversary's downfall. Now, he needed to figure out exactly how far she would turn before breaking. His thoughts wandered back to his encounters with her. He couldn't remember her name and didn't really care to alter that statement. She was a tool and tools didn't need titles. They had functions; and hers was to destroy Anton. It was long past time to get rid of that particular thorn in his side. Throughout the centuries, no matter the conflict, that righteous prick wedged his way between Claude and his desires for power. Perhaps, his earlier attempts at Anton's annihilation would finally pay off.

Boris had suggested turning her to their cause. As intriguing as Claude found the idea, he was not so sure she would fall under the lash. To sow the seeds of chaos, there needed to be rules, unyielding and rigid in design. The spitfire who defended herself with ease did not seem to be one to toe any kind of party line. He rubbed his jaw, the sting of her right hook gone but far from forgotten.

"Broken can be just as useful, sir."

Claude ground his teeth to maintain his temper. *I'm going to put a bell around his damned neck.*

"Didn't your mother ever tell you it was rude to listen in on people's thoughts?" His gaze remained fixed on his dreary surroundings as Boris stepped up to his right. The man moved like a shadow, silently avoiding the light. While this skill made him infinitely beneficial as a spy and an assassin, it was extremely unnerving to his allies.

"No. She was too busy servicing the men in the army to pay much mind to what I did."

There was no plea for sympathy in Boris' voice, only bland facts repeated in rote boredom. Claude recalled hearing that his father was unknown to him, but given the company his mother kept, he must have been a real bastard to spawn such a sociopath as his second-in-command.

Behind him, the rustle of activity stirred, his soldiers returning at the end of their tasks to make reports and steal some sustenance. At the thought of food, his insides churned. One of the lovely by-products of becoming a Rogue Warrior was the inability to gain anything more than momentary pleasure from eating.

Claude let his mind wander as he fondly remembered dining on the finest the world had to offer. As a son of noble birth during a time when nobility stood for something, he had never wanted for anything. The best meats money could buy, the rare, soft flesh melting on his tongue, washed down with a floral burgundy wine. Buttery lobster caught fresh from the ocean and ripe, juicy berries from exotic lands.

Now, he would indulge his decadence on rare occasions when he needed the act of chewing. The In-Between provided all the sustenance any Rogue Warrior needed in the form of essence. Stolen from the fallen or the innocent, essence is the living force driving humans to excel and to reach for the stars. Some call it the soul, others refer to it as the spirit.

To Claude and his fellow Rogues, they simply called it dinner.

The silent shadow hovering over his shoulder refused to give any more details, and Claude opted to resume his original train of thought.

"You spoke to her," he remarked, still transfixed on the garden view. "What truly are the chances that she would turn on Dudley Do-Right?"

Eerie quiet had him second-guessing his earlier assumption that he wasn't alone. Frowning, he shifted his gaze from the vanishing sun and glanced behind him, staring perplexed at Boris' pensive expression.

"To be honest, she seems to have no loyalty to anyone. She fights for survival alone. So, if we offer her what she needs, it is possible she could be twisted enough to join us."

He chuckled, his lips curling into a delightful smirk. Twisted. Yes, that was the correct word indeed. Even the new recruits who thought themselves to be tough discovered that, to be of use in the pursuit of chaos, a certain degree of corruption needed to take place. Not only did values get cranked to the dark side, so did the physical form. During the transition, fledgling Rogues were filled with the

Void, the deep and oily blackness removing any remaining humanity and kindness still lingering in their souls.

Claude recalled his own initiation and again his stomach revolted. He shook his head, banishing the memories, and returned to stare at the bleak scenery. Darkness crept in silently while he was lost in a reverie, the distant glow of the moon washing the wintery trees with muted silver. Yet, in this harsh cold, hope shone brightly in the fragile green sprouts.

Quelling the urge to yank the innocent blades of grass out by their tiny roots, he turned and marched back inside.

"Turn her, Boris. I want this over. Now."

SIXTEEN

"Come stay with me, Danika. If only for a day. Both you and Liam. Please, you could use at least one good night of sleep."

Helpless to do more than bear witness to her agonizing struggle, Anton breathed out his offer and held her tenderly.

After Danika finally emerged from the tattered remains of the closet victorious, rifling the pants at his head, he nearly leaped for joy. With the Calling Card still protected by the pocket of her threadbare denims, he easily banished it back to the Void and rushed to her aide. He cradled her gently as the words of his sworn oath boomed in his mind. *Protect and defend the free will of humanity.*

But that did not mean he had to uphold his duties in enemy territory. She froze in his embrace after he whispered his heartfelt plea. He feared she would shore herself back up behind her high walls. If she did, he would be obligated to honor her wishes. The choice must be hers.

She nodded timidly, her affirmation nothing more than a bump of her forehead against his chest. Releasing the tension in his shoulders, he leaned away and guided her eyes up to his. "Is that a yes?" He dipped his chin slowly, a hint of smile touching her lips as she responded with another nod.

It took no time to convince Liam to join in their journey. Truth be told, he had grown quite fond of the boy in such a short amount of time. He was bright and kind, two qualities saved through the loving strength and sheer willpower of his aunt. The ride to his Forest Hill home was over far too soon, miles disappearing during the rapid-fire interrogation of an inquisitive four-year-old. Anton laughed, patiently answered each of Liam's curious questions as he maneuvered in and out of the light early afternoon traffic.

Yet, the silence of his other companion piqued his attention. He sneaked sidelong glances, catching only glimpses of her face, her focus intent on their path. She eyeballed off-ramps and street signs. His heart sank as she repeated the same purposeful concentration as he led them inside his home. While Liam dashed about, gawking and pointing out everything that caught his eye, she scanned and cataloged each door and hall, as if determining the fastest way out should the need arise.

During their short trip, he discovered much about the fierce yet skittish woman curled up on his couch. Liam was safe in one of the spare rooms on the ground floor, deep in his innocent dreams. Éamon remained cloistered upstairs, leaving him in relative peace. Anton trailed his fingertips along the thick woolen blanket sheltering his beautiful warrior, his thoughts swirling about as she slept.

Another point of curious information was her somewhat forgotten bad habit. During his previous visit, he remembered her nearly decimating a full pack of cigarettes in one sitting. However, not once did she reach inside her pocket, nor did she ask to smoke on the drive to his house. He thought on it, realizing it truly was nothing more than something to do when she was nervous.

Perched on the edge of the deep walnut and glass coffee table, he continued his quiet study of his sleeping guest. At rest, many of the harsh lines on her forehead softened. Pale evening light cast an ethereal glow on her ivory skin. The playful dusting of freckles across the bridge of her pert nose spilled onto the apples of her high cheeks. However, the brutal evidence of her harsh mistreatment still lingered. Slender silvery scars traced haphazard patterns along her fair flesh while garish purples and blues mottled her jawline before disappearing beneath the blanket's edges.

He clamped his jaw shut, stifling the growing growl. The more his thoughts strayed to the hateful place she and her innocent nephew were forced to call home, the stronger the desire to tear it down to its foundation. Despair shrouded each room and every wall hid secrets of rage and abuse.

Anton pushed the low table away, giving him some much-needed space. Near enough to stroke her cheek, but not so close to hover over her, he knelt beside her and closed his eyes. With an exhale, he slipped into her thoughts and stood on the edge of her conscious mind. He recalled the ease with which she ousted him yesterday and opted to merely observe. Pain, overwhelming and unending, surrounded him. Yowling and rabid, it bit into her soul and offered no reprieve. He stared aghast as deep bruises and unhealed fractures crippled her psyche. Red fist-shaped contusions and angry handprints of purple created a collage of violence, highlighted by sickly yellows and faded greens. Blackened circular burns and razor-thin cuts added definition to the amorphous, swirling mass.

Nowhere could he find a bright spark or a glimmer of peace. Only faint traces lingered around the captured images of a certain smiling four-year-old boy. Anger grappled with grief as he continued to stare at the horrors that had marked her life. But the image that would haunt him the most involved Danika, her uncle, and a slamming door. The sheer terror reflecting in her defiant brown eyes tore at his spirit.

"What are you doing?"

Her voice was calm and curious, sleep coloring her gravelly tones. Behind his closed lids, he pictured her furtive frown. She deserved so much more than life had given her. Taking a slow breath, he returned to his body and opened his eyes, meeting the expectant gaze of his beautiful warrior. Intelligence and strength radiated in her brown eyes, and desire stirred in his blood.

Here was no gentle maiden, no fairy-tale damsel cowering timidly beneath the covers. His Danika was the dragon, fiercely protecting the few precious belongings that mattered.

But even dragons need rescuing.

His gaze dropped to her full lips, unable to resist the urge any longer. His mouth watered in anticipation. He took his time, deliberate and slow as he trailed his eyes back to hers. Her cheeks warmed to a delightful shade of pink and the deep chocolate pools receded from the encroaching black.

"I was thinking about kissing you." His attempt at a whisper turned into more of a hungered growl. Blood thundered in his ears as it raced through his veins, deserting his brain and fleeing gleefully below his belt line. The edge of the table bit into his spine, but moving was not an option.

Her jaw dropped and he forced his body to remain still.

"Do you usually announce your intentions?" Her husky voice breathed warm and tempting against his face. His denims shrunk another inch and he leaned in.

"A gentleman never takes what is not freely offered." With hesitant care, he raised his hand and stroked her flushed cheek with the back of his knuckles. Healing pulses seeped into her skin and the sickening bruises began to fade. The purple ring around her eye lessened until it was only a memory.

He thought of the staggering amount of healing possible if he was buried deep inside of her, and a deep, possessive rumble slipped out.

"S-s-s-so I have a choice, huh?"

Her soft and stuttered words nearly shattered his teetering control. Desire scented the air and swallowed the nutbrown of her eyes. He tuned in to her rising heart rate, each beat matching his in perfect harmony.

A slow smile tugged at his lips, her timid strength a source of both delight and amazement.

"Always, *koxána*. Your voice will always be the last." Careful to hold her gaze, he edged close and dared a chaste kiss on her cheek. Her heady scent assaulted his senses and he trailed his lips along her jaw, nuzzling his nose into the hollow of her neck.

"Wh-what if-f-f-f...Ah, fuck it."

Drunk on her intoxicating fragrance, he sensed her initial movement after the fact. He dragged his head up as she slid off the couch and landed in his lap. His eyebrow arched up, tugging the corners of his mouth into a smirk. He was ready to let her take the lead and he loosely encircled her shoulders.

However, he wasn't prepared for her fierce response. She threaded her fingers through his hair an instant before slamming her mouth against his. Encouraged, he tightened his embrace, cradling the back of her head and tilting her mouth for better access. She forced her tongue beyond his teeth and dug her nails into his hair. He frowned even as she clenched her legs tight around his waist.

This was wrong. As happy as his body was to have her straddling his painfully erect cock, there was a terrified desperation to her actions. This was not the response of a woman in the heat of passion; this was frightened dominance. With delicate care, he shifted gears slowly, guiding her movements away from the frenetic while still allowing her to retain control. He dropped his jaw, inviting her to deepen the kiss. He encouraged her tongue to dance and twirl with his, dipping and receding between their fused mouths. He did not fight her. Instead, he steered her. A caress across her back here, a tickle along her ribs there.

Tense seconds slipped into impassioned moments as she gradually gave into his seduction. Relaxed and languid, she melted against his chest, the battle of sexual supremacy ending in a tie. She rolled her hips in sensual circles and the diamond hard tips of her full breasts cut through her thin shirt, pressing into his chest. He hungered to inch his fingertips beneath the hateful cloth and test the weight of each fleshy mound.

He chose the safer, and slightly more painful, path and kept his hands in the skin-free zones. But that did not mean he couldn't get a good grip on other hidden parts. The edges of his lips tilted up as his playful squeeze of her ass earned a throaty groan. Only when the need to breathe reared its head did he break the seal of their first kiss.

She drew in ragged gasps, resting her damp forehead against his shoulder.

"Well," he huffed out, smiling as he sucked down gulps of air. "Should things go further, I don't think I need to ask who's going to be on top."

DANIKA STRUGGLED to form coherent thoughts, but her brain was too busy spinning from the touch of his lips. Hell, knowing Liam slept in the room just down the hall wasn't enough to cool her jets. She wasn't sure if it was his accent, his proper manners, or the simple fact he was absolutely drop-dead gorgeous, that made her lose any and all self-control.

And what did she do at the first sign of interest from him? She friggin' attacked him. Her heart pounded hard against her rib cage, panic and self-preservation trampling the frail, fluttering wings of hope and something deeper she feared to name. She scratched and clawed, wishing she truly knew how to respond to his tender touch.

In her pea brain, she figured if she scared him away, he could get on with his life. As far as she was concerned, he had more than repaid her tiny kindness. The sooner he learned she was not worth the effort, the better off he would be.

But some tiny corner of her still wished for the impossible. In her dreams, she imagined a compassionate lover, someone who cared about her wants and needs. A real man who put her desires at the top of his list, not at the bottom of the food chain. Strong arms to fight away the dark, not to pummel her into pained submission. Caresses and love nips, not punches and bite marks.

And here he was, her own personal superhero.

During her show of aggression, he did not turn away. To her surprise, he did not throw her across the room. What he did was far more terrifying.

He gave her a reason to believe in the possibility of love.

Did heroes truly exist?

He met her anger and with some kind of magic, he made it into something else. He willingly allowed her to take the lead, but never relinquished control. With one hand cradling the back of her head and the other with a healthy grip on her ass, he gave in to her fumbling kiss.

An unfamiliar warmth tiptoed along her skin, slow and hot like maple syrup. Delicious and decadent, it flowed from where their lips met and covered every inch of her being. She lost the desire to fight and savored the taste of passion. His tongue danced and twirled with hers, teasing and tempting. She relaxed her jaw and a heady sigh slipped into his mouth. His soft hair tickled the palm of her hand and she trailed her fingers through the thick waves.

All sense fled when she rocked her hips against the coiled python tucked into his expensive looking jeans. Not to mention every ounce of moisture in her body. When her panic began to rise again, he slowed things down and pulled his lips away. Air rushed in, releasing her fears and she attempted some degree of rational thought.

She panted heavily and rested her ear against his chest. The downy wool cocooned her cheek, muffling the steady thump of his heart. The strong rhythm soothed her jangled nerves, giving her courage to speak.

"Go further? What makes you think it's gonna go any further than this?" Smoky gravel coated her words and she cleared her throat.

Again, his response threw her for a loop. His deep rumbling laugh sent lightning zinging through her veins and she was primed for round two.

"Call it a dream of mine, *koxána*."

She stared off into nothingness as she sat, curled in his lap. Only the ticking of an incredibly large watch face on the wall cut through the soft silence. His hand made circuits up and down her spine, the pace languid and soothing. If she closed her eyes, she could almost forget how bad things truly were. If she relaxed her guard a fraction, she could pretend heaven existed on earth, even for a minute or two more.

This couldn't last.

Reality was a harsh bastard, and Danika knew it was only a matter of time before the shitstorm outside ruined this fantasy.

Shoring up her internal walls, she squeezed her arms between them and with hateful and deliberate pressure, pushed away from him. The sooner she ripped the Band-Aid off whatever this was, the better. Liam had already bonded ridiculously fast, and it would destroy him when Anton came to his senses and dumped her.

Her own feelings were less than secondary. She was used to rejection and knew the sting of it well. The knit pattern of his charcoal sweater was not that interesting, but it was safer than meeting the sea-green eyes she could feel staring at the top of her head.

Don't look up. Don't look up.

Her mental mantra weakened and crumbled at the gentle touch of his knuckles under her chin. Encouraged to raise her gaze, she blinked rapidly and swallowed hard. She had to be sure her emotions were safely in check when she finally met his seductive eyes.

Yeah, that was a big negative. Fire burned in those pale green depths. Heat and the promise of forever. She glanced away, unable to get too invested in the impossible. She rested her fingertips in his massive palm and prayed for the strength to speak.

"Trust me, I'm not the girl guys like you dream about."

Hoping it didn't sound as pathetic as it felt to say the words aloud, she untwined her legs and took to her feet.

Ever the gentleman, Anton lifted her out of his lap and rose up alongside her. Moment broken, she plopped down on the couch, tossing the blanket over her legs. Not that she was cold, but the more layers between her and him might send the message to her body to dial down the sexy thoughts.

"Are you certain of that?"

Without switching her gaze, she pictured the smile on his face. Mirth colored his richly accented voice and she heaved a resigned sigh. Dragging her nails against her scalp, she nodded.

"I just don't know why a smart, good looking guy like you can't see it. Look, I appreciate all you've done for me and for Liam." She studied the pale wood at her feet and rested her forearms on her knees. "But I am no good and I still don't know who you are."

Images flashed before her vacant stare. Two titans pounding the crap out of each other with swords, one of the blades weighing twice as much as her. Steeling her resolve, she snapped her gaze up and captured his sad eyes. "What were you doing in that alley the other night, anyway?"

SEVENTEEN

Oh, boy. Here it comes.

Anton raked his hand through his tousled hair and cringed as his beautiful warrior posed the question he had been dreading. As a Guardian Warrior, he was forbidden to tell falsehoods. As a man of integrity, he believed in the power of the truth. Yet, as the potential lover of a female prone to tread a dangerous path, he had an obligation to keep her safe. All three stood in a disharmonious balance. Three edges to the same blade, all equally sharp and lethal if one mistake was made.

"Can't we go back to the kissing?"

The passionate spark in her warm chocolate eyes disappeared into the dark and she straightened her spine. Apparently not.

"I see. So, I'm supposed to trust you implicitly, drop down and suck your dick, but you can't answer one simple question." She folded her arms across her chest, moving farther away from him.

His heart sank, the venom in her words striking a painful blow. He knelt at her feet, his palms lightly cupping her knees. Refusing to fail, he held her gaze and spoke honestly.

"No, Danika. That is not what I meant at all." He poured every ounce of compassion into his voice, praying it would bring her back to him. "My reasons for being in that alley are...complicated."

Her eyes narrowed, a deep furrow between her shapely brows cutting a channel of doubtful aggravation.

He groaned, flinching in mortified retrospection and lowered his forehead onto the backs of his hands. "Dammit. That didn't come out right, either. I didn't mean that you aren't smart enough to follow it." Daring a glance up, he peered at her from under the veil of his embarrassment. "I really do know how to talk. I...I just don't know what to say so you don't run screaming from me."

With his skills as a Conduit, it would be so easy to search her mind and find the correct words that would make her stay. But that would make him no better than his enemy.

Free will.

Guardians fought to ensure all humans had the freedom to choose their life path.

The frown relaxed a fraction as she blinked quickly in contemplation. Her arms lost some of their rigidity, easing her guarded pose, but she remained apart.

"I'm not a child. I know what a shit hole this world is. All I want to know is why were you and that Satan bastard from my nightmare going all Lord of the Rings on each other?"

He bit the inside of his cheek to hold back a prideful smile. She was intelligent and direct, two qualities he valued and were sadly lacking in many of his partners. That might explain why he was so attracted to her from the moment he saw her silhouetted in the early sun's light.

He rose up slightly and placed his hands on her shoulders. He took his time as he trailed his fingers down the length of her arms. She watched expectantly but did not stop him. Encouraged by her lack of pushback, he slipped her hands into his, guiding her to uncross her tense limbs. As much as he wanted to pull her into his lap, he opted to remain the gentleman and was satisfied to lace his fingers with hers as he sorted through his thoughts.

"He is my enemy and it is my duty."

She arched a brow. "Really? Is that your final answer? 'It's my duty.' What are you, the sword-swinging police?"

The situation spun from bad to worse, and all his attempts at couching the truth were backfiring in rapid succession. Defeat loomed close, and he sighed in heavy resignation.

"In a sense, yes. Please know that I am only trying to protect you and—"

"Protect me?" Her voice cracked as she yanked her hands away from him. "How? Tell me how the fuck refusing to give me a straight answer is protecting me?" She clamored to her feet, nearly knocking him over in the process. "I see two guys hammering away at each other in the middle of the friggin' night. I think I have the right to know more than the party line."

A door closed above his head, recognizable footfalls moving down the hall and toward the stairs. Shit.

"And you still haven't told me what the big deal was about that dumbass card."

"What card?"

Anton hung his head, cushioning his frustrated mind in the palm of his hand. Of all times for Éamon to make his grand entrance, it had to be at that precise moment.

How much worse could this get?

DANIKA SPUN HER GAZE AROUND, shocked at the familiar lilt of this new player. The man descended the steps like he owned the place. He had that purposefully messy hair only the ridiculously gorgeous could pull off. Blond and copper hues wove through the GQ style, and he oozed power.

He was easy on the eyes, and from his loping gate, he knew it. Bright blue eyes framed by long feathery lashes, perfectly tanned skin, and muscles visible even through his clothes. But the boyish smile hid something deeper, something dangerous. He strolled over, inviting himself into the conversation without so much as a hello.

She opened her mouth, a smartass comment hanging on the tip of her tongue, when he extended his hand. Lightness and mirth danced in his impossible blue eyes.

"Éamon Alasdair Pádraig McClearon, at your service." His brogue was thicker than her father's, so she guessed him to be pretty fresh off the boat. She studied him as she reached for his waiting greeting. A strange jolt raced along her arm the instant she grazed his palm, and she quickly yanked her tingling fingers away.

"What the hell was that?" Needing space, she moved away, using the length of the coffee table as no man's land. She split her glare between the two guys and stood alone in calculated defiance.

The polished smile across from her vanished in a wave of confusion and Éamon dipped his chin. "Sorry. Next time, I'll be sure to pick up my feet."

A static shock? Doubtful. Her gaze searched the hard wood floors but did spy thick carpet lining the steps leading to the second level. She gave her wrist a good flick, encouraging the pins and needles to subside. "Yeah, sure."

"So, you were saying something about a card?"

Her frown returned in earnest, with a slight headache creeping up in its wake. She reset her arms in shield mode across her chest and sat back into her right hip.

"You always eavesdrop on people's conversations?"

A pained groan from her necking partner off to her left wasn't enough of a deterrent. She tilted her chin up a notch and refused to back down. Sure, the pair of them weighed as much as her block, and she had no real chance if things went bad. But she was tired of being tossed around without any say.

"It's not hard when you're trying to out shout each other."

The Mick did have a point, which only aggravated her more. "Oh, so it's a volume thing. Next time, I'll try to get pissed a little quieter."

Anton was strangely silent. She glanced over in his general direction, his gaze locked with the other guy. The air crackled with that same electricity that zapped her earlier.

"You boys wanna share with the rest of the class?"

He opened his mouth but Mr. Friendly jumped in. "Only if you go first, *acushla*."

Her forehead was starting to ache from all the frowning exercise it was getting during this interrogation. "So, what? I show you mine and you show me yours? Sorry, *bod*. Played that game and trust me, you ain't got anything I haven't seen before."

The Irishman's bright blue eyes hardened to icy shards. Insulting Anton's bestie probably wasn't the smartest decision she'd made all day, but the dumbass train had already left the station. Her back was against the proverbial wall and she was not about to lose.

"Seen a few in your time, have ya' then?"

She tipped her chin up a bit more. "Enough to know yours ain't gonna scare me." Well, maybe a little. The bastard was big enough to bench press a Buick, but she also knew a genuine good guy when she saw one. They were few and very far between. However, something in the way he carried himself told her she was treading on thin ice.

"You always try to bully girls into giving you what you want, boyo?"

A dangerous tic started at the corner of his tight-lipped smirk.

"Only when my friends' lives are involved, darlin'."

Whether he intended to sound like a complete condescending asshole or not, he hit the mark in spades and she was done. She took two steps and stopped when she was up close and personal.

"How can a card be a life or death object, *shinach*?" She poked the Irish bear in the chest before swiveling around to face her speechless angel, daring him to steal her ire. "Both of you have such a hard-on for the damned thing, but neither of you have the balls to tell me why."

"Who gave it to you?" The lilt was absent and the words cut sharply through the strained air. She clenched her jaw and climbed her gaze back up to Éamon's eerie blue eyes. She thought she caught a freaky glow somewhere buried deep in those pools, but she chalked it up to a passing car's headlights and lack of real sleep.

"Why? You need a date?"

A hint of amusement flickered in his piercing blue eyes, one corner of his full lips dancing up and down.

"Do you even own a filter, darlin'?"

Undaunted, she shook her head. "And deprive the world of some much needed honesty? Not bloody likely."

The tension melted a degree or two, but she wasn't ready to concede just yet. "So both of you are going to keep deflecting my question? Awesome. Who taught who that trick?"

That seemed to knock a little of the wind out of the Irish giant's sails. Something akin to regret flashed across his handsome face and disappeared in a blink. "That would be me. Taught him all he knows."

The playful wink and sad smile sat at odds with the commanding stance. Exhaustion drained her desire to continue her statue impression, and she dropped her arms to her sides. "Congrats. You both deserve a friggin' award for that one." She sidestepped into the testosterone-free zone and stalked down the hall.

"Danika, wait." Anton called after her.

The unexpected presence at her back threw her into survival mode. His gentle caress on her shoulder zinged through her body, and she snapped her arms up, knocking away his comforting touch. Glaring in his general direction, she continued on her path toward the room where Liam slept.

"Wait? Wait for what? More bullshit half-truths?" She opened the door and flipped on the lights. Leaning inside, she smacked the wall, shattering the peaceful silence. "C'mon, peanut. We gotta go."

It killed her to wake him so abruptly, especially when she knew the hell she would be returning him to face. She headed to the bed, jostling the slumbering lump gently while trying to ignore the magnetic shadow hugging the doorway. Liam's pleading whimpers tugged at her heartstrings, but her mind was made up.

"No buts, mister. Get going."

It didn't matter how great the house was, or how sexy the company. No way was she going to stay where she wasn't getting a straight answer. Not when she had the choice. She kept her eyes glued to the floor, searching for the shoes she was certain Liam kicked off before crawling under the warm covers. The voices in her head screamed in warning, shouting for her to let him stay. He would be safer if he remained. In her heart, she knew the big strong men living here would keep him out of harm's way.

But what about her? Who is going to protect her?

She dashed her arm across her damp eyes, cursing herself for her moment of weakness, and spun right into Anton's arms. His strong hands steadied her with fragile care and nearly shattered her resolve.

Nearly, but not quite.

"Danika, please stay." Terrifyingly tender emotions thickened his voice, and she wanted nothing more than to give in. Instead, she shook her head harshly and shrugged out of his embrace. Strength laid somewhere away from those intoxicating green eyes, so she refused to seek them out.

"Huh uh. Not until you're ready to fill in some important blanks." She placed her hand on Liam's back as the little guy shuffled his socked feet out into the hall. With her quickest escape route clear in her mind, she steered his tired steps toward the front door. Anton followed, a silent wall.

"Let me at least drive you home." His pleading tone was more tempting than she was willing to admit.

When she reached the living room and caught the stern and emotionless stare from his buddy, she clenched her jaw so tight her teeth ached. "No thanks. I know how to find my way home."

Before Liam could see Éamon, she guided him out onto the stoop, staying one step behind. "Thanks for nothing."

She tossed the words over her shoulder and latched the door at her back. The sooner she put this day out of the present and into the past where it belonged, the sooner she could go back to living without hope.

"Auntie Nika? Did Unka Ant'n do something bad?"

She swallowed hard, coughing as her unshed tears choked her. "Nah, peanut. We just needed to go. He's, uh, got stuff to do. It's okay."

She hated lying to him, but the truth was such a mystery, and if she spent another second in Anton's magnetic presence, she feared she'd lose herself in an impossible dream forever. Resting her hand on Liam's bony little shoulder, she started the long trek homeward, trudging out of heaven and back into hell.

EIGHTEEN

"WHAT THE HELL IS YOUR PROBLEM?" Anton swiveled, pinning Éamon with an angry stare. "Why did you have to treat her like that? You don't—" The rest of his sentence, as well as his entire body, locked, the giant pause button in the sky firmly pressed and held.

"No, my friend. *You* don't. You don't know anything about her." Éamon stalked over as Anton struggled to move from his frozen pose. Only his eyeballs seemed to be under his control, and all they could do was follow his mentor's slow approach. "You see a damsel in distress and you jump in with both feet. You never look around to see if you're gonna land on solid ground or in a viper's pit."

Anton's jaw ached as he fought to speak, and his muscles trembled in barely controlled rage.

<*And I'm supposed to do what? Sit by and wait until she's dead before I give her a hand?*>

Éamon tossed his hands into the air and grabbed hold of Anton's shoulders. The biting force of his fingers snapped the spell, giving him power over his limbs again.

"No. But you do need to listen and to think."

He attempted to shrug out of the man's vice-like grip and met with little success. Stunned at the lack of empathy from Éamon, he glared perplexed at him. Instead of the easy-going friend, here stood the ruthless taskmaster who first trained him all those centuries ago. He staggered as memories overtook his mind.

Anton collapsed to his knees, blood dripping from his nose. His opponent had not laid a hand on him, yet he ached as though he'd received a brutal beating. He forced his gaze up from the dusty ground and squinted in the late afternoon sun. Even in the dim silhouette, he felt the disappointed stare from his mentor.

"Your enemies will use every weapon in their arsenal to defeat you. The deadliest is the one we do not see."

Anton hung his heavy head and crawled again to his feet. He had lost track of how many hours they trained today, as well as how many times he knocked the dust off his ass climbing back to standing. "So you keep reminding me, tovarysh. But how can I see what I cannot see?"

An exasperated growl and a sharp cuff to the back of his head served as a temporary answer. "By opening your mind, idiot. You trust far too easily. You see good in all who surround you. It will be your undoing."

Taking a page from an earlier lesson, Anton whipped his leg about and swept the feet out from under the hulking man. Sidestepping quickly, he avoided his falling friend and lifted his tired arms in a loose guard.

"Then why did you recruit me?" he roared, frustration clouding his judgment. "I stood before those steps, staring into the face of God, and you sought me out! Why?"

He didn't register the movement but something slammed into his chest and he was again staring at the sky. Defeated and drained, he chose to stay grounded.

"Because you believe, my friend." Éamon knelt beside him, a comforting hand resting gently on his shoulder. "You fight when needed and only for what you believe is right."

Calm cut through his anger and eased his weary body. He inhaled past the catch in his side, his ribs mending with each breath.

"I am confused. I believe in people and the promise of peace, but that is also my downfall?"

"No." The single word whispered through his mind. "It is not your belief in the good of humanity. It is your inability to believe in man's evil."

"I have seen evil. I have participated in war, not war fought against a stronger foe, but decimation of a weaker opponent for the sake of power." He closed his eyes, hiding from the stark truth of his own actions.

"You ordered your men to protect your homeland." A pair of strong hands guided him to a seated position. "Nothing you have ever done was motivated by greed, or lust, or pride. Your heart is pure."

The pause drew Anton's attention. "But?"

Éamon sighed, shaking his head. "But I fear your innocence may be your undoing."

Anton stood squarely before his mentor, the timely lesson fading back into remembrance. Since that long-ago lecture, he'd fought to keep his eyes open and his actions honest. He walked the path of the Guardian Warrior and battled against the darkness in the hearts of his enemies. He did not interfere; he guided humanity, steering them to be their best selves. He lived in the light of truth and honor. Never once had he faltered. He had made love to thousands of women, yet none held a candle to the untamed and wild beauty of his Danika.

"This has nothing to do with my innocence. Why don't you trust her?"

"Why do you?" Éamon's response shot like a bullet, aimed straight for his heart. "You yourself said you know almost nothing about her."

"I...I just do. I can't explain why I trust her. You didn't see her standing up to that French fucker. In my gut, I know she's—"

"That's not your gut talking, boyo."

Anton growled and his hand throbbed. It took a couple seconds to realize he'd decked Éamon. Releasing his clenched fist, he paced away from his friend and shook out his aching fingers. What was wrong with him? Shoot first and ask questions later was not his style. He was patient, studying all possible outcomes before he made the first move. Methodical to a fault, he strategized and weighed his options.

Then what was it about Danika that had him throw caution to the wind? Éamon was right about one factor; it was more than his gut talking. Each time he thought her name or pictured her behind his closed lids, a good portion of his blood took a slight southerly detour. With his eyes squeezed shut, he couldn't stop the desire from rising.

"She is different, *tovarysh*."

"That's what I'm afraid of, *dearthair*." Éamon wiped the lingering crimson off his lower lip, stroking his jaw. A sad light flared in his peacock blue eyes, and it chilled Anton to the bone. "I do hope she is your match, I honestly do. She's got you thinking all the right things and you deserve the love of a good woman. But I don't want to be the one to say 'I told you so' when she destroys you."

Words failed him as he stared at his former teacher. *Please, God. Tell me I am not wrong about her.*

NINETEEN

Boris sipped snobbishly on his average vodka tonic as he eyed the blue-collar crowd. Raucous conversations fought for supremacy against the volumes of the various sporting games on the myriad of flat screens. The scents of cheap bar food, sweat, and bargain basement perfume blended into a stomach-churning miasma.

An overly perky blonde tapped his shoulder and wiggled her fingers, as well as her ample assets, in greeting. Shifting his sneer into an acceptable smile, he shook his head. When she stuck out her bottom lip in an immature pout, he rolled his eyes and lifted his glass. The ice cubes served as a decent screen and with little effort, he twisted her suggestive offer. Her mind was so vacuous and self-absorbed, it was child's play to warp her simple thoughts.

Her painted-on grin fell and she hurriedly excused herself, racing toward the bathroom in tears. He chuckled darkly. Sure, the young girl's mother had been ill, but planting the added guilt over deserting the elderly woman during her hour of need definitely sweetened the pot.

Once again alone, he returned to his survey of the faces. In his brief contact with the female in question, he gathered this was her hangout of choice. She was Irish and this was an Irish bar. The connection was obvious. Yet this would be the second night without a sign. For the opportunity to coerce Anton's intended, he would spend every waking hour in this dive, but only if it was the correct venue. Perhaps he guessed wrong.

He glanced down at his watch, contemplating calling it a night, when the object of his attentions walked through the front doors. Black hair with bold blue streaks moved with purpose through the thick crowd. The rest of the patrons might discount her baggy clothing, but he knew the lope of a predator when he saw it. Barely tempered rage oozed off Danika in delicious waves as she shouldered her way to the bar. She wore her pain and anger like a coat, her gaze darting around the room as if she were measuring up her next opponent. She tipped her chin toward the bartender and slapped down cash in front of her.

Boris licked his lips in hungered anticipation. She was a prime contestant for his team. Jaded, no stranger to violence, and willing to get her hands dirty. She would indeed make a formidable Rogue.

Now to see how far the dreamer got with her.

A shot glass filled to the brim with thick amber liquor arrived before her just as he sidled up next to her.

"How fortuitous," he crooned.

She reached for the drink and tossed it down in one swallow, motioning for another.

"I had hoped we would meet again."

She stared into nothingness as she waited for the next round. "Bully for you."

He smiled and took the vacant seat beside her. "It looks like you are trying to forget something. Mind if I join you?"

She downed the shot as easily as the previous one. "It's a free country," she grumbled.

"How strange to use that phrase." He paused, hoping his comment drew her attention away from her thoughts. Success was achieved and she pinned him with a bland stare. "A free country. Freedom is what this land is built on, even if it is only an illusion."

"We gonna have a political or philosophical debate? 'Cuz, honestly, pal, ain't in the mood for either." She turned her gaze back to the refill and sighed, extending her hand.

Boris intercepted her reach. "Perhaps we can find something you are in the mood for?"

The contact was brief yet powerful. Through her eyes, he glimpsed a battered room, a sleeping child, and fear of retribution. Anguish gripped her heart as she sneaked out the fire escape. Traces of Anton's attempts at seduction stirred within her, yet she banished the promise of love and opted to survive in purgatory.

She slipped her fingers out from under his hand and snatched the beckoning drink.

Armed with dangerous knowledge, he feigned manners, if only to set the pieces in motion. "I am sorry. I did not mean to startle you."

She lifted one shoulder and took a slow sip. "No harm, no foul." The glass touched her lips again and she paused. She shifted her gaze toward him, a beautiful sadness buried deep in her brown eyes. "Look. Why not find a more willing partner? I'm never good company."

"On the contrary, I find your company quite intriguing."

She blinked deliberately and her bored expression returned.

He laughed, the sound grating and fake to his ears, but he needed to detain her for a little longer. Focusing on the distance, he honed in on the exact building and apartment. The drunk inside was easy to find and even easier to coax into a violent rage. If he could keep her occupied for a few more minutes, the deal would be sealed with the sweetest prize: vengeance.

Something odd flashed across her face and she took to her feet, slamming back the last of her drink. "Uh, I gotta go."

He frowned. Could she have intercepted his intentions? *Was she a Latent Conduit, like me?*

"Wait." He grabbed a pen near the cash register and took her hand in his. Smiling slyly, he turned her wrist and exposed her open palm. "Here is my number. Please call me should you wish to have another philosophical discussion on the merits of freedom." He wrote slowly and with deliberate care, temporarily tattooing her palm with the numbers of the current burner phone in his pocket.

He added his name as an afterthought before releasing her. "Call anytime. I don't sleep much."

A furtive frown creased her forehead and she nodded, mumbling some half-polite response before dashing out.

Boris smirked and finished the weak dredges of his cocktail. He dropped a bill large enough to cover his drink, plus those of half the bar, and whistled an ancient lullaby as he stepped into the night.

Guess good things do come to those willing to wait.

DANIKA FLIPPED up the collar on her jacket as another cold breeze kicked up. She had only intended on a quick stop at the pub to straighten her thoughts, and for her, three drinks was a short night. She froze, fear stealing the heat from her blood.

Was she turning into her uncle? The rage, the alcohol, the fighting.

Her stomach churned as the possibility spun in her mind. She forced her legs to continue toward home, still sifting through the ever-growing pile of evidence. Panic numbed her fingers as she searched in her pocket for a smoke.

She only fought when she was sober and used alcohol to calm her anger.

Liar.

She never drank to excess.

Liar.

She raged at the world because she was trying to protect Liam from the horrors of it all.

Liar.

"Stop it!" she screamed, covering her ears. Her lighter clattered on the asphalt, her pack ending up in a melted snowdrift by the curb. But there was nowhere to run from the voice inside her head. For each rational explanation she formulated, the dark part of her called her on it.

If you're such a good girl, why didn't you stay with Anton? It whispered.

"Because he deserves better," she muttered under her breath, fishing her keys out of her pocket. That silenced her alter ego. Plodding up five flights with only her inner bitch as company was a long and uncomfortable walk. The closer she got to her apartment, the greater the dread in her gut. Panic amped up her steps and she hit the barrier at a dead run.

Trembling, she fumbled with her jangling keys. The right one finally slid into place, and she yanked the door open.

She blinked rapidly, attempting to make sense of the surreal scene. Splintered wood littered the hall and fist-shaped holes decorated the walls. Nothing new there, but the fresh deep crimson splatters sprinkling the scene froze her blood. Liam. A dark emptiness swallowed her when she found his bruised and battered body sprawled on the floor.

"No no no no no no no..."

A gentle shake on her shoulder dragged her out of her hellish reverie. She focused on the moving mouth of the bald doctor standing in front of her. In the sterile white and chrome room, pointless words fell from his thin lips, while soft smiles and patient nods accompanying some of the practiced phrases. His hand remained, apparently giving some sort of compassionate advice, and her gaze swung back to the pinging machines surrounding her tiny nephew. Bandages wrapped around his head, masking his wild blond spikes. Concealed were his bright green eyes, hidden by the swollen lids. Purplish fist-shaped bruises and angry cuts decorated his cheeks. One cast reached from wrist to shoulder while another peeked out from beneath the blanket at the foot of the bed.

A pair of rubbered soles squeaked into the distance and once again, she was alone with the only family member she cared about. Trapped in her own dark thoughts, anger rose and the desire to destroy the world blinded her. A distant, sensual voice warned of caution and restraint, but she was beyond reasoning.

Retribution.

Revenge.

Those were the driving forces in her mind.

A strange sting tickled the center of her left palm. She stared at the black squiggles until they became legible numbers. Numbly, she reached for the white phone next to the bed and dialed.

Alarms shrieked and screamed in her head, begging her to stop and hang up. Two rings passed and the noise grew so loud, she nearly missed the questioning voice on the other end of the line. What would she say? Should she hang up before it was too late?

The rhythmic mechanical beeps surrounding her and pinging off the sterile walls sliced through her indecision.

"Meet me at Donovan's." She blurted out the short phrase and hung up before whoever answered had a chance to respond. The beating of her own heart kept pace with the machinery.

Her fault. This was all her fault.

Guilt crept up her spine and sat smugly on her shoulder. Maybe she couldn't take back what had happened, but she sure as hell was going to make sure it never happened again. She leaned down and placed a tender kiss on an unwrapped bit of forehead.

"Rest easy, peanut. I've got this."

Without looking back, she headed out into the night.

TWENTY

Anton paced in ever tightening circles, his massive kitchen no match for his frantic thoughts. Why couldn't he get a hold of Danika?

After their earlier disagreement, he and Éamon settled into a tentative calm. Perhaps the beers did aid in the peace process, not to mention the hot and fresh quattro stagioni pizza from Antico Forno. Yet through their amiable and superficial chatter, he kept one ear to the whispering Void. One of the perks of being a Conduit was the ability to eavesdrop on the entire world. The comic book writers were not too far off when they created Professor Xavier and his telepathic device, Cerebro. The skill to be in everyone's head at the same time had paid off on numerous occasions.

Except this one. Each time he searched for Danika, she was able to shield herself from his questing mind. He attributed her thick walls to her violent living environment, but now he was beginning to think it might be something more. Something learned from a teacher he shuddered to even consider.

He had been sitting on the edges of her awareness, a silent presence just beyond her consciousness. From his vantage point, he could only glean broad emotions from her. Anger, hurt, confusion, and defeat jumbled and tumbled around, each one seeking dominance from moment to moment. Brief glimpses of happiness tempered with regret flashed into her mind when she thought of her nephew.

He gained a modicum of satisfaction from the conflicting emotions when her thoughts turned toward him. Desire and passion sadly blended with dismal resignation and his heart ached.

Then nothing. As if a giant door had slammed shut, she simply vanished from his senses.

"Why not just call her? You do have her phone number, right?"

He bit down, holding his tongue behind his teeth while he came up with a less snarky response. "As far as I can tell, she didn't have one. There was no landline in the house, nor did she seem to have the means to pay for a mobile."

His circuit widened, and for some inexplicable reason, he ended up in the living room, staring out the picture window onto an empty street. She could be anywhere between there and the rest of the city, for all he knew. "I do know where she lives and—"

"You planning on stalking her house?"

"NO!" Anton slammed his fist against the wall, his anger so powerful the entire room shook. The fragile centerpiece on a nearby end table jumped in fright and teetered precariously on spindly legs. If the ancient glass sculpture did not have such sentimental value, he would have let it shatter. Instead, he scrambled to catch the blue and green figurine before his rage destroyed another valuable item.

Deflated, he slumped into the nearby chair. "Éamon, she is my spiritmate. I cannot let her fall into darkness."

Éamon sighed heavily and joined him in the living room, bringing up the points he had made only hours earlier. "Anton, you need to think this through. You yourself felt her rage. She is a prime target for the Rogue recruiters. Her life, the hatred of those surrounding her, all the violence. It's shaped her into the perfect agent of chaos. There is no remorse in her actions and—"

"But you haven't seen her with her nephew." He sat up and leaned forward, resting his elbows on his knees. "When Liam is around, she's patient and kind. He is her anchor into the world. She fights to protect him. She has suffered to keep his innocence. I just know it."

Compassion gave him strength and he held his ground. Éamon's penetrating stare threatened to burn straight through him, but he refused to give up his faith in her. As knowledgeable as his friend was, Éamon wasn't the one who'd walked through her mind.

Anton alone had seen the horrors she faced. He knew the degradations and tortures she suffered to keep her nephew innocent.

Was she beyond redemption?

"Everyone deserves the chance to choose the path their own life takes."

Éamon groaned, pinching the bridge of his nose as he shook his head. "I hate when you use my sage advice against me. You do know that, right?"

"I would say I'm sorry, but too much is at stake. I need to find her. Please, I need your help."

Anton stared at the top of Éamon's head, locked in silent prayer while his mentor weighed his request. All of his own skills came up with zero. He didn't even know if she was still alive. His stomach clenched in fear as he shoved that possibility far from his mind.

A resigned sigh gave Anton much-needed hope. Éamon lifted his gaze, pinning him with a cautious glare. "No shooting the messenger if you don't like where this leads."

Anton smiled, relieved. He clasped his mentor on the shoulder and took to his feet. "I make no such promise, *tovarysh*, but I will try." He sent the exact location of Danika's building to Éamon's mind and headed for the door. He needed to be ready to fly out as soon as Éamon found her.

The seconds ticked by in an uncharacteristic snail's pace. Anton frowned, confused by the lengthening silence and fear began to grow.

"Uhhh...where did you say she lived?" Éamon's eyes remained closed. Not good.

His heart sank as he rattled off the address again. Ice thickened his blood and he dragged his damp palms down the leg of his denims.

"There's a lot of activity there. Police. Fire. Ambulances. It's hard to pinpoint just one person in the noise. But none are female. That trail goes off in a completely different direction."

Anton swallowed hard, forcing down the rising panic. "Can you give me a general guess?"

Creases appeared and disappeared across Éamon's forehead as he peered deeper into the Black. "Shot in the dark? Head toward Boston Medical. But I want..."

Anton didn't hear anything after the announcement of a hospital. He threw open the door and *moved* across the miles, stopping only once he reached the shadowed alley looking out onto the main entrance. He took one step out of the darkness and smacked into a swirling mass of fragmented emotions wrapped in a package his body immediately recognized. Before she could escape, he tightened his hold on her arms.

"Danika? *Koxána?* What happened?"

Self-hatred, internalized blame, and thick waves of uncontrolled vengeance rolled off her. He cupped her cheeks in his hands and pressed his forehead against hers. She struggled and kicked, her attacks unfocused and lacking power. She flattened her palms against his chest, refusing his comfort.

Daring the possible consequences, he pressed his forehead against hers and delved into her troubled mind. Images of Liam lying in a large hospital bed stole his breath, the sight of him cocooned and hooked to machines like a punch to the gut.

<Éamon. Boston Medical pediatric ICU. Hurry, please. His name is Liam.>

He needed no reply; if a child was involved, Éamon would move heaven and earth to get there. Knowing the boy was in safe hands, he turned his attention back to his beautiful warrior. He navigated through the chaos of her thoughts, sifting through her rage and despair as he desperately searched for her true spirit. A shadow in the shape of Danika stood just out of reach. Cautiously, he slowly approached the hunched figure.

<*Danika, moja ljubov.*> He poured all the love in his heart into the tender words. <*My love, I am here, with you now. Please, come back to me.*> Instead of his strong and fierce warrior, a dark beast spun around, affixing him with a lethal stare. Her brown eyes burned with an amber glow, and her flowing silken hair whipped around with the fury of a hurricane.

<*For what? To continue to be a chew toy for life? To sit idly by as the only person in my family I care about is destroyed?*>

Dark fire licked at his heels, trying to force him to give ground. But he knew the tricks of his enemy too well. Standing tall, he peeled away the layers of loathing. With tender patience and care, he dismissed each new furious rage that rose up. He waded through her frantic blockade, never losing sight of the glimmer of love he knew was there.

<*No, my beautiful warrior. I ask you to come back to me and be my spiritmate. My beloved one.*>

The angry visage shimmered. He pushed on.

<*I know who you are, and I know why you have touched me as no other ever has. Nor ever shall. You alone call to my soul.*> Behind the waning façade, he glimpsed a fragment of her true self. Tears coursed down her cheek, but the darkness was determined. So was he, and this was not a battle he was willing to lose.

<*She chose to follow the path of revenge. That makes her mine.*>

The whispered voice was faint, yet somehow familiar, as though the speaker called to him from a time long ago. Anton was so close, the walls of anguish crumbling away as he continued to approach. He would think on the voice later, once she was out of harm's way. At the gates of her heart, he placed a hand against the weakening veil separating him from his love.

<*No. She belongs to no one but herself. She lives by her rules and will not be tamed.*>

He strode past the final barrier, confident and sure. There she stood, trembling as she cowered, hidden behind the veil of her hands. A proud smile touched his lips as he wrapped his arms around her. He placed his knuckles under her chin and guided her eyes toward his. No matter how tight the stranglehold of the Void, Anton saw through the lies, seeking the spark of truth and hope deep within her chocolate eyes.

<She is stronger than you can comprehend. Love drives her actions, not hatred. Beyond that, she is my heart. My love. My Danika.>

With his unwavering pledge, he pressed his lips to hers and the remaining darkness vanished. Once again in the world of the real, he cradled her close to him as she sobbed. He kissed the top of her head, savoring the brush of her soft hair against his skin.

"I've got you, koxána. I've got you."

He repeated the tender phrase as he led her toward the secluded alley. He held her tight and returned to his house, careful to ensure that no humans saw his mysterious passing.

TWENTY-ONE

ÉAMON RESTED his elbows on his knees, pensive as he sat on the uncomfortable stool and watched over the sleeping child. Anton had only given him a name, one which he recalled hearing before. His friend made mention of a Liam when defending his lady love. He expected to hit the hospital and find the standard sick kid routine.

He was not prepared to see such a horrific degree of savage brutality inflicted on an innocent. Bruises and blood-stained bandages covered most of the visible boy, while oxygen wheezed in and out through a tube. As much as he wanted to jump to the obvious conclusion, and justify his opinion of Anton's current obsession, he reserved judgment until all the facts were in. He reminded himself that his side viewed the world with open eyes. That meant him, too.

Taking a deep centering breath, he dragged the swiveling seat the scant distance between the wall and the bed. He settled in beside the pinging machinery and laid his palm across the young boy's forehead.

Fists slammed into the frail body, his attacker much larger and definitely male. The stench of stale alcohol polluted the air, and slurred curses rang through his ears. Rage directed toward everything and nothing found a lethal focus, and tiny arms offered little protection

against the onslaught of hate. Words the child's mind could not deci-
pher were shouted at no one in particular.

"Fucking cunt! Think she owns the damned place?" In the
distance, a bottle shattered and a sharp sting raced down his cheek.
"Well, she ain't here to protect you now, boy."

Blow after blow rained down while obscenities filled the ensuing
void. A loud snap echoed in the night, and he collapsed onto the floor.
Terrified, the child clawed feebly at the ground, frantic to crawl away
from the violence, his leg shattered and useless.

"Why, Papa? Why?"

He cried until his throat was raw. A giant boot collided with his
head and darkness offered a place to hide.

Éamon blinked rapidly and slipped back into his body.

"Goddammit." He choked out the harsh words, dashing the back
of his hand across his leaking eyes. Looked like he was going to be
eating crow for dinner tonight.

"Can I help you?"

He took to his feet, brushing off his leathers, and prepared his
speech before leaving with the boy.

"No. I was just coming to see..." Éamon turned and froze, words
drying up as he stared into a face from the distant past. "What the
fuck are you doing here?"

The man in the white lab coat blinked, perplexed. He adjusted
his glasses and tucked his hands into the large front pockets. "I am
this boy's attending—"

Éamon waved off the rest of the impending lie, and the thin veil
of the In-Between the man was using as a mask shimmered. "Bullshit,
Krishenko. Don't bother hiding. I know what you are. What are you
doing here?"

The mousy, bland face melted away with a sickening smile. "I
don't think we've met, so I would be ever so curious to know how you
recognized me." He slipped off the glasses, shedding the remaining
fakery and leaned his hip into the wall.

Éamon folded his arms across his chest, his senses on high alert for any more surprise visitors. "Because I can smell your kind from a mile away." He narrowed his eyes, burying the dread growing in the pit of his stomach. "You're the one who keeps running interference on Anton."

Boris bowed, accepting the honor with egotistical flair. "Guilty as charged. Which begs the question once again, who are you and why should you care?"

"I am the one who will stop you. That is all you need to know." Unsure of how much his asshole brother, Cabal, told his Rogue soldiers about their opposition, he erred on the side of caution and stayed anonymous. His feelers detected no other enemy in the vicinity, but he refused to lower his guard.

Boris' smug smirk faltered, losing a fraction of its evil intent. "I find that ha—" His blue eyes flew wide and soon, his face took on a matching hue.

Éamon smirked as his stunned companion clawed at his throat, prying at invisible fingers. With a patronizing shake of his head, he tsked, unlocking his arms, and crossed to the bed separating them. "Oh, I don't care what it is you're believing." Once again in control of the situation, his lilt returned in earnest, as did his easy smile. He leaned over and tenderly scooped the young boy into his arms.

Disconnecting the wires and tubes was simple, done with barely a thought. The child stirred fitfully, pain threatening to awaken him mid-rescue.

"Shh. *Codladh, éinín.*"

Éamon purposefully ignored the gasps and wheezes from the staggering man to his left. He hummed soft lullabies, swaying and bouncing his steps toward the room's only door. At the threshold, he paused, listening for the heavy thump behind him. The clattering of a tray as it was yanked to the linoleum under his feet verified success.

"Be sure to tell your boss some rules are not meant to be broken," he added, directing the words over his shoulder. "And I will unleash hell on those who harm the innocent."

An agonized grunt was all the response he needed. Pleased with himself, Éamon grinned and whistled happily as he strolled out.

TWENTY-TWO

The world took a dizzying turn, and if Danika really gave two shits, she would have looked up. But the iron barrier of her mental threshold had been decimated and there was no stopping the rush of her tears. Each time she pictured Liam in that damned humongous hospital bed, she almost lost it in the dark behind her closed lids. Only a gentle voice calling through her rage calmed her frantic thoughts. It whispered of loving acceptance and refused to let her fall into the pit of despair.

A tiny part of her wished she could tell that voice to go suck an egg, but the vast majority of her psyche was not interested. Duct tape was used, and that tough bitch got tossed in the closest closet. For the first time in her life, Danika just wanted to be a girl and be held by a big strong man who told her she was worth a damn.

The sirens and car horns mysteriously fell silent, replaced by a soothing nothingness. Between sobs, she caught the subtle hint of earthy scents and spices overriding the familiar aroma of diesel and burning rubber. Even the ground under her feet shifted from concrete to cushioned.

Too bad she hadn't been paying attention. She might have even been impressed, but her reality consisted of the two strong arms around her shoulders and the steadily beating heart beneath her ear. Other parts began to pique her interest as well, desire stirring in a long-forgotten corner of her soul. However, fear continued to stand in the way, a looming wall of self-doubt blocking her path to love.

"You're safe now, *koxána*. There is no reason to fear."

Anton's delicious and exotic voice flowed down her back, each word stroking her skin. Had she gotten naked and not realized it?

Hell, at this rate, anything was possible. A warm chuckle rumbled in his chest, thrumming against her cheek and his arms tightened around her. He pressed his hand in a broad circle up and down her back, and she felt the distinctive scratch of her threadbare shirt.

The dream was too nice to disturb, and she opted to keep her lids sealed shut. "Where are we?"

"You can open your eyes. I promise I'm not going anywhere." His warm breath tickled her neck as he whispered in her ear. "We're in my home."

Confused and incredibly curious, she willed her eyelid to peel back. Sure enough, she stood in the one place she never thought she would see again. She had only seen the living room and the hall, but she recognized the architecture and knew it to be true. She swiveled her gaze in every direction, in awe. Somehow, without ever getting into a car, she was now physically in an impossible place halfway across town.

Rubbing the back of her hand across her eyes, she wiped away the remnants of her breakdown and struggled to put the pieces together.

"But, but how?" As much as she was interested to go exploring, that would mean stepping out of his embrace. She turned her face up to Anton. Speechless, her jaw dropped and words locked in her throat. Powerfully tender and tempting emotions lit his unfathomable sea green eyes and she would happily drown.

She caught fragments of a half-remembered conversation, phrases drifting around in the maelstrom of her thoughts. Falling in the dark of her soul, she swore she heard him calling to her. He spoke of things like love and forever, things more dangerous than the hatred of her normal life. And they terrified her. She feared the weakness such soft emotions would bring. If she cared for something, it could become a weapon against her.

But not Anton. He was the weapon, prepared to fight off any predators; a pure alpha male with arms like steel. When she looked at him, weakness wasn't the word jumping into her mind. He was strength, unabashed and unashamed. He was her Superman, fending off the demons in the shadows and protecting her with all his heart.

Her arms trembled, the urge to wrap herself around him unlike anything she had ever experienced. What would it be like to hold someone, to be cherished?

In a word, heaven.

The selfish thought barely took root when another truth slammed hard into her.

Liam.

As if he read her mind, Anton released his hold on her, sliding his hands down the length of her arms. His smile never wavered as he laced his fingers through hers.

"Come. There is much I need to tell you." He glided backward, encouraging her rubbery legs to follow suit. Her steps, wooden and clunky, shuffled along the hall until they reached the room she had so rudely yanked Liam out of just the other night. She huffed and swallowed shallow gasps of air to stay conscious as they stood before the semi-closed door.

"But first..." He disentangled one hand and knocked softly. "I think there's something you'd want to see."

A muffled reply from behind the barrier gave needed permission and he reached for the doorknob.

Danika wasn't sure what she would find as Anton moved aside, but nothing could prepare her for the sight of her nephew, tucked beneath the covers. No machines beeped around him, and missing were the bandages and casts that had held him together only moments ago. Her breathing ratcheted higher and the threat of passing out seemed a definite possibility.

Only the steadying hands on her shoulders kept her upright. She blinked repeatedly, thinking to dismiss the vision and praying for things to remain at the same time. When she refocused her eyes, the happy image did not change. Next to the bed sat Éamon, the big, leather-clad warrior looking somewhat out of place as he read softly. She recognized the cover as one of Liam's favorites, but she had no idea how it managed to make its way into Anton's house.

"I figured you'd want to know he was okay." The press of his cheek against her ear warmed her soul and she trembled under the weight of his compassion.

"How is this possible?" Her harsh whisper barely broke the serene scene, and her brain scrambled to dissect the information her eyes were feeding it. Éamon raised his head, an oddly sad smile on his firm lips as he continued to read. He nodded in silent response, the gesture conveying an apology she never expected.

"Because magic *is* real." The delicious accent at her back coupled with his strange statement pulled her out of her stupor, and she glanced over her shoulder. His smile was honest, betraying no cruel humor. Light and hope shimmered in his pure green eyes, and she turned to face him.

"As I said, I have much to tell you."

TWENTY-THREE

Anton waited with patience honed from years of endless campaigns. Yet this battle far outweighed any skirmish in his past. His beautiful warrior deserved the truth, and she deserved to hear it from him directly. No more vague references and superficial answers. Love required trust, and if he was to be worthy of the heart of the strong, but scared female standing before him, he needed to prove it.

<Tend to her, brother. I'm not going anywhere. We can all talk later.>

He glanced at Éamon and tipped his chin. He sensed the moment his friend had arrived with the child's broken body, anger and remorse thrumming through the walls. His powerful friend made short work of healing the boy's injuries, and Anton was confident that the memory of the incident was most likely erased as well.

Now for the more difficult job.

With a tender smile, he captured her confused gaze and placed a soft kiss on her forehead. The chaste touch fired his blood and he breathed deep, drawing her wild scent into his soul. She squeezed his fingers and he stilled. Yet as he attempted to release her hand, her grip tightened and refused to let go.

Elated beyond words, he guided her toward the stairs leading to his room. He kept his gaze on her as his body backtracked on its familiar route. Even if he was unable to begin the Claiming Ritual tonight, he wanted her to be close to his side. He needed her to believe she could trust him and that he would be there for her. She followed his lead, her gaze darting around. He recalled their initial meeting and her innate survival skills; the wall at her back with an eye on the quickest escape route. Words would not work in this moment. He could tell her she was safe until he was blue in the face. Only his actions would speak the truth of his intentions.

After his dive into her psyche, he retained the link, a trail no wider than a cat's whisker. The sliver connected her innermost thoughts to his, vibrating with cautious curiosity as they moved closer to the master bedroom. Fear trembled along the fragile thread, but it didn't deter her from finishing her path.

His brave, beautiful warrior.

His heart swelled with pride and he sent a thankful prayer to the heavens. God truly did exist and now, it was his happy obligation to prove it to her. A smile touched his lips, looking forward to the upcoming opportunity to be completely alone with her.

He pushed open the door and stood back, allowing her to decide to walk through. He kept a gentlemanly distance while he listened in to her swirling thoughts. Her ideas ranged from flying back down the steps, hiding in the massive bathroom they just passed, or his favorite, pinning him against the nearest wall and screwing him until neither of them could walk right.

A certain part of his anatomy also enjoyed that option, his cock pressing painfully against his zipper.

"This is my room. But if you would prefer another room, there are several from which you may choose. I...I would only ask that..." Once again, words failed him. With his free hand, he brushed the back of his knuckles along her jaw. "I'm sorry, koxána. I'm usually much better at speaking. I don't want to scare you, but I would feel better if you would stay with me tonight."

Her cheek warmed under his skin and her chocolate brown eyes darkened. Holding his gaze, she lifted her hand and rested her fingertips gently on his palm. The need to feel more than her hesitant touch slammed through him. Fire, powerful and inescapable, coursed in his veins and he prayed with all his soul she felt the same.

"Can I, I mean, um, are you...why..." Her stuttered response disarmed him and he was helpless. He closed the scant distance between them and peered deep into her wide eyes.

"I will give you all you ever desire. Love, tenderness, safety for you and your nephew for as long as you wish. Even answers."

Entranced, he tore his gaze away from her parting lips.

"I will never take more than you are willing to give. I ask only for your consent."

Her chin quivered and tears pooled in her nut-brown eyes. "Why? No one's ever cared about that before."

With the pads of his thumbs, he wiped away the threatening drops clinging to her lashes. "Because there must be only honesty between a Guardian and his beloved, his spiritmate."

He pressed his lips to hers, drinking in her silent sobs. He breathed in her pain and doubt, locking it up inside of him and returned to her peace and understanding. Her lips parted, inviting him and he gratefully accepted. He swept his tongue along the warm confines of her mouth, her wild fragrance overshadowed by the lingering oily dark.

Patient and thorough, he delved into each corner until he banished the smoky aftertaste. He slipped his fingers through her loose hair, the silky strands tickling his rough palm. Tilting her head, he left her lips and nipped along her jaw, burying his nose in the hollow behind her ear. Her heavy groan encouraged him, but only words would give him the final answer.

"G-g-guardian?"

He teased the delicate shell, tracing its curve with butterfly kisses. "It is what I am, *koxána*. I am Antonius Mykola Yurchenko, Boyar under Prince Yaroslav the Wise." He pulled back and gazed at her flushed cheek. Her eyes fluttered behind her drooped lids, her kiss-swollen lips trembling as she dragged in shallow gulps of air. Bending down, he hooked one arm under her knees and scooped her up, cradling her against his chest.

Without missing a beat, she grabbed onto his neck, clinging tight to his sweater. Hypnotized, he stared at the rapid jump of her pulse just beneath the surface of her ivory skin. "I was born in the Year of Our Lord one thousand and ten."

She tensed in his embrace and raised passion-darkened eyes up at him, wide in disbelief.

"And I have waited a hundred lifetimes to find you."

"But why? I...I'm...broken."

He strode inside, treading his booted feet against the ecru carpet, smooth and deliberate. He held her gaze as he lowered her onto the massive dark walnut sleigh bed. As in his dream, her black hair spread out like a silk canopy across the deep forest comforter.

"Then I hope you will let me make you whole."

She ducked her head quickly, but he caught the glimmer of one silvery tear. Bending close, he trailed his lips along the damp path. A heavy sigh escaped her, her body arching off the bed. His rough sweater scratched at his chest, but he had to suffer the itchy wool until she responded. The tentative press of her breasts against him did seem a point in his favor. As did the firm grip of her fingers on his bicep.

Cautious, he studied her grasp, determining if it was a panicked push or a positive pull. Everything hinged on the next few moments and his body was eager should she accept his offer. When she released his arm and dug her fingers into his hair, dragging him closer, he nearly wept in joyful glee.

"Is that a yes?" He nuzzled her ear, his voice breathy and soft.

"I still think you're crazy," she groaned, needy.

He chuckled wickedly and she shuddered beneath him. "That may very well be true." Nipping along her jaw, he delighted in the stolen peace. "Definitely crazy about you."

The bed vibrated, and he lifted his head to discover the cause of the tremor. To his surprise, she hid under the shield of her arm as she laughed. The throaty mirth kicked his libido into overdrive. Joining in, he rolled onto his back, carrying her to straddle his raging erection.

"Dear God, Danika. You have the most beautiful smile." A sexy blush painted her skin, and she rested her palms flat on his chest. He held onto her hips and gazed up. The spark he glimpsed in a fleeting moment now shone brighter than the sun. "You should smile more often."

She swallowed, his gaze fixating on the flexing of her delicate neck. "Haven't had much reason to do it."

He reached up and cupped her flushed cheek. "Maybe it's time for a change, *koxána*."

She captured his hand, holding his calloused palm against her silken skin. "Please tell me I'm not dreaming all this, Anton. I...I don't think I can take it if this isn't real."

"Say it again." He breathed the request, grinding his hardened cock against her cocooned core.

His name. The corners of his lips curled up, his heart soaring at the simple word.

An adorable frown tugged her eyebrows together for only a moment before melting into another disarming smile.

"Anton?"

He growled hungrily. "Again."

Her eyes darkened, passion churning her deep brown eyes. "Anton."

He levered himself off the bed, and she leaned down to meet him in a tender kiss. Her touch was timid, much different than the frantic attack of their first embrace. He softened his lips and dropped his jaw, inviting her to explore. Allowing her time and freedom, he folded his legs in, providing a more stable seat for her. It did not stop him from wrapping his arms around her. He snaked one hand down to rest on the curve of her ass as the other cupped the back of her head. Her thick hair flowed like water between his fingers. If he could stay in that moment, he would die a happy man.

Breathy moans poured out of her and he devoured each sound with fervor. He felt her hands slide across his ribs until they came to a stop just shy of his shoulders. Blood thundered through his ears and he broke away from her lips.

He vaguely remembered her query and his promise to tell her everything. As she rocked in his lap to gaze up at him, he bit down hard on his molars, suppressing a pained groan. Rational thought fled along with the majority of his blood supply, both streaking to the sweet spot where she rested on his straining zipper.

Her eyes flared wide. He guessed she felt the press of his groin against her thin jeans.

He grinned sheepishly. "I would apologize, but the thing has a mind of its own. And in this matter, we are both in complete agreement."

To say her responding smile was breathtaking would be an understatement. His heart stuttered the longer he gazed at her. One delectable corner of her mouth tilted up and a mischievous glint sparkled in her chocolate eyes. Missing was the angry, jaded girl, mad at the world, who'd stood with her back to him in the morning sun. In her place was his beautiful warrior, strong and fierce. He grazed his knuckles along her jaw, savoring her soft skin. Entwining his fingers through her midnight tresses, he thanked the heavens for this exquisite blessing.

Her lips parted and he shook his head. "I know, I have many more answers for you." He kissed away the furrow starting on her forehead. "And the first one is yes. I can read your mind."

The frown remained, tempered little by his admission. "How long have you been doing it?"

"For as long as I can truly remember. But for you, I only began to look when I found you outside the hospital. No," he added quickly, taking a gentle hold on her chin to keep her focused on the present. "Please. Stay in this moment with me."

He sweetened the deal, leaning in to press his cheek against hers. "We will worry about other things later, *koxána*. I promise."

"Do you always keep your word?" Her leery tone was a heavy weight on his soul. He squeezed his eyes shut, forcing back the remembered images from his walk through her mind. The men in her life had given her little reason to trust another, but he was determined to change her outlook.

He brushed his lips along the sculpted line of her jaw, savoring her heady and wild scent. "Only death could stop me from fulfilling my word to you."

She melted in his arms, the tension in her body fading into memory. "Oh."

He dragged his tongue down the column of her neck as his hands explored the breadth of her back.

"Will you stay? Here? With me?" God, he was so hard for her, he feared the metal teeth of his denims were going to leave a permanent zig-zag pattern on his cock.

"I...Yes," she sighed her timid reply.

Anton paused, his mouth an inch away from a nasty looking scar on her collarbone. With deliberate slowness, he lifted his gaze and found her eyes. Passion had devoured most of the nut-brown eyes. He sensed her lingering fear and apprehension, but he could not dismiss her steadfast strength.

He cradled her face and kissed her tenderly. "Thank you, Danika. I hope I prove myself worthy of your trust. But right now, I hope you don't mind if I rip your clothes off."

He felt the curl of her lips under his, the temperature of the room rising ever so slightly. "If you have something else for me to wear, it's all right by me."

Her playful response signaled a major change. His rumbling chuckle was her only warning and with a graceful twist, he laid her back onto the bed.

"*Koxána*, I would be perfectly happy for you to parade around naked at all times."

Her smile faltered. "You say that now but—"

He swallowed the rest of her personal dig, thrusting his tongue into the hot recesses of her mouth. He wanted to banish her doubt and to show her love. The shirt she wore slunk away from her waist-line, his hands greedily wadding the offending fabric. He broke the seal of their lips long enough to yank it over her head. With a quick tug, he added his sweater to the clothes discard pile and turned his gaze back to his beautiful warrior.

In the growing predawn glow, he stared in rapt awe at the truth of her life as she lay bare before him. The scar close to her throat that had intrigued him only moments ago was merely the tip of the iceberg. Thin welts, parallel scratches, and buckle shaped bruises marred her porcelain skin. Ample breasts, strapped down and contained by the worn-out scraps of spandex, begged to be released and he was more than happy to oblige.

He licked his lips, anticipating the feast laid out for him. So entranced by her powerful body, he failed to notice she had drawn her arms to cross her head, attempting to hide from his gaze.

Words would be meaningless in that moment, so he acted instead. He spied an especially ugly contusion on her ribs and leaned down. With a breath and a thought, he blew softly against the painful discoloration. He closed the scant distance and kissed the now flaw-less flesh.

"What are you doing?" By the hushed but clear tones, he could imagine her stunned expression. The dig of her nails on his shoulders also hinted at her surprise. He was too engrossed in the tantalizing texture of her skin, dragging his tongue toward another nasty mark, to lift his head from his current task. Instead, he chose to pour the answer directly onto her bare stomach.

"Keeping my promise."

TWENTY-FOUR

Danika nearly jack-knifed off the bed when he kissed her hideous scars. The mere fact he didn't vomit at the sight of her half naked was a true testament to his courage. Yet his unexpected and thorough treatment was mind-blowing to say the least. Every nerve ending fired and exploded, overloaded and hungry for more.

A tingling heat built at the junction of her thighs and she rolled her spine, desperate for some release. Her brain opted to sit this one out and let her body take the lead. It was still trying to make sense of his earlier information.

Guardian.

Hundreds of years old.

That might explain why he was so kickass with a sword. Not to mention how talented he was with his tongue. With each sweeping pass, the aches she had lived with for the whole of her life seemed to vanish. The pinch in her side from a crookedly healed spiral fractured rib eased, air flowing pain-free into her starving lungs. Her shoulder, her arms, her everything. As if someone with a magic eraser wiped away all evidence of her violent past.

But not a mysterious, nameless someone. Someone with soulful green eyes and an accent that turned her bones to jelly and her blood to lava.

She ground her ass against the softest bed she'd ever touched. Muscles flexed beneath her hands, solid and strong. Hungry for more, she relaxed her clenched fingers and trailed them down his sculpted back. Scars tickled her palms, the rough texture forming distinctive patterns and shapes. Straight lines from slashes, circles from gunshots. It was simple to determine the cause for each ripple she found, experience a cruel teacher.

A hungry growl, the recognizable sound of fabric tearing, and cool air kissed her breasts. She gasped and when his mouth sucked on her diamond hard nipple, she cried out. In her hidden hopes, she imagined sex as something beautiful. Two bodies, two hearts, two beings becoming one. Granted, her own experiences proved time and time again sex was nothing more than pain inflicted on a weaker victim. Her stomach knotted and churned as the vicious memories threatened to ruin this cherished moment.

<Stay with me, koxána. Stay in the now.>

His exotic voice banished the remembered screams and past agonies, bathing her in warmth. The words were poured straight into her head since his mouth was still working its magic on her bare skin. He nuzzled his stubbled cheek in the sensitive valley moving from one nipple to the other. She dug her short nails into his broad back. In the dark behind her closed lids, she reveled in the unfamiliar and intense sensations. Swallowing hard, she fought with her mind, forcing it to follow his direction.

Too bad fear had long since put a stranglehold on her dreams.

"I...I can't."

She squirmed under his weight, disgusted by her own weakness. The press of tears pricked at her scratchy eyes and she dragged her hands away from his tempting muscles. He lifted his head and met her gaze, raw concern mixed with feral hunger in his sea green eyes.

"Did I hurt you?"

His breathy words hit her like a fist. She scooted down, pinning herself willingly under him.

"No. No, you didn't, but..."

But what? *But I'm too far past fucked-up for saving. Why can't I just say that?*

He rolled off her, coming to rest on one elbow as he leaned against her side. The heat from his body disappeared, the cold morning air stealing away the much-needed warmth. Regret reared its ugly head as he caressed her cheek with the back of his knuckles.

"You *are* worth saving, *koxána*," he whispered, a devastating smile on his kissable lips.

She gaped, the brain-vocal connection lost in the heat of his gaze.

"Can I get a word in, or are you just gonna grab the thoughts from right out of my head?" In truth, she was terrified he was going to discover how weak and stupid she really was. And each time he stepped into her gray matter, the closer he was to finding it out. Clamping down on her molars, she shifted her eyes away from the gorgeous face hovering above her.

"Danika?"

She continued to stubbornly study an interesting crease in the covers. Her fight was pointless, more so because she honestly didn't want to win. His gentle touch along her chin coaxed her gaze away from nothingness.

"*Koxána?*"

She blinked away the tears that refused to disappear.

"You don't get it. I'm...Shit." She yanked her gaze away, unable to speak under the intensity of his searching eyes and shielded herself weakly with one arm. Maybe the answers she sought dwelled in the darkness. "To say that I have trust issues would be an understatement."

His lips pressed soft kisses along her exposed throat, the day-old stubble on his cheek driving her wild. The embers she thought had been doused by her own stupid self-incrimination sparked anew, heat creeping stealthy through her veins. She groaned sharply as he dragged his tongue across her racing pulse.

"And?"

The single word snapped her libido to an eleven. Her breasts grew heavy and ached for his touch once again. She dropped her arm as a shield and placed her hand on his broad shoulders. His back bowed, his rock-hard chest tickling her sensitive nipples.

Why was she even arguing? Logical reasoning was fading into the distance as desire gained momentum.

"And I don't know how to not be a disappointment to you."

There. She said it.

He stroked his rough hand along her ribs, the tips of his long fingers teasing the under curve of her breast. Her ensuing sigh was an embarrassing cross between a groan and a whine. She felt his lips curl into a smile as he nipped at her collarbone.

"My beautiful warrior, the only way you could ever disappoint me is by keeping silent. I am yours to command, Danika. Say the word and I will move heaven and earth to fulfill your wish."

The powerful conviction in his voice shook her to her core. She trembled and held on tight, whispering the scariest words she had ever uttered.

"Can... Can you show me what it feels like to...to have someone care?"

ANTON PAUSED MID-LICK, processing her naked request. Her words, honest and stripped bare, filled him with hope. He lifted his gaze, drinking in the fearful apprehension reflected in her deep chocolate eyes and pushed himself up to hover above her. Deliberate and controlled, he slipped his hand down to rest on her narrow hip. Only the band of her tattered denims separated him from heaven.

"Thank you for your trust in me, *koxána*." He dipped his chin in reverence. As the sun crept beyond the horizon, he took the time to truly see her. His skills as a healer had removed the evidence of her recent bouts, but the deep scars were beyond him. However, the pale patterns did not mar her beauty in his eyes. Instead, they enhanced it. Here was a female who had stood against hatred and ignorance and come out the other side.

Lean muscle covered her slender frame, clearly defining the shift from feminine curve to warrior's strength. Shadowy channels scored the lines separating each rib. He shoved his anger at her lack of proper food into a corner. That would be for another time.

Entranced, he followed the nervous trembling of her abs, his mouth watering in hungered longing.

"Would you object to me tearing these jeans off your body?"

The porcelain skin took on a lovely shade of pink, and his cock knocked hard against his zipper.

"I can be more careful if you'd like."

She scissored her legs, arching her back as she clamped her fingers around his wrist.

"I don't care how you get them off. Just get them off. Now," she moaned urgently.

He knew that tone well. Not wasting another moment, he grabbed the helpless fabric with both hands and split the seams with ease. Yanking off the ragged remnants of both pants and panties, he revealed a pair of toned ivory legs, mottled with discolored circles. Again, he filed away his rage, focusing instead on her pleasure.

Her startled gasp spurred him on. Starting from her delicate arch, he kissed his way up the length of her legs, certain to give each limb the same devout attention. With each pass of his tongue, another bruise faded into obscurity. She bucked and cried out, her short nails cutting tiny crescents into his back. Once her wounds were healed, he turned his attention to her damp core. He settled his weight onto his elbows and rested her knees on his shoulders.

Her thoughts had become nothing more than images and sensations. Fire and need, desire and passion. She asked him to show her how it felt to be cared about. Thinking of nothing but her, he lowered his mouth and nuzzled the sweet juncture of her thighs.

Panic flared in a tiny corner of her mind and he slowed his eager pace. As he placed tender kisses on the edges of her core, he widened their mental link. He refused to control her, but he did not want her to fear his intentions. With loving and sensual care, he gave her access to his every sense. Stroking her sweat-slick skin, he sent waves of cascading pleasure, tantalizing her body and spirit.

"Oh God. Is...is that what...what you feel?"

<It is, and so much more.>

He splayed his hands across her flat stomach, making sure to keep his hold loving and light. Her pounding heart fell in time with his and he dragged his tongue along her damp folds. A rough inhale bowed her spine, lifting her off the bed, and honey flowed from her shuddering core. His eyes rolled back into his head and he lapped at her sweet juices. The mounting pleasure nearly overtook the dizziness he attributed to the growing lack of blood to his brain.

Daring for more, he walked his fingers around her hipbone and cupped her ass. One hand remained occupied kneading one rounded cheek while he busied his free hand with his strangling buttoned fly. He growled, frustration tempered with fervor and the end product was a satisfying snap. Not once did his mouth ease from his loving ministrations as he slithered out of his jeans. His cock sprang free, primed and ready but he remained focused on her desires.

His mental tether shivered, her panic climbing an inch. Recollections of her previous partners fired his need to assure her. He slid his hand back up the length of her leg and placed one final kiss on her inner thigh before working his way back up her body. Her postorgasmic shudders rippled across her toned abs, the undulating waves too tempting to resist.

"You are so beautiful," he remarked, his gaze following each tantalizing flex and bunch.

"H-how can you even say that?" Her rough, smoky voice warmed his heart. Pressing his lips along a trio of slender scars along her ribs, he glanced up the length of her body. He pushed onto his locked elbows, the added height giving him a clear view of her face. Or at least, he would have, if she weren't hiding beneath her crossed arms.

Lightly, he trailed his fingertips from her crooked elbow to her wrist, encouraging her to lower her shield. His patience paid off and his reward was a pair of sad brown eyes.

"I cannot lie, *koxána*." A curious frown teased her eyebrows closer together. "For any Guardian to speak falsely would cause him physical pain. But more importantly, I say it because it's true. Your fierce spirit, your will to make things better for Liam. All of it is a testament to your strength." He toyed with her hair spread out like a blanket across the sheets. "And I find that sexy as hell."

His scorching words sent a delicious blush over her entire bare body. Need hammered at his soul, as well as other parts of his anatomy. Smiling, he rolled onto his back, carrying her with him to straddle his hips. The heat of her wet core hovering so close to the straining head of his cock was sweet agony. Her eyes flared wide and her knees dug into his sides. He lazily held her hips, his grip light and designed only to keep her stable. She flattened her palms against his chest. Through her trembling arms, she telegraphed her deep-seated fear.

Damn. He swallowed past the lump in his throat, forcing his raging desires back into their cage. He slid his hand up her flushed skin and cupped her cheek.

"This is all for you. Even if you say to stop right now, your wish and your desires rule this moment and every moment to follow."

Her eyelids fluttered down and she leaned into his touch. "That doesn't sound very fair to you. Get you all hot and bothered, then not seal the deal."

He rose up, wrapping his free arm low about her waist, his wrist balanced above her ass. "Danika, look at me," he implored. She took a slow breath and met his gaze. "I have waited lifetimes to find you. To see you bathed in pleasure is worth it for me."

His brain knew the truth of his words. Too bad, his cock had much different plans, the painful erection twitching beneath the slight weight of her.

A sly smile tilted her full lips. "Are you sure about that?" Her gaze flicked down to his lap. "'Cuz I'm thinking another part might not be too happy with that idea."

He chuckled, leaning in to tease the hollow of her throat. "Well, he does tend to have a mind of his own."

Wicked laughter bubbled up and flowed down his back. "I can tell."

He groaned as she rolled her ass against his groin.

One final kiss on her neck and he laid down again. Holding her darkening gaze, he hooked his thumbs into the waistband of his constraining denims and slipped them past the base of his aching shaft. Her fingers clawed into his pecs as she rubbed her slick folds against his cock. With a loose grip on her thighs, he massaged and kneaded his way up until his hands rested on her slender waist.

With patient care, he let her set the pace. The air grew thick, the scent of her growing arousal the sweetest perfume to him. Her spine bowed as she stroked herself against him, her head lolling back. Just as he had imagined, her hair flowed like silk across his skin. He fisted a handful of strands and buried his face into its beckoning midnight shimmers. Each inhale drove his need higher and higher, his hips meeting her hungry pace.

She threw back her head and cried out, dampness seeping onto his engorged shaft. He pried his eyes open, drinking in the intoxicating sight of her in orgasmic pleasure. Her firm breasts jutted to the heavens, nipples like pink and rosy nubs bobbing on twin seas of creamy flesh. Short nails dug into the meat of his quads as she rode the cresting wave.

"*Garnij.*" Beautiful.

TWENTY-FIVE

Danika sucked air into her burning lungs. Every nerve ending sparked and her skin felt two sizes too small. *If this is what love feels like, sign me up.*

So many sensations coursed through her blood, but there was one mystery yet to discover. Curiosity and fear shared the stage and her hand moved off his muscular thigh. She dropped her head forward while she reached for his massive erection between her legs. Her fingers slipped easily around the slick head, wet with her own juices, and she explored the full length.

Her heart quickened, contemplating possibilities and impossibilities. Could she fit him inside her? Was she too broken to feel anything if she did?

<I don't want to hurt you, koxána. I...I healed some of your past injuries.>

She lifted her gaze, disbelief dropping her jaw. "What? How? And when?" Her mind might have been reeling from his shy confession, but her body was more interested in the truth of the miracle. As if driven by some primal need, she rose onto her knees and aimed the bulbous tip at her trembling core.

His hands gripped her hips, holding her poised just at the moment of surrender. "Are you sure this is what you want?"

She peered deep into his eyes, searching for the source of his pause. She sensed no hidden agenda, his touch was meant as a security measure. For her? Even now, in this most intimate moment, his thoughts were directed to her well-being. And the walls around her soul shattered.

Locked in the glow of his sea green eyes, she gently lowered herself onto his rigid shaft. She groaned heavily, gasping as her channel opened wider, his slow invasion pushing her beyond any earlier measure of pleasure. Fire lanced through her blood and sweat slicked her skin. His hungered growl sent shivers straight to her core and she came.

"H-how are you, ah, doing this?" she moaned, her voice a harsh whisper. She had only imagined sex this fantastic, but her dreams didn't hold a candle to the real thing. Heat raged through her, sweet friction sparking new fires with each loving stroke. He lifted her up, sliding out until only the thick tip stayed buried inside her.

"Making love to you is easy, *koxána*." His hips flexed and he sank further into the stretching walls of her body. Stars danced behind her fluttering lids and she clung to his shoulders. "You speak through your actions and I only need to listen."

Her head lolled as she savored the languid pace of his thrusts. Drunk on the sensations coursing through her from head to toe, she splayed her fingers across his chest and reveled in the pleasure. In and out, shallow and deep, she rode him, their hips rolling and dipping in perfect synchronicity. Sweat trickled between her breasts, adding to the damp puddle between their legs.

"More." The single word shocked her as it tumbled from her lips, mid-sigh. She slid her hands along the slick planes of his chiseled abs, across his hard pecs, and grabbed onto his shoulders. Her spine curved as she pressed her forehead against his.

His breath huffed in warm bursts, sending chills down the length of her hot skin. "Take all you need, *koxána*."

She wished her mouth was more willing to make word stuffs, but sadly, all her faculties were focused on the inferno raging deep inside her hot core. A surviving rational brain cell recalled him talking about her use of actions to speak for her. Time to test the theory. Bowing forward and pressing her forehead against his, she clasped her hands around his wrists resting on her waistline, encouraging him to quicken his strokes.

Wired and past the point of no return, she sat upright and slammed her hips against his. Her fingers clenched, digging her short nails into his cut muscles as she impaled herself over and over again. Electricity zinged wherever their flesh met, but nothing compared to the lightning storm brewing beneath her skin centered just south of her belly button. She was spiraling higher and higher, beyond all sense of reason and she didn't care. It was as if each of his powerful and loving strokes banished the pain of her past experiences, burning away the disgust and leaving her somehow clean.

His gruff, masculine voice murmured exotic words. Their mysterious meanings were lost on her, but their tone was fiercely possessive.

She captured his gaze and the world around her exploded. She gasped, only to shove the needed air back out in a scream ripped straight from her soul. Flames of erotic sensation coursed through her as she climaxed hard. Her body quivered and spasmed uncontrollably as he stilled beneath her, gripping her hips tightly. His cock tensed deep inside her an instant before flooding her hot core.

Every part of her body shook and she collapsed onto his chest. Her sensation threshold had not only been crossed; it had been smashed, burned, and left on the side of the road. Tiny convulsions twitched along her limbs and she struggled to draw in more than a staggered breath. Even her lips tingled as air passed over them. This went beyond intense. His heart pounded beneath her ear, his skin warm and damp.

Compassion and warmth colored his unknown words while he

gathered her listless arms into his tender embrace. He pressed a soft kiss on the top of her head.

"Sleep safe, my beautiful warrior." She swore he said something more, but exhaustion took control and her eyelids refused to remain open. One thought swirled through her mind before sleep completely took over.

So this is what it feels like.

Her lips curled into a drowsy grin and she snuggled deeper into his arms.

TWENTY-SIX

CLAUDE GLANCED at the Rolex on his wrist, taking a break from glaring daggers at his agitated second. Boris growled and paced in an uncharacteristic manner. In truth, he found the man's frustration refreshing. He was beginning to wonder if anything could rattle the man. Turns out, it only took one pain in the ass Irishman.

Yawning loudly, Claude rested one leg over the arm of his regal throne and tapped his toes against nothing while his underling's petulant tantrum continued. Half listening to the ongoing rant, he sipped at an especially smooth brandy. Granted, the liqueur had once served as someone's conscience, but that was not important. The idea to age the essence much like alcohol did actually work and he was grateful for the dulling effect. Especially in moments such as these.

Bored by the lengthy scene, he waved off the next bout of whining about to fall from his lieutenant's lips.

"Spare me your bruised ego and tell me what else the man said."

He may have been impressed by the wintery stare if he were a lesser man. Right now, he needed more usable information. The clock was ticking and not in their favor.

Boris stalled his current circuit. "He knows who I am, I mean who I was. I had never laid eyes on the man until yesterday and he knew my name. Knew my history with Yurchenko."

Claude sighed with vocal ennui. "So you have said. Numerous times, if you must know. But none of it gets us no closer to knowing who *he* is." He rose and crossed to the small table, needing a refill of his drink. "You said he gave no name but mentioned something about rules." He paused mid-pour. "It could be you had the rare opportunity to meet the true leader of the Guardians."

The silence at his back encouraged him to continue without further interruption. He smiled to himself and topped off his glass. Turning around, he aimed his gaze at his second, and the man's beady blue eyes flared wide.

"It is only a rumor, but stories have been circulating for as long as I can remember about an ancient Celt who trained the first of the Guardian Warriors. He is spoken of in whispers, much like the boogeyman. It is said he is the lone man to be a full Triumvirate." The slack-jawed response would have been amusing in another situation. "A Conduit, Channeler, and Marshall all wrapped up in one enemy who fights for humanity. Again, it is only a rumor."

Claude recalled the first time he'd heard the legends. Their sire, Cabal, was known to all, since each of his soldiers was required to pass his test as well as surrender any lingering traces of humanity found within their souls. He wondered if his Boy Scout of a counterpart had a similar initiation rite. Since the knowledge did not matter in this moment, he quickly banished the query and returned his mind to the task at hand.

"He did carry himself like a man used to being obeyed, but I did not get any kind of all-powerful vibe from him." A fraction of doubt clouded the normal arrogance in Boris' voice. Another useful chunk to file away for future use.

"He managed to knock you on your ass quite handily, if your recounting of the event is accurate."

A flick of his wrist and the impending excuse halted. "But that's neither here nor there. The boy was nothing more than a tool. A very effective one, but a tool nonetheless. There are more buttons on that female to push. She does have a father in that hovel, does she not?"

Boris closed his mouth, his thin lips pulling into a tight line, and he nodded sharply.

"Good. Find a way to use the father and report back to me. No doubt she is with that fucking Ruskie in his fortress, so we will need to draw her out."

"He's Ukrainian, not Russian."

He shook his head, vaguely apologetic given the angered growl from his second.

"As you have repeatedly reminded me. I meant no disrespect toward you."

Claude turned and stared at the dingy garden path beyond the thick window. Twists and turns in the rocky trail cut through the dormant forest, but all led to the same destination. He only needed to navigate the curves and the end game would be his.

This time, mon ami, victory will be mine. You have no real stomach for the true brutality of the humans you claim to serve so reverently. Loyalties are so easily twisted and soon, I will shove the truth of it down your throat.

TWENTY-SEVEN

MUFFLED groans roused Anton and he peeled open his eyes. He had watched over her after she fell into a deep slumber, ensuring his in-depth healing session mended her broken pieces and smoothed over the raw edges. How he managed to concentrate on her injuries while buried balls deep into her welcoming sheath was still beyond him. Yet, a part of him knew locked in their loving embrace, he had access to not only her body but her spirit as well.

He focused on her loving heart, the small, tender corner hidden away from the violence of her life. Dwelling within was hope and a timid romantic ideal of happiness. She wondered how he could care for her, while he wondered why she didn't realize how rare and amazing she truly was. As he peered behind the veil, he discovered a woman unafraid to stand up for herself or for those weaker than herself. Unbeknownst to her, she'd had the beating heart of a Guardian before she'd even met one.

I claim you, body and spirit.

I claim you, heart and soul.

Your life I tie to mine, your joy and your sorrow.

When the Claiming Ritual words had tumbled out as she rode

him to ecstasy, tranquility had filled his soul. Maybe his peaceful spirit could balance her mercurial nature. Until things were completed, he would simply do his best to show her love.

Lethargic, he lifted his head off the pillow and searched the room for the cause of the disturbance. Still deep in sleep and sprawled across his chest, Danika thrashed and mumbled, her lean legs kicking as she fought some imaginary foe. He tightened his loose hold on her slender body and kissed the top of her head. Her silky hair, still damp, blanketed his skin, the wild fragrance stoking the smoldering embers of last night's fire.

Her twitching became more violent and he trailed his hand along her slick back.

"Shhh, *koxána*. I've got you."

The innocent friction starting from his fingertips lanced straight to his hardening shaft. Ready for round two, but uncertain of her level of interest, he reined in his libido and slipped into her dream.

Horrific images of Liam's broken body and fists landing devastating blows surrounded her psyche in a world full of blackness and pain. She fought against the shadowy opponents, tired rage burning in her eyes, yet she refused to be defeated.

His beautiful warrior.

She'd stood apart for far too long, battling against life and those who were meant to protect her with no one at her side.

No more.

He strode through her dreamland's demons, banishing the hateful visages in the wake of his purposeful steps.

<I promised to keep you safe, my love. You will never have to face the day, or night, alone again.>

Within her mind, he pulled her to his side. She stirred in his embrace and he opened his eyes. Her chocolate eyes blinked up at him, curiosity and confusion painting an adorable frown on her sweet face. He smiled and brushed his thumb across her forehead, wiping away the deep crease.

"Is this really gonna last?"

He cocked his head and cupped her pale cheek. "For as long as I draw breath."

"Oh." Her blush warmed his palm, kicking his grin into overdrive. Eager as he was to delve once again into her welcoming body, he had caught a faint unvoiced desire in the back of her thoughts. He scooted into a seated position and cradled her in his arms.

"Oh, and so much more. But first, can I tempt you into a shower?"

TWENTY-EIGHT

DANIKA WASN'T sure which saint to pray to, but one of them definitely thought she deserved a break and sent her an angel. It didn't hurt that her heavenly protector came wrapped in the body of a total Adonis who drove her to peaks she had only heard of in fairy tales. All through their morning marathon, he didn't tire. He was thorough, to say the least. And now, he offered her a real shower.

If the size of the bedroom was any hint, the bathroom had to be ginormous.

Also, she was certain she stunk on ice. Failing to recall the last time she really even changed her clothes, once again, she marveled at him.

"Geez, I must look like ten miles of bad road and smell like something died. How come you haven't run screaming away from me yet?"

The warm chuckle pouring down her back nearly sent her into an orgasmic spin. "You look like a woman who has been well loved, *koxána*." He rose with her still tucked against his chest. She felt light as a feather in his arms, delicate and fragile. So many parts of her warred against each other during their short trip across the room. Her mind whirled so fast she thought she was going to throw up.

Cool ground met the bottom of her bare feet. She glanced down curiously. Deep walnut wood covered the cavernous space. Her jaw dropped as she stared.

"Sweet Mother of God. This thing is bigger than my whole apartment."

A sunken tub sat tucked against the far corner. Across from it was a huge glass-encased chamber. A giant round showerhead coupled with a hand-held massaging nozzle looked down from above. Accents of burgundy and dark green gave her the feeling she just stepped into some secluded forest glen. As cool as the shower looked, something about that giant bathtub continued to draw her wandering eyes. Honestly, she couldn't remember the last time she took a bath. The faucet in her uncle's place had broken years ago, not to mention she didn't like the idea of being naked for longer than she needed to be even in her own home.

She searched for a toilet, but it was mysteriously absent. This truly was only a room for bathing. A small inset door to her right was cracked open and revealed the hidden john.

"It's not quite that big." He kissed the top of her head. "I'll get the water warm while you tend to your needs."

She watched him stroll toward the massive tub. Damn, that man had a body. Scars traced battle lines across his muscular back, showing testament to his skill as a warrior. Powerful broad shoulders and thighs like tree trunks, and don't even get her started on that ass.

He paused, stopping just shy of the stylish silver faucet and glanced back at her.

Holy fuck.

His sea green eyes danced with impish glee.

<The sooner you're done, the sooner we can get to round two.>

Never before had she peed so fast. His laughter bled through the wooden barrier, but she opted to give her teeth an extremely necessary once-over. Her fingertip doubled as an impromptu toothbrush. After a quick swish, she took a centering breath and opened the door. A thick cloud of fragrant steam met her as she reemerged, clean, heady, and definitely masculine. She closed her eyes for a moment and let the strange sensation of luxurious warmth invade her being.

<Come, koxána. The water will feel even better.>

Peeling back her lids, she tucked her hands under her armpits and shuffled toward the sunken hot tub.

"I thought you said shower." The surface of the water rippled with hidden jets, beckoning her to join her earthbound angel in the large whirlpool. He extended his hand as he lounged, one elbow propped lazily against the curved rim.

"I did, but I changed my mind," he smirked. "Or, should I say, you changed it for me. Your gaze did seem more interested here than on the shower." She smiled shyly and accepted his offer. Cautious, she reached for his steadying arm and dipped one toe into the frothy water. A second passed and her foot remained unscalded. She took a deep breath and carefully sank into the welcoming warmth. Opting for discretion for some dumb reason, she sat across from him, keeping her knees to herself. Heat and heavenly aromas wrapped around her as the focused streams soothed her aching muscles. Unable to stop the heavy groan, she hung her head and allowed pounding water to massage her lower back.

"Oh, wow."

Her juvenile response earned her a sensual chuckle. Her heart picked up the pace and she lifted her head, dragging her gaze away from the interesting bubbles. She had no idea why she felt the need to hide. Hell, a few hours ago, she'd climbed all over his delicious body like a jungle gym.

Now, she was what? Ashamed? Embarrassed? Afraid?

"I completely agree."

Steam filled the scant space between them and she wasn't sure if the source was the hot water or his searing look. She started to tuck her hands under her armpits, until she caught a whiff of herself. Hoping not to gag, she scooted away from him.

"Um, are you sure this is a good idea? I mean, I really need to hose myself down."

The corners of his lips curled up and her tongue froze. He scooted forward, brushing his palms against her knees. "I promise, *koxána*. This is a bathtub, just like the one in most houses." Her flat stare encouraged him to continue. "Maybe a little bigger, but a tub all the same."

He twisted around, giving her a peek at his gorgeous muscular back, and grabbed a bottle of shampoo. "It's got a constant filtration system so the water stays quite clear." Her gaze trailed down to the hint of his ass and all the liquid in her body congregated between her thighs. Groaning to herself, she slunk beneath the water, even knowing the warmth would do nothing to cool the fire under her skin.

Panic clenched her lungs and she quickly resurfaced, sputtering and coughing. Being underwater brought back too many bad memories and she fought her momentary freak out. She didn't want any of her damned demons spoiling her mood, but it seemed her wish wasn't getting granted today. A new form of embarrassment urged her arms to move and she set to washing her hair, using her frantic nerves to fuel her fingers.

He stilled her hands with a tender touch. "Danika? You're safe here."

She peered at him through the blur of bubbles. Even without sharp edges and defined lines, he was sexy. Once the soap started to sting her eyes, she finally glanced away and dunked her head under the water, just enough to rinse out the cleansing lather. The earlier fear didn't return and she hid in the cocooning silence. His words swirled through her head, but she had a hard time bringing herself to believe them. Safe was a word in a children's game; not part of real life.

She slid back to her side of the wide tub and took out some pent-up frustrations on her hair, twisting and squeezing out the thick, damp rope.

"*Koxána?* You can say anything you like." She paused, shifting her gaze to him. Water trickled down his face, clinging to the scruffy stubble along his jaw. She stopped strangling her ponytail and dropped her hands to her sides.

"Yeah, you say that now. What if all I have to say is just a load of crap? I'm not good with polite conversation, if you couldn't tell already."

His smile ignited every nerve ending and sent delicious chills from heels to hairline. "I wouldn't mind some impolite talk."

Her shoulders drooped as a light sigh slipped from her lips. "Well, that I can do in spades. I...I've never...had anything like last night." He took her hand, encouraging her to continue. "I don't want to sit here and cry about how tough my life has been. It is what it is and nothing can fix that. But," she paused, praying for some verbal guidance from above. "But for a while, you...you made me think there might be some reason for it all." She scoffed, shaking her head. "Gah. Listen to me, will you? I sound like I should be in a freakin' sappy romance movie."

"Is that wrong?"

She leveled her gaze at him.

He wasn't teasing her. Instead, he openly accepted her ramblings. "I have seen much in this world and not all of it is beautiful. You seem to think because you've dealt with terrible things, it makes you a terrible person." He dragged his fingertip across her lips, silencing the staunch refusal in her thoughts. "Nothing you can ever say will convince me of this. You have survived with more honesty and integrity than any man I've met."

Her cheeks warmed under the directed heat of his sea green eyes. "You make it sound like I'm a good person. Trust me on this, I'm no angel." *Not like you.* She opted to keep that last part to herself. Judging by the arched eyebrow across from her, she was less than successful. His hand trailed down her arm, his light touch sending fiery chills along her skin. The surrounding water wasn't helping much either, the blissful heat stealing her ability to think clearly.

"You do realize angels were sent down from heaven to punish or bring destruction?"

She smirked, one corner of her mouth tilting upward. "Well, yeah. But that's just Old Testament stuff there."

He joined in, smiling back at her. Damn, he was handsome in ways she didn't even have words to explain. "True, but being a good person isn't an easy task. Good doesn't mean you allow life to use you as its doormat."

He did have a point there. But would it truly justify all of her actions?

He continued as she mulled over his earlier words. "Good means not backing down, even if the odds aren't in your favor, if you believe what you're doing is best. I have seen brief glimpses of your life, *koxána*."

Her blood thickened, fear lining her veins. "So you know?"

"Know what? Know you go beyond good?"

With a sullen shake of her head, she dropped her gaze. No way could she say this and still maintain eye contact. "No. I've...done things." Images of hundreds of brawls leaped into her mind and she struggled to banish them, as well as the brutal couplings entangled within those memories.

"Danika?"

She flinched at his soft and understanding tone. His fingers remained still, resting slightly north of her kneecaps. Why did she bother trying to resist him? If she was honest with herself, she didn't know why she was fighting anymore. He was everything any woman could ever ask for. And for some bizarre reason, he thought she was worth a damn.

He grazed his knuckles against her jaw, his rough skin tantalizing. She closed her eyes, savoring his tender touch.

"You only see half of those events. In each and every fight, you were battling because someone weaker was being taken advantage of. You stepped up because it was the right thing to do. And as to the... other incidents," his voice deepened, becoming an angry growl as even he refused to give her experiences their true name. Rapes. "You did not do those things. Those vile and violent acts were perpetrated by cowards. I wish I could reach through your memories to find each one of those dogs and destroy them."

A weak grin tugged at her lips at his gallantry. "That would be one hell of trick."

"For you, *koxána*, anything."

"Really?" She had aimed for more sarcasm and less desperation. Maybe all his heartfelt promises had her believing in fairy tales, even for just a moment. Her eyes fluttered open and tried vainly to focus on the world beyond the thick steam and the comforting male presence inches away.

"If it would allow me to hold you in my arms? Definitely."

Trying to play off his compliment, she opted for a safe bit of bantering. "I bet you say that to all the girls." She barely recognized her own voice, the normal bitterness missing, replaced by hopeful mirth.

He tilted her chin up and her gaze followed. A smile hotter than the sun warmed his face, and she was helpless to stop her lips from responding in kind.

"Pretty much, but I sometimes change up the ending."

Her jaw fell open and he laughed hard, scooping his hands under her ass and carrying her to his straddle his lap. Even as she slung her legs across his thighs, she still struggled weakly against his embrace.

"You have to admit, you had that one coming." He kissed the tip of her nose, and his powerfully male scent surrounded her. She inhaled his strong, clean spice, pulling it into her soul, and relaxed. Curling her arms against his chest, she rested her head on his shoulder, enjoying the unexpected peace of a good laugh. Her hair fluttered with his easy breathing, his cheek warm on the crown of her head.

"I have never said that to another, *koxána*. Nor have I felt one tenth of what I feel right now." Delightful thrills ran after his fingertips as they trailed up and down her spine. He pressed his full lips against her forehead. "You are the only one who holds my heart."

His whispered words shot straight to her soul. Too good to last.

But what if it wasn't? What if, just this once, things actually did go in her favor?

TWENTY-NINE

THE HEAVY DOUBT and frail hope battled in her telegraphed fears and Anton held her tighter. She deserved far better than life had given her, and he would give his last breath to ensure she would never live in squalor again.

As honorable as his thoughts were, his body was more interested in another taste of the sweet heaven currently perched above his crotch. His cock twitched in eager anticipation of round two. He would deny his urges until she again gave him the green light.

His remaining brain cells reminded him she asked about getting clean. With a wink and a kiss on her nose, he reached for the soap. Her hard nipples scraped lightly against his chest, and a pained growl slipped from his clenched jaw. Heat radiated from her deep blush as she retreated to the opposite side of the tub and he chuckled.

"Of all the surprises being with you has given me, the most refreshing is your shyness." He lathered his hands as he closed the scant distance between them. Kneeling before her, he took one of her arms in his foamy grasp. She didn't flinch or pull away from his touch, but her eyes spoke of an intrigued curiosity. He massaged her fingers, working up the length of her strong arm. Carefully, he kneaded the thick knots and the tension eased out of her bit by bit.

"I still don't know why you haven't run screaming from me. I'm no fashion model like I'm sure you normally date and—"

He silenced her with a searing kiss, pouring his heart and his open acceptance of her into it. She linked her arms behind his neck and wrapped her legs around his waist, unlocking her jaw to draw him in deeper. His cock jerked, brushing against her soft folds. Water sloshed in sloppy waves as he shifted less than gracefully from kneeling to sitting. He gripped her strong ass, digging his fingers into the taut muscles, and ground his hard shaft greedily against her damp heat.

She shuddered in his embrace, her knees clenching around his waist. Something deeper than need drove her, and he caressed her back, easing into her mind. Ghosts of her past assaulted her fragile spirit, alcohol laced breath burning her skin and cruel hands seizing her tender flesh.

<Koxána, those days are gone. Never again will they harm you.> With a wave of his hand, he banished the hateful images and infused new memories built on the passion of their previous night. He pictured her beautiful face at the peak of her orgasm, the delicate blush blanketing her body. Each vision he conjuring pushed her ragged history further into the dark reaches of her mind. Later, he would talk to her about removing them completely.

Until then, he would help her create better things to remember.

He kissed his way along her jaw and returned to the now. Her frantic pace slowed to a sensual crawl, and his lips curved in happy response. She groaned, the throaty sigh firing his blood and sending his cock into erection overdrive. Tension disappeared from her shoulders and her body bowed and arched, her taut nipples scraping against his chest. He growled in hungry response, nipping playfully at her tempting collarbone.

She shifted her weight, rising onto her knees. He happily accepted the offer of her firm breast, suckling on the plump mound as she carefully lowered herself onto his aching shaft. His fingers gripped her hips, holding her poised at the moment of invasion. He popped her luscious peak from his mouth and turned his face upward. Passion darkened her chocolate brown eyes and an unguarded smile tugged at one corner of her seductive mouth.

He swallowed hard and guided her further down his hard length. Enraptured, he focused on her fluttering lids as a needy sigh slipped from her slightly parted lips. Her tight sheath welcomed him, inch by delicious inch. He retreated and flexed his hips, driving farther inside. She tossed her head back, flinging droplets of sweet rain from her soaked tresses. Her nails dug into his shoulders as she swayed and rocked, pulling him deeper inside her. The surrounding water lubricated each thrust and glide, the temperate damp holding them in a state of perfect warmth. Sweat glistened and dripped between her breasts and he hunched over, eagerly lapping up the salty droplets.

One final thrust and his hips knocked against her ass. She gasped and he stilled, savoring the feel of her hot channel holding his entire length with loving care. He trailed his hands along her back and made a beautiful discovery. With his fingers splayed and intertwined, his thumbs reached the outside edges of her narrow shoulders. For all her strength, he found the feminine and fragile heart of a tender warrior.

I love you, Danika. He kept the tender sentiment locked within his mind, afraid his avowal might shatter the delicate moment. Instead, he cradled her cheek in the palm of his hand and rocked his hips languidly. His gaze didn't waver, drinking in the sensual play of emotions on her face. Tiny creases formed and disappeared between her slender brows and she gnawed her plump lower lip, her groans soft and breathy. She matched his deliberate pace, shudders rippling down her spine with each keening moan.

Time stretched to infinity as he sank again and again into the hot gripping channel. Her muscles clenched and tightened, milking his cock as she cried out in ecstasy. Unable to resist, he growled and joined her, flooding her with his hot seed. Sucking down air in greedy gulps, he pressed his lips to her forehead as her body shook. He cradled her against his chest, savoring the calm after the storm and breathed two tender words into her ear.

"Thank you."

"F-f-for what?" He smiled at her stuttered response and turned his gaze toward her. Her eyelids dragged up, exposing her dark brown pools.

"For being you and for trusting me with you." Her flushed skin took on a rosier hue and he smiled, tracing her chin with his knuckles. "And for the mind-blowing sex."

He placed a chaste kiss on the tip of her nose as she laughed. "Oh, hon. I think that was all on you. I was only along for the ride. No pun intended."

He chuckled, tightening his ass and twitching his cock still buried between her soft folds. Her eyes flared wide, her giggle growing heavier. "Care for another trip? Just to make sure?"

As interested as his body was in the idea, he read her desire to check on things beyond these walls. Guess it was time to return to the real world, if only to make sure it was still spinning. Forcing away the pained grimace, he lifted her from his lap, slipping free from her body with a contented sigh, and set her down next to him.

"I think Liam might be awake now and I think food might be good for everyone."

At the mention of her nephew, she ducked her head, but not before he caught the guilt-ridden expression flashing across her face. He frowned and gently raised her chin.

"*Koxána*, he is safe and alive, because of you. Don't bear the weight of someone else's hateful actions. You didn't do this to him." He paused, pressing a finger to her parted lips. "And before you can say it, had you been home last night, you would have ended up next to him in that hospital, or worse, in an early grave. Justice will be meted out; that I can promise you. But let's focus on the now and on your needs."

"But that bastard needs to pay." The venom he had worked so

hard to banish crept back into her voice, but it was tempered with something new, something beyond simple vengeance. He cupped her cheek, threading his fingers through her slick hair.

"And he will. You have my word on it. It is a Guardian's duty to protect his spiritmate and all she holds dear. As long as I draw breath, I will ensure you never want for anything."

His palm warmed, her pink skin hot against his. He wagged his eyebrows devilishly. "And I do mean anything."

"I kinda gathered that," she purred.

He stared into her eyes, peering into her soul with wonder. How long would it take for her to realize how amazing she was?

He winked and smiled. "Come on. If we stay here any longer, I think Éamon might send up a search party and that would be a very bad thing." His light banter earned an answering grin. "Besides, I might start gnawing on your leg."

Her velvety laugh washed over him and his cock jerked to attention. Too bad his early warning system was triggered the moment Éamon stepped off the top stair.

"Are you two ever gonna come up for air?"

Anton smirked, scooping Danika into his arms before she disappeared beneath the water's surface. "He can't see through the walls, beautiful," he whispered. Shifting gears, he called over his shoulder. "We'll be right down."

<Is Liam awake?>

"All right, hurry up. Coffee's getting cold."

<He is. He's a great kid. Looks like I need to make one hell of an apology.>

Silence returned, nervous and confining. Afraid she'd fortified her internal armor, he pulled her in close and kissed the top of her head. Words were not what she needed now. Instead, he translated all the things he couldn't say into pure and loving sensations and sent them down their personal link. Comfort and acceptance, peace and passion, became tangible entities and he promised them to her with each touch.

She relaxed in his embrace, leaning her head against his shoulder. He savored the rare peace, searing this captured moment into his heart. His eyes drifted shut as his fingers slipped through her thick silken hair. Éamon would return soon, but Anton wanted to linger in this perfect serenity as long as he dared.

"We can't stay here, can we?"

Her simple request warmed his soul and a contended smile tugged at his lips. "Well, we could, but we'd end up looking like a couple of dead, dried up raisins." Her body bounced against his chest. "And Éamon is nothing if not relentless. I'm surprised he waited as long as he did before interrupting us."

Still giggling, she crawled off his lap and turned to face him. "Yeah, I thought you were gonna say something like that."

His cheeks cramped from overuse and he handed her a bar of soap. "Well, we have known each other for quite a few years." Grabbing the washcloths, he tossed one her direction and lathered up quickly. "I'll have to tell you about the time he caught another Guardian in a compromising position."

"Really?" She arched a brow, waiting for him to elaborate.

"Yeah." He dragged out the single syllable, thinking how best to begin the embarrassing anecdote. With the advent of modern technology, it was much easier for the general public to share captured blunders worldwide. His brethren, however, were able to link to a communal, hive mind. This translated into mortifying secrets racing across the globe long before the Internet was invented.

"You know how some waitresses manage to show up to the table just as you've taken a huge bite?" He shifted his gaze, catching the sparkle in her beautiful brown eyes. Her impish smirk and nod encouraged him to finish the tale. "Well, let's just say both parties, um, had their mouths quite full."

She tossed her head back, laughing and he joined in the mirth. Hope beamed in the radiance of her easy smile and he sent a prayer of thanks to the heavens. The light mood remained while they finished cleaning up.

He stepped out first, offering his hand out of habit. She narrowed her eyes, contemplating his aid and to his surprise, she placed her fingers into his. As she climbed out of the water, he stared enrapt. In the light of day, she was truly stunning. Strong lean limbs, narrow waist with generous curves both above and below. Gone were the bruises that mottled her skin the night before, but not the scars she had earned during her life. Those she would carry with her, unless he could convince her to allow Éamon to help her. His friend was the strongest healer he had ever known. It was rumored even death took a backseat to his skills on occasion.

She pulled her hand away and tried to cover her nakedness. He shook his head, stilling her. "Please, let me look on you for a little longer."

"Why?"

He lifted his gaze to her face, meeting her confusion with pure adoration. "Because you are beautiful, *koxána*, and I want to carry this image with me for all time."

Her gaze slipped away, darting around the room in search of a safe landing spot. He retrieved a large towel from the open rack and draped it around her shoulders, bundling her in the rich burgundy terrycloth. "You might as well get used to it, because I will tell you this every day until you finally believe me."

Her sarcastic scoff was swallowed up by the thick towel. His first urge was to give her a playful swat on her delicious ass, but his arm locked before the tap landed. He opted to place a kiss on the visible crown of her head as he avoided her flailing elbows. The gentle gesture had the desired effect, her frantic movements pausing and resuming at a more controlled speed. He grabbed another bath sheet and made short work of toweling off.

"There's a spare toothbrush in the cabinet over the sink." Quickly wrapping the thick material around his waist, he headed back into the bedroom to procure something which might fit her.

"You keep spares for a reason?"

He laughed, unwilling to take the bait. "Yes, and he's downstairs waiting rather impatiently right now." Her incredulous disbelief thrummed along their mental link. <*As sad as it sounds, it's true. He, along with any other Guardian who needs a safe place to bed for the night, is the reason I keep a stash on hand. It's part of our code.*>

"Code?" she repeated.

He chuckled, entertained by her muffled inquiry. He continued to search, shifting through hangers and raised his voice enough to be heard. Since he had already begun the Claiming Ritual, he might as well begin sharing some trade secrets.

"Yes. It's quite long and seems to change with the times. But most of all, it's a solid set of principles guiding us through the crazy maze of shoulds and should nots."

His hand stilled as he recalled the day Éamon spoke the words that would forever alter his destiny.

Éamon placed his hand on his shoulder, the light touch rocketing along his limbs, and his muscles clenched, locking him fast to the spot.

"You have been chosen to take up the mantle of the Guardian Warriors. It is an ancient honor, given to those who have sworn to protect and defend the free will of humanity. You were chosen for your skills and for your valor."

A loud cacophony of voices filled his mind, none of them his own. Cries for help, screams of the wicked, and whispers of lovers meshed and entangled, all vying for supremacy in his head.

"The world is a dangerous place, with many mysteries veiled from the eyes of man. Creatures of evil, bent of turmoil and destruction, hide within the souls of the Rogue Warriors. You have been called to do battle with your sword, your wits, and your soul. No untruth shall pass your lips. To this arsenal, we give you an extended life in your current form and the ability to move with the wind. You can hear the thoughts of any mortal and can heal with a touch."

Little by little, the volume subsided until only the voice of his foreign friend remained. Power coursed through his veins. Gone were the lingering pains of old wounds and fatigue from battle. Color sharpened and distant images gained clarity.

"*Many miles will you travel, and many lands will you discover. No place will you call home for more than two score and ten years. You will be drawn to your enemy across time and space. Your enemy will hide within the heart of men and within the realm of the In-Between, the void betwixt the land of the living and the land of the dead. They will influence dreams and move in shadows.*

"*You will vanquish your foes, sending them back into oblivion. You will fight until you find your spiritmate. She will bring you balance and quiet your restless soul. Once you have made her your own, you will choose to find another to take up the battle in your stead or to bring her into the service of the Guardians.*"

As Éamon paused, Anton returned his gaze to the speaker. A brilliant aura of shimmering blue and gold surrounded him. His knees nearly buckled in reverent benediction. Only the gentle but unyielding hold on his shoulder kept him on his feet. The angelic light faded and once again, he stood beside his smiling friend.

"Do you accept?"

A door closed downstairs and Anton shook his head, grounding himself firmly in the present. His search had stopped on a long-sleeved button-down that could double as a dress with the addition of a belt. He guessed it would have to do for now. He laid the shirt on the bed and returned to grab a pair of jeans.

He emerged from the closet and was still zipping his fly when she joined him. His cock knocked against the metal teeth as she stood before him, the long sleeves swallowing up her arms.

"Damn. That shirt has never looked that good."

She blushed, doubling up the cuffs. "Umm, thanks."

He took her hand, lacing her fingers with his. "C'mon. Let's get you some food."

THIRTY

The rich scent of fresh coffee wafted up the steps and slapped Danika right in the face. Her stomach gurgled and growled at the heavenly aroma and she glared at her loud middle. Anton chuckled beside her as they walked hand in hand toward the stairs.

"But I have to warn you, Éamon's coffee has been known to eat holes through mugs, stomachs, and I think we even used it once to melt through a door lock."

She opened her mouth, but a voice from around the corner beat her to the punch. "Oy. Comments like that will not get you served any faster."

Survival instincts had her gaze scanning the set-up, but instead of scoping out exit points and escape routes, she marveled at the beauty of his home. Pale wooden floors and earthy colors adorned the living room, while sleek chrome glittered in the sunlight from the kitchen area. She followed her nose to the sparkling silver and marble and was nearly dropped on her ass by a tiny freight train in a ginormous T-shirt.

"Auntie Nika!"

Liam clamped onto her thighs and she wrapped her arms around his spindly shoulders. Her questing fingers discovered no bandage or cast or anything as guilty tears slipped down her cheeks.

"Hey, peanut," she croaked. Dashing her hand across her eyes, she knelt down to get a better look at him. His bright green eyes danced with innocent joy, but his expression shifted in a blink. A deep furrow cut across his tiny forehead.

"Auntie, why you crying? Is you okay?"

She choked out a sharp laugh, forcing a smile through her grief. "I am now. How about you?"

Liam beamed. "I am. I'm glad Unka Ant'n let us stay here. Can we stay here forever? I really like my room. It's got a big bed and a— Oh, look!" He stepped back, modeling his new wardrobe. "Did you see the cool shirt Unka Éamon got me? Isn't it neat?" He tugged at the giant shirt, twisting the white letters proudly proclaiming, *Not only am I cute, I'm Irish too.* Unable to speak, she nodded and yanked him close, hugging him tight.

She held on for dear life, thanking every saint she remembered and a couple she conjured up from her imagination. If she continued this strangling embrace, Liam would freak out. But she needed the extra couple of seconds, if only to convince herself this was real.

"Unka Ant'n? Is Nika okay?"

She sniffed back the rest of her blubbering, chuckling at his accusatory tone toward her lover. Lover? Yes. To call him anything else would sound insincere. Although other words did come to mind.

Guardian.

Angel.

Savior.

Sex god.

Yup, those worked too.

She leaned back and met the serious eyes of a four-year-old. Ruffling his hair, she winked at him. "You ask him if I'm okay?"

His little mouth twisted into a sardonic smirk. "Well, I have to ask someone. *You're* being all weird and Unka Éamon was with me."

The room erupted in raucous laughter. "Gotta love kid logic," Éamon piped up from somewhere in the vast space.

Anton patted her shoulder in feigned sympathy. "He does have a point there, *koxána*."

She slid her gaze to the gorgeous hunk standing so close she could feel the heat lingering on his skin. "Smart ass," she quipped. Needing to be back on somewhat equal ground, she rose to her feet and glared at the giggling giants in the kitchen. Neither looked particularly sheepish about their outburst and she was soon dragged into their playful mood.

A cup of sanity appeared before her, and she nodded in thanks to the bearer. Looking up, prepared with a tender smile, she blinked in curious surprise to see Anton's friend. The snarky Irishman she traded barbs with was strangely absent. Understanding reflected from his peacock blue eyes and compassion pulled up one corner of his full lips.

"So, I guess I need to say thank you for this?" She wasn't sure if she meant the coffee, the T-shirt, or Liam's life. The truth: it was all of the above.

His shy grin masked an odd sadness. "No. It was my pleasure. That's a great kid you got there, *mo chara*."

Cautious, she accepted the peace offering, taken slightly aback by his attitudinal one-eighty. She took a hesitant sniff but detected nothing more than strong coffee. A frown tugged her eyebrows together as she studied him. Why was he being nice to her, even calling her friend?

"Yeah, um. Thanks." She retreated a step but he kept his distance.

He rested a hand on her shoulder and an eerie calm settled into her. *<He no longer has any memory of what happened to him.>*

She blinked at the unfamiliar voice ringing in her head. Her gaze snapped up as she stumbled, her chin raised in proud defiance. His sympathetic smile eased her rattled nerves at his uninvited nearness.

"And for what it's worth; I was wrong and I'm sorry."

Anton's low whistle dragged her attention away from her current view. "Someone get me a calendar. This has to go down in the record books." His teasing tone garnered a half-hearted smirk. Her angel folded his arms across his broad bare chest, a sly grin warming his handsome face. "I think I can count on one hand the number of times I've heard him say those words without being intoxicated."

"And who says I'm not right now, boyo?"

Light laughter filled the room again, but this time, she didn't join in. Her brain was still reeling from its informational overload. All she could do was stare at the surreal scene as it unfolded. Liam spun around, giggling as the huge shirt flared around his spindly legs. Anton lounged casually, his hip resting on the counter near the massive silver fridge. Éamon had taken a seat on the open edge of the breakfast nook, his impossible blue eyes studying her intently. Was this what normal felt like?

Coffee splashed onto her bare foot and the floor, her arms rigid and trembling. The mug slipped out of her grip yet she heard no tell-tale smash. She spied more movement out of the corner of her dimming vision and Anton guided her to the nearest seat. Her heart and lungs raced to keep her conscious and she swallowed hard.

"Breathe, *koxána*. Take it slow and easy, and just breathe."

With her face so close to the wood floor she could count the rings, she struggled with each stuttering inhale. Gentle fingers traced languid circles on her back as someone knelt beside her. Her body immediately recognized Anton by more than his unique cologne that still clung to her skin.

Fuck. She didn't want to appear weak in front of Liam, or worse, scare the crap out of the kid.

Why can't I deal with this?

<*Because so much has happened and you need time.*> Even in her head, his voice held the same sensual accent. <*Liam is young and will forget this momentary lapse from his protective aunt soon, without any help from Éamon.*>

She lifted the bowling ball on her shoulders, dragging her gaze upward. Tilting her head, she glanced sidelong at the shirtless god crouched by her side. How much longer would he be so tolerant with her laundry list of issues?

~

ANTON GAZED into the face of his beautiful warrior, forcing a calm smile as she unraveled before his eyes. Too much, too fast. He realized the truth of the simple phrase as he watched helplessly as she nearly drowned in the recent joys. Silently, he berated himself, angered by his rush to show her happiness.

He didn't notice exactly when her meltdown began. After her initial reunion with Liam, she seemed fine, even venturing to join in their light bantering. But soon, her panic slammed into him, the fierce emotion a physical blow against his chest. He led her to the closest chair and crouched at her side. Calmly and with patient care, he drew centering swirls on her back as he encouraged her lungs to follow his steady lead. His gaze snapped up and warned off Éamon as he stepped in behind her chair. His friend frowned but backed away.

<*I know you are only wanting to help, brother, but she panics worse when someone stands at her back.*>

Éamon nodded, understanding hardening his expression. Without skipping a beat, his friend crossed to Liam, assuring the frightened young boy and bringing him back to the breakfast nook and his unfinished bowl of cereal.

Grateful for the solitude, he returned his attention to his spirit-mate. Conflicting emotions oozed from her, jumbling into a paralyzing anxiety. When she raised her head, his heart nearly broke.

Lost.

Her brown eyes focused on something distant and melancholy.

"I've got you, *koxána*. I've got you." Snaking his fingers beneath the still-damp curtain of midnight silk, he cupped the back of her head and leaned in. As he pressed his forehead against hers, he blanketed her with calming serenity. He whispered encouraging words, letting them filter through the frantic noise of her thoughts. Patience learned from centuries of campaigns paid off and her breathing evened out, each inhale smooth and steady.

"Feeling a little better?" He asked, easing out of her immediate space, yet still remaining near enough should she need him.

The tension in her shoulders seeped out and she nodded slowly. "Yeah, I think so."

Her voice cracked and he placed a soft kiss on her forehead, banishing the remaining creases. "You ready for some food?" He leaned back to read her eyes. Her lids fluttered up and he heaved a sigh of relief. In her deep chocolate eyes, he recognized the beautiful warrior who stood proud and powerful before her enemies.

Another dip of her chin paired with a slight smile and he beamed in response. He lightly grasped her fingers and led her to her feet. When the crown of her head bumped against his chest, he wrapped her in his embrace. Her arms snaked around his waist, and he cherished the simple gesture.

Éamon cleared his throat, breaking the peaceful mood. "Are you two lovebirds gonna come and join us or what?"

"Lovebirds?" Liam quipped curiously. "What's that mean?"

"Well, éinín, it means your aunt and my friend there...care deeply about each other."

Anton chuckled at Éamon's innocent and abbreviated definition. "We'd better get over there before things get any more detailed."

"Does that mean I might be getting a baby brother or sister to—"

"Whoa there, peanut." Danika spun out of Anton's arms and made a beeline to the smiling cherub, his little feet thumping against the bench seat. "Baby what? Where do you get these crazy ideas?"

Liam shrugged, grinning happily at the prospect. "But Auntie Nika, isn't that how baby brothers are made? When a mommy person and a daddy person—"

She covered his mouth gently as the two hyenas in the room nearly doubled over laughing. "That's about all the info you're gonna be getting. At least, not until you're a whole hell of a lot older. Like thirty." She ruffled his wild blond spikes and scooted next to him.

Anton waited a moment, watching the tender interchange from the safety of the dining table. Éamon had taken up residence near the stove, silent as he stood guard over the picturesque scene.

<How bad was he, Éamon?>

His friend inclined his head toward the empty room to his left. Anton frowned, glancing back toward his fiery warrior and her giggling nephew. Nowhere in the world would they be safer, yet he hesitated to leave them alone. He raised his troubled gaze back to Éamon. His mentor clearly read his unease and dipped his chin in response.

<Bad was only the tip of the iceberg. The doctors bandaged his immediate wounds, but with his internal injuries, and the long list of needed donors, he would've died before the week was out.>

Pinpricks of pain radiated from the center of his palms and only a conscious flick of his wrists released the tension in his coiled fingers. He dared not imagine the brutality his spiritmate would have suffered had she been home as well.

<How much do you know about the uncle?>

Anton clamped his jaw shut, holding in an angered growl. <Enough to wish the man a swift and painful death. He did this to him, didn't he?> He knew it in his gut but asked the question anyway.

Éamon nodded, moving to refill his empty mug. <And before you even think it, yes, any and all memories of the night have been wiped clean. He believes he remained here, sleeping the day away. It was the simplest solution.>

Anton heaved a heavy sigh of relief, grateful beyond words until he met Éamon's stony expression.

<If the man's such a bastard, why do they stay with him?>

Anton blew out a long, slow breath, searching for an answer. He understood the difficulty when family was involved. While he pondered, his gaze wandered toward his enigmatic female. Her crooked grin buoyed his spirit. He winked in sly reply, chuckling as her cheeks pinked.

Éamon cleared his throat, fixing him with a bland stare.

<Sorry. From what I gathered, it didn't seem like they had much of a choice. She did tell me her mother died many years before and her father...>

His thoughts fled. Crap. Where was her father? He launched himself toward the pile of keys, snatching his set. He quickly stomped into the River Roads sans socks, snatched his jacket off the hook, and headed to the back door.

"Anton, wait! Where are you going?"

He doubled back and kissed Danika tenderly. "I'll be back in a flash." One final caress of her cheek and he faced Éamon with a serious gaze, shrugging on his trench. <Keep them here. I won't be long. I have to check this for her.>

<Wait. I have something you have to hear.>

Too focused on the task at hand, Anton dashed out the door and jumped into his car, then sped back toward the city. Whatever Éamon needed to tell him would keep. But first, he had a promise to fulfill.

THIRTY-ONE

ÉAMON SWORE in as many languages as he could think of, then invented some new ones just for the occasion. Damned stubborn idiot. His continued attempts to get through went unheeded. As he rummaged around in his pocket, he spied Anton's phone still plugged into the wall charging unit. He tossed his hands skyward and growled at the useless device. Only a gentle tug on his sleeve brought his tirade to a halt.

"Unka Éamon? What's wrong? Why are you mad?" Liam's concerned voice doused his anger with arctic precision. He paused, dropping his shoulders, and he knelt beside the inquisitive youth.

"I'm not mad, little one. I'm just worried that my friend might have gone off without all the information he needs."

Bright green eyes blinked up at him innocently. "Is that bad?"

He ruffled the wild blond tufts and hoped his smile was convincing enough. "I sure hope not, *éinín*." He regained his feet and shifted his gaze to the only girl in the room, her silence speaking volumes. There were uncomfortable questions he needed to ask, but her guarded stoicism might make this more difficult than he wanted to admit. He opened his mouth only to be preempted by her direct inquiry.

"What do you want to know?" Her voice belied calm, but her fidgeting fingers told a vastly different story. If he pushed her too far, he could damage the fledgling relationship. But this was about more than two people falling in love. Other lives were tangled into this web, and Éamon would need to balance the scales as he went along.

"Can I get you something to eat first?"

She arched a brow. "That good, huh?" His jaw dropped to respond, but she beat him to the punch. "Bad news is always best on an empty stomach."

The blatant cynicism of her words was like a punch in the gut, hitting almost as hard as the faint scars peeking out from the edges of Anton's dress shirt. Again, he reevaluated his original impression of the serious female.

"True, but personally, I think better after I've had some food. I could whip up a quick omelette for you. Honest, it's no trouble t'all."

She frowned, contemplating his offer as she gnawed on her lower lip. She answered with a timid nod and he grabbed the needed ingredients. He tuned in his Channeler skills in her general direction as he fixed the simple meal. Either she felt nothing, or the walls surrounding her emotions were so impenetrable nothing escaped.

Liam, on the other hand, exuded life and joy with every breath he took. Innocent curiosity encouraged him to explore and question each new discovery as he moved around the room. Bright warmth followed him through the house and Éamon smiled in spite of himself. Appearing engrossed in his cooking, he tuned into Danika's reactions, fully expecting gruff and harsh commands while the young boy danced and frolicked about. To his surprise, she only gave gentle warnings when his little fingers got too close to the sharp weapons or the fragile breakables decorating the walls. Not once did she raise her voice as she sipped her coffee and remained cocooned in her private thoughts.

"Where's his mother?" He flinched at his breach of protocol. "If ya don't mind me asking, that is," he amended. Plate in hand, he crossed to the corner bench and joined her, giving her the lion's share of the space. Not an easy task given the cozy nature of the nook, but he managed.

"Nah, it's fine." Her words masked her unease. "He's my cousin's kid and she decided motherhood wasn't for her." She shrugged and polished off the dregs of her mug. "She dumped him on...on my uncle's door when he was barely a year old."

"Were you living there at the time?" A brief nod was her only reply. Suppressing the urge to give physical comfort, he offered her a warm smile instead. "He's lucky to have you, Danika."

She pinned him with a sardonic stare. "Yeah, 'cuz getting the shit beat out of you and nearly being killed is an awesome way to spend your childhood. Best thing for a four-year-old."

This time, he did not hesitate. With a light touch, he covered her hand, his fingers splayed wide in case she needed to escape. "You're right. But he's alive. If you weren't in his life, I can guarantee he would not have lasted this long." Her arm jerked but she didn't budge. "What happened to him the other night was unforgivable, but the act was not yours." He sensed the impending fall of tears and switched tactics. "You protected him better than any mother, helped him get this far, and now he's got two more people to watch over him."

She screwed up her face, the deep crease on her forehead yanking her brows together. "Two?"

"I'd say we come as a package deal," he shrugged, "but it might sound a bit creepy." His smirk earned an apropos eye-rolled response and he chuckled. "But it is kinda the truth. I think I can speak for Anton on this one, saying neither of you will have to want for anything ever again."

She started to shake her head, but he stopped her with a similar gesture. "Ya think you can talk him out of this? Hell, I've known him for more years than I care to count and I couldn't convince him to stay in the bloody house."

Her contemplative frown returned in a flash. "Just what the hell was so important that you didn't want him to go, anyway?"

Great. *Why did all of his guys have to pick such smart ladies?*

Easy. They were Guardians, the strongest and easily the most stubborn bunch of males on the planet. Only the sharpest females would ever match them.

He groaned out a resigned sigh, raking his hand through his hair as he leaned back. "How much do you know about him?"

She lifted one shoulder and finally took a bite. "He told me a little. He talked about the Ukraine and some prince guy. He's got Old School manners about him. Opening doors for me and shit like that." Bit by bit, the omelet vanished from the plate. "I haven't seen many Southie boys with chivalrous intentions. You know, honor and right-eousness. And those blades of his are wicked sharp."

Éamon nodded slowly in the lengthening silence, giving her time to eat and him time to think. She paused mid-mouthful, noticing the eerie quiet. He smiled and glanced off to his right. She followed his gaze, relief washing over her face as she spied Liam fast asleep, tucked into one of the overstuffed loungers in the living room. "He wore himself out good."

Knowing their privacy would be undisturbed until Anton's return, Éamon let down his guard. "I first met Anton in 1039."

Her jaw popped open, the fork clattering onto the plate before she covered her mouth, banishing both her surprise and breach of etiquette.

He shrugged carelessly. "What can I say? I age well."

She blinked deliberately, rattling her head and returned to her meal.

"Normally, Guardians are recruited on the battlefield, but him, I found standing in front of a church."

Images appeared as he recalled that fateful meeting. Anton oozed protectiveness as he gazed up at the spires of Saint Sophia. He had been studying the enigmatic young boyar for months, watching as the man chose the honorable path, even if it wasn't the easy one, time and time again. He bore all the hallmarks of a true Guardian and Éamon recruited him without hesitation. Eons had passed since he had first been tasked with creating the Guardians, warriors to preserve free will, while his brother was given reign over the Rogues. And he thought modern parenting needed help.

Among many of Éamon's particular skills allowed him to find those special few, the fellow members of the Guardians' Triumvirate living among humanity. Auras of Conduits, Channelers and Marshals flared brighter, their colors clearer and more pronounced. And Anton practically glowed, sparkling more than the golden dome of the cathedral before them. The reverence on his upturned face gave Éamon all the answers he needed about the truth of his character.

Since then, he never once doubted his friend. However, even after years of battles, there was still an unbroken sense of naïveté in Anton. He always believed in the inherent good in the hearts of all, and not once did he falter in his quest to save any and all he happened upon. For centuries, Éamon feared this blind trust would bite him on the ass.

Sadly, today might be that long-awaited day.

Drawing out of his reverie, he blinked and returned to the present conversation. "Hmm?"

She set down her fork onto her mostly finished meal and repeated her missed query. "But you knew he was a fighter, right?"

He dipped his chin. "Pretty much. It was easy to tell, and the way he commanded his men proved he had some skill with tact and diplomacy. He's what we call a Conduit. It means he can influence people's thoughts."

She leaned away, cautious. He waved off her rising concerns. "Not like that. Well, since he is one of the good guys, that is. He would never force anyone to do anything against their natures, if that's what you're thinking. I'm what's called a Channeler, which means I can do the same to people's emotions."

"So, is that why when you put your hand on my shoulder, things got all weird and fuzzy?"

He chuckled, lifting a shoulder sheepishly. "I haven't heard it called exactly that, but yeah. It helps to diffuse some tense situations, like when people might get news a little hard to accept."

"Or if someone needs a clear head." There was no accusation in her direct words; only understanding. He peered into her dark brown eyes and nodded.

"Anton is lucky to have found you, *mo chara*." She blushed and looked away, scoffing in disbelief. He took a deep breath before adding the tough part. "And he's gonna need a clear head when he finds out the bad news."

Danika glanced sidelong at him from narrowed eyes. "Does this have anything to do with the business card you both were so freaked out about?"

Damn, and perceptive to boot.

"It does. What can you tell me about it?"

She fidgeted before shrugging. "About the same as I told Anton." Her fingers twitched, as if searching for something. She barked out a harsh laugh and dragged her hands through her hair. "Damn, I could really use a smoke about now."

He opted to test the waters. "Or a drink?"

"Yeah," she replied with a heavy sigh. Instead of acting on her vices, her shoulders drooped and she reached for her empty mug. "On second thought, how about some more coffee? It's time I started fighting my demons with a sober head."

He smiled, impressed by her inner strength and gladly refilled her cup. "We can go outside, if you want."

She shook her head, her decision well and truly made. "Nah, it's all good." Her hand trembled slightly as she took a delicate sip. "I don't know what all I can tell you about it. Some guy showed up looking for directions and gave me the thing."

Éamon laced his fingers together and rested his elbows on the table. "Do you remember anything about him? What he looked like? His name, maybe?"

"He didn't say his name that time. To tell you the truth, the guy kinda gave me the creeps. But then he showed up again while I was at the bar the night..."

Éamon lifted his gaze from his musings at her pause. "The night?" He prompted, edging closer.

She raised her frightened eyes, anguish weakening her voice. "The night my uncle sent Liam to the hospital. Fuck, this is all my fault." Éamon quickly grabbed the mug before it shattered on the floor, slipping forgotten from her hands. "I went to Donovan's to grab a drink and clear my head and that same guy was there. He wrote his number on my hand and told me to call if I needed anything. And while I was there...and then when I...when I got..."

Her breathing became shallow gasps as her pale skin turned ashen. Éamon knelt beside her and enveloped her in a comforting wave. He guided her lungs to keep the air flowing as she continued.

"And when I got home, and found Liam, I...I was...If I had been home, I could've protected him. I should've been home, but—"

"*Tóg go bog é, mo chara.* Breathe. You did not do this, trust me. Had you been home, they simply would have waited until another opportunity presented itself, or things would have been far worse." He reached out and touched her chin to still her bobblehead impression. "Our enemies, the Rogue Warriors, believe that mankind is at its peak of invention when placed in horrific and deadly crises. And they delight in manipulating innocents to bring them what they want. It kinda skirts the rules, but when you're out for chaos and mayhem, who gives a shit about following the law, right? Now, Anton told me you two first met after you stumbled onto him and another battling. Was he the one you saw at the bar?"

"Satan with the fucked-up orange eyes? Hell, no." She shuddered and her Irish soul took physical form as she rushed through the Stations of the Cross, even kissing an invisible crucifix around her throat. "The only other time I saw that douchebag was in a nightmare. Nah, this guy was a lot scrawnier. Weird pale blue eyes, slicked back black hair and a hipster goatee/'stache thing." She rubbed the back of her neck and stared at the floor. "Do these bastards hunt in packs or what?"

"You have no idea," he groaned. "But to answer your question, yes, they do tend to run in large circles. The more, the merrier, I suppose." He leaned back, sitting on his haunches as he determined the best way to couch the next fun tidbit. "You weren't supposed to see the fight, much less be able to join in. By doing that, you made yourself a candidate worthy of both sides."

"Wait. You mean...you mean this is a recruitment? So I'm what, supposed to pick a friggin' side?"

Panic and paranoia bled from her, spiraling quickly into a fearful frenzy. "No, not in the way you're thinking. Well, yes, on the part of the other guys. The one you fought, Claude, is the resident leader of the Rogues and he and Anton have been fighting for years. Seemed the damned Frenchman always had it in for our boy. Hell, I think this row's been going on for near on two hundred years. I..." This time, the pause was on his end. "I never realized why until very recently."

"This is all some sort of sick, twisted game?" The flood of dormant emotions threatened to consume her and Éamon struggled to hold her terror in check.

"I know you don't have much of a reason to trust me; you hardly know me. But Guardians cannot lie. It's part of our code. To speak falsely causes pain. Actual, physical pain, even for the smallest untruth. While I can't say you wouldn't be a boon to our side, Anton's actions have been pure and driven by only one thing: love."

His calm and level words clicked the tension down a notch or two, but he sensed she had many more questions. He opted to leave those for the one who claimed her. Nodding slowly, he waited until she responded in kind and he stepped out of her personal space.

"But the guy in the alley and the guy at the bar were two different people, right? They can't, I don't know, shape-shift or something like that?"

Éamon returned to his seat, shaking his head sadly. "God forbid, no. They do have the ability to cloak their appearance, shroud themselves in unremarkable guises."

Her flat stare encouraged him to continue. "Think of it as wearing a mask that makes you look like anyone else. It allows them to blend in, not stand out. But sadly no. No, this is much worse. The Rogue at the bar is actually a very old friend of Anton's." *And it's gonna destroy him when he finds out.*

She frowned, the wheels in her head spinning behind her intelligent brown eyes. "So he was using me and Liam to hurt Anton." Her spot-on assessment needed no answer. Without a word, she slipped out of the booth and moved toward the stairs.

"Now where do you think you're going?"

Danika turned, her chin lifted in determination. "No way I'm gonna let him go and have all the fun."

"Fun? You call what's coming fun?" Éamon cautiously took to his feet.

She stalled, holding his gaze. "Honestly, I don't know what the hell to call it. All I know is that I won't hide while..." The lost yet fiercely protective gleam in her eyes conveyed the words she feared to speak.

"Are you sure you know where he was going?" Judging by her defiant stance, there would be little chance of changing her mind. But perhaps, he could alter her course.

"I have a good guess." She climbed up two steps before glancing back over her shoulder. "Keep an eye on Liam?"

He shook his head violently. "You're joking, right? Anton'd be clamoring for my family jewels if I let you out of my sight." He crossed to where Liam slept peacefully, lost in the innocent dreams only children have. With a light touch and a whisper, he deepened the dream state. "He'll be safe here and won't awaken until we all get back."

She eyed him for a heartbeat. A sharp nod later, she dashed up and out of sight. Éamon paced the floor, trying once again to connect with his friend, but to no avail. He was going to smack some sense into that thick head when he got the chance.

He sent up a silent prayer, shrugging into his thick leather trench as she came back down. Blinking slowly, he stared at her ingenuity. A pair of Anton's boxers, the button-down hastily tied around her waist as a makeshift belt and a black undershirt completed her ensemble. She padded the final steps, a pair of Anton's socks looking more like boots on her petite feet and shrugged as she passed him.

"Beggars can't be choosers. C'mon. Hope you've got a fast car."

Éamon reached for her hand before she made it out the door. She slipped easily from his loose grasp and faced him.

"I have a very fast car, but I have a better idea to get us there even quicker. But I'm gonna need two things." The crown of her head might've barely topped his shoulders, yet she stood tall and unafraid. "First, I need to know where."

She nodded sharply. "All right. My building isn't far from the BAC. Just go to—"

He waved off her verbal directions. "Just hold the place in your mind. To be on the safe side, think about the hall or corridor leading to your front door."

Danika narrowed her eyes but dipped her chin slowly and uncertainly. "Oh-kay. And the second?"

He smiled weakly, opening his arms. "Can I get a hug?"

She remained a cat's whisker away, contemplating his request. "No funny business?"

Éamon pressed a hand to his heart. "On my honor as an Irishman, I—"

Her raucous laughter encouraged him to amend his earlier pledge. He dropped his hand and lifted a shoulder. "Then on my honor as a Guardian." Giving her a second, he retrieved his concealed weapon of choice from inside his jacket pocket. She pursed her lips, eying him from a safe distance. With a playful wink, he flicked his wrist, snapping the innocuous baton into a seven-foot staff. A delicate brow arched upward, impressed but still she stayed out of his reach.

"Please." He held out his hand and waited. She took a deep breath and nodded, closing the distance. He plucked the address from her mind as she approached the final steps.

Spinning the staff over his head in a practiced flourish, he channeled the momentum and tapped the butt onto the ground beneath his feet. A shimmering crack in space opened and he wrapped his arm around her. As Anton had warned him, she tensed in his embrace, the nearly overwhelming urge to flee oozing from her.

But she refused to back down, earning more of his respect.

"Hang on tight."

All right, Anton. No getting pissed off when the cavalry arrives.

THIRTY-TWO

"Ah, what a beautiful morning. I do believe I will have cup of coffee."

Claude stood at the kitchen window, watching the empty street outside with calm anticipation as feet behind him shuffled through the debris. With the amount of dried blood splattering the dingy wallpaper, he was surprised anyone got out alive. He glanced over his shoulder, studied the home's remaining occupants. No use calling either of them living dwellers since they were nothing more than meat puppets, pawns moving about the board, oblivious to their true purpose.

The burly bully stare vacantly at him, helpless to do more than follow orders like a dutiful dog on a leash. Life had fled from his body faster than a dream at dawn. The man didn't even put up much of a fight to continue his existence. Pity. From the way he abused the children of the home, Claude had anticipated more of a challenge.

"Oh now. Don't look so glum." Claude pushed off the counter and crossed to retrieve the offered mug. "I gave you a chance to join, but you opted for oblivion. Soon enough, all of this will be over and you can go back to living..." He chuckled, amused at his own choice of words. "Oh, I almost forgot. You don't get to go back to truly anything."

<He's here.>

Perfect. The message he had been hoping to hear finally arrived. Painting on a self-satisfied grin, he sat down at the grimy dinner table, shifting his chair to face the apartment's main hallway. "Now, look your best. Company's coming."

The door splintered off its rusty hinges and Anton swaggered inside. "Fournier!"

Claude cringed, pressing a delicate finger to his aching ear. "No need to yell. I'm right here."

"What have you done with her father?"

Waves of pious anger moved down the narrow corridor in his foe's wake. Blinking calmly, he brushed aside the ineffective verbal attack and sipped at the ghastly excuse for caffeine. "Ugh. I would offer you a cup, but even I'm not that cruel."

Claude lounged as Anton growled, his direct path playing right into his trap. "Enough talk, you piece of shit." He stormed into the tiny kitchen, slamming his palms against the flimsy table. "Where the fuck is Danika's father?"

"Come, come, now," he tsked. "Manners, *s'il vous plaît.*" He gestured to an empty seat and waited. The hairs on his arm stood at attention, the barely restrained violence becoming a palpable force in the confined kitchen. Never before had he seen his opponent so unbalanced. This final game of cat and mouse would truly be deserving of song.

Anton narrowed his eyes menacingly. "Did you show manners when you nearly slaughtered an innocent child?"

Aghast, Claude splayed his fingers across his heart. "Me?" He laughed as he rose to his feet. "*Non, non, mon ami.* I did not raise a hand against the child. Nor did I twist the mind that did. That is not where my talents lie. Have you ever known me to employ such base strategies?"

The anger morphed for an instant into blatant disbelief as Anton stared flatly at him. "Yes."

"Be that as it may," he growled through clenched teeth. "I pride myself on being a man of greater vision." Anton scoffed, momentarily interrupting his train of thought. He glared in the hulking do-gooder's general direction and continued. "Mundane manipulation to kill one person? Child's play. You see, that kind of sport is over far too quickly for my tastes."

Claude's furtive gaze darted over his enemy's shoulder a second too early. Anton jerked his head around, narrowly escaping the death blow. Instead of impaling him, the sharp silver tip emerged from the Guardian's side a fraction of an inch below his rib cage. The trap worked beautifully, even if the Rogue assassin didn't succeed in killing his mark. Claude grinned proudly and stepped aside as Anton howled in agony.

"My eyes have been on the long play, one you have been blind to for centuries. Soon, I will have my grand prize. Come." He beckoned to the cloaked figure at Anton's back. "I'm sure the two of you have much to talk about."

The weakened warrior slipped to his knees, his hand feebly wrapping around his midsection in an attempt to hold back his escaping life's blood.

"Greetings, *tovarysh*." Horror and disbelief shifted the once-proud expression on Anton's face. "I see the years have not been good to you."

~

"BORYSKO?"

Anton wasn't sure what hurt more; the vicious pain slicing through his insides, or the unbelievable shock cutting through his heart. He coughed, clamping down on the nauseating wave threatening to steal his consciousness and he staggered around in a sloppy circle.

No. Not possible.

His ears might deceive him, but his eyes did not have the same courtesy. Standing before him was his lieutenant from so many campaigns. He had lost the long shaggy beard, but he would never forget those hawkish blue eyes for as long as he lived.

"How? Why?"

Both questions seemed moot and unimportant, but he wanted some answers in his last few hours. A powerful left cross landed on his jaw and his knee buckled, slamming his back against the unyielding stove. He sucked in short gasps and blinked up at the man he had called friend.

Boris sneered, using a discarded towel to wipe the flat of his blade clean. "Truly? Those are the only things you want to know at the end? You never could see farther than your own sanctimonious pride. After you vanished without a word, I took command. It was easy enough to get most of the men to follow me. They hungered for a decent fight."

Images accompanied the explanation, displaying in graphic detail the continued years of useless battles. Familiar faces faded and vanished, their lives squandered for nothing more than a lust for destruction.

"A decade or so went by before the bastards at the top realized peace was more profitable. Peace." He spat out the word, his lip curling up as if trying to banish the taste from his mouth. "I wandered the vast continent, searching for something to give my life meaning. Battlefields are easy enough to find when you have a reputation preceding you. Not too long after that, before the Byzantine Empire finally gave up the ghost, I met Claude, who presented me with an interesting proposal."

"It seems your comrade has a unique skill set." Claude's cultured and smug accent bled through Anton's shock. Gulping in pained swallows of air, he struggled to keep his unbelieving gaze on the hellish specter from a lifetime ago. "A Latent Conduit. Very rare indeed. You see, he can mask his presence, as well as any he chooses to hide. That last little bit comes in quite handy, especially with a foe who can pry information from anyone's mind." The arrogant voice of the Rogue leader moved in the darkness at his back, circling like a shark in crimson waters.

How could he have been so blind?

Boris tilted his chin, nodding toward his new ally. "And all for the price of my soul."

"Why?" Anton choked on the meaningless query, but his shattered heart required an answer. "How could you turn your back on—"

The back of his head bounced off the oven door and he saw stars from the staggering blow. "You. Deserted. Me. How dare you sit here and spout piety at me?" Fingers dug into his hair and yanked his fuzzy gaze away from the floor. He struggled to focus on only one Boris, so he opted to stare at the one in the middle. "He showed me the meaning of true power," he growled, gesturing to Anton's enemy. "Not the 'God and country' crap you tried to shove down my throat."

Two more painful collisions with the solid surface at his back and Boris jerked his hand away. Anton fell forward and rolled onto his uninjured side, collapsing under the weight of his grief.

"I think it was in Morocco, maybe Turkey. I don't really remember, but I will never forget the day I saw your smug face." He snapped his fingers, grinning as his eyes sparkled with malicious intent. "Wait, it was Morocco. It was August in 1726 and there you were, Mr. Peacemaker himself."

His stomach churned as he flipped through his memories, frantic to find that one specific event. Ismail Ibn Sharif, with his army of slaves, was fighting to do what no leader had done before. He had ousted the British and the Spanish and was on the verge of unifying the Bedouins into one nation. While Anton did not condone the man's use of conquered enemies to enforce his ideals, for the sake of unification, he would try and negotiate peace. He had been sent as envoy to many of the Berbers, speaking as the voice of reason to the tribal leaders in the hopes of avoiding conflicts. Since tales of the blood-thirsty army of slaves preceded his visits, many tribes opted to submit to Sharif's rule rather than become a memory.

"You were awkwardly dancing around some bimbo. It was pathetic, really. She was ready to drop to her knees in the street, but, ever the gentleman, you sent her away to meet later."

Anton heaved and levered into a seated heap, the sting of breathing dulled by the painful realization. The girl had been eager to say thank you, and he had suggested a more private hook-up after he cleaned up. She never arrived. Instead, he was attacked by a handful of adolescent Rogues. At the time, he was grateful she was not present, believing fate had spared her from the brutal scene.

"Did you ever wonder why she didn't show?" Boris whispered, his face so close his breath tickled his skin. "You ever wonder why ALL OF THEM didn't?"

Ice lined his veins as the full force of the vicious truth shattered his soul. A sea of feminine faces swarmed into his fading vision, their beautiful smiles and passionate kisses swallowed up by pleas for aide and agonizing screams. He dug the heel of one hand into his temple, howling in impotent rage as echoes from the past flooded his mind. Unheard cries crashed into his heart and he broke under the pressure. Tortured. Violated. Dead.

All because of his interest.

"Yes. Let that sink in."

Anton was vaguely aware of one male voice ferreting through the din.

"Did you think to check on them? Oh no. *You* took the high road, egotistically believing the further your presence was from them, the safer they would be. Well, your theory might have proven sound, if they weren't already dead."

Anton shook his head in disbelief, unwilling to accept this level of depravity possible at the hands of someone he once trusted with his life. But at each turn, another missed fact flashed into his mind. Blinders forged by years of avoidance fell away and the ugliness of the world converged in this moment. Holding in useless tears, he dragged his head up, forcing down the rising bile as he scanned the room with new eyes. Boris and Claude reveled in the chaotic swirling emotions oozing from the very foundations of the space. Grief, torment, and heavy sadness drowned the brief moments of joy created by a pair of haunting nutbrown eyes and the heart of a child. The dark abyss threatened to swallow him the longer he lingered, his gaze caught in its deadly undertow.

"Those were merely finger foods, nothing more than a quick bite to whet the appetite. The real *pièce de résistance* will be watching you die as your female joins us." His eyes flared wide as Claude strolled near. "All the pieces are in play, so you won't need to wait too long for sweet oblivion."

Roaring, he launched off the floor, tunnel vision focused on the architect of this horrific scene. From off to his left, a freight train collided with him and he drove his elbow down between Boris' shoulder blades, digging his heels into the cracked linoleum. A fierce blow to his damaged rib cage nearly dropped him to the floor. Fury redirected his energy and sent his knee up into Boris' gut.

This was more than centuries of pent-up frustration getting unleashed. This was a fight for the life of his spiritmate. She deserved more than to meet her end at the hands of his enemies. He refused to consider the other possible outcome. Since he had begun the Claiming Ritual, their souls were tied together, the knot loose but real. If she were to fall into the clutches of the Rogues, his existence would blink out. No heaven, no angels, no chance at rebirth or renewal. Just the infinite nothingness of the In-Between.

At least, if he died fighting to save her, his death would have some meaning. He held on to the fragile notion as he fought tooth and nail. Punch after punch rained down and he struggled to give as good as he was getting. But the deep wound drained his strength, his remaining will leaking out and coating the floor. A bone-shattering right cross spun him about and he stumbled into the table, the spindly legs teetering and collapsing under him.

"You...you stay away from her!" He glared with one good eyes at his smirking opponent. His heart raced, fear and panic feeding the waning adrenaline as Boris swung his gaze down the hall toward the missing front door. Over the stench of death, he caught the unmistakable scent of his spiritmate.

"What the flying fuck..." The soft voice of his beautiful warrior boomed, drowning out the thundering blood pounding in his ears.

No.

His arms trembled as he fought to regain his feet. Unlocking his mind, he reached out for her, begging her to turn around and run for her life. He heard no footfalls, but he felt her coming closer and closer. Tears slipped down his cheek as he shifted frequencies and shouted to Éamon.

Nothing. Empty static and white noise were his only response.

A malicious grin coated his old friend's face as he snapped his beady blue eyes back, licking his lips lasciviously.

"Right on schedule. Try not to die before all the fun."

THIRTY-THREE

THE MISSING front door should have been Danika's first sign something was deeply wrong. The scattered debris in the hall was a little familiar. She even remembered the splattered traces of Liam's blood on the walls. But the two uninvited guests in her kitchen and the crimson polka-dotted paint nailed the coffin shut. Not to mention the sight of her personal Superman laying in a battered heap on the remnants of the cheap pressed wood table.

"You planning on paying to replace that?" She gestured toward the splinters spread beneath her feet as well as the dinged and broken appliances.

"Danika..."

She swallowed hard at the hollow voice coming from Anton. Hell, she picked up the rattle of his chest from across the room. So much wrong kept getting piled onto her plate, her legs threatened to buckle and dump her on her ass. Yet the smug expressions of the two douchebags steeled her resolve and she continued to glare, waiting for an answer.

"Don't worry, hon. I know you didn't do it on purpose." Fucking hell. She must have "STUPID" permanently stamped on her forehead, but no way was she going to back down. "But you," she said, shifting her gaze back and forth between Satan and his minion. "I don't remember giving you permission to come inside."

The skinnier one, who she'd met on the stoop, snickered and slunk toward her. "I think you're getting your myths confused, my dear. The permission thing only works for vampires."

"I'm not your dear anything, cock jockey."

A tic started in his mustache, twisting his smirk in the heat of his restrained rage.

"Now get the fuck out before I forget my manners."

"Oh, but the party is just getting interesting." The Devil spoke and she forced her body to stay still.

Her blood chugged through her icy veins, fear cooling her tongue. The hairs along her bare arms stood at attention and she wished she was armored in more than oversize underwear.

"Leave it to you, Fournier, to pick on a girl." Éamon had lost his lilt and that wicked looking staff somewhere between Anton's mansion and the shadows of her building. When the big guy asked for a hug, she thought he was only looking to offer her a friendly squeeze to bolster her nerve. But nothing prepared her for the sickening weightless sensation followed immediately by the familiar gray cinder blocks spinning in front of her blurry vision.

If she survived the next five minutes, she had some serious questions that needed answering.

"DANIKA!"

Her head snapped around at her uncle's bellowed voice, freezing as he stalked toward her. In his wake, he dragged what appeared to be a life-sized, and incredibly limp puppet. Shock nearly stopped her heat. She barely recognized her father through the blood. She rushed out of the kitchen as Cian dropped the remnants of a man at his feet. Balling up her fingers, she launched herself forward and drove her fist into her uncle's smug face. Worry over the repercussions of direct violence against the bastard had always stilled her attacks. But not today. Today, Liam was safely far away, and her father looked to be inches from crossing the Rainbow Bridge.

No, today, she would have some fucking retribution.

The hit landed solid and spun him away. Unwilling to give up her momentary lead, she swung again and again, dealing two vicious body blows. A powerful right cross caught her temple and she staggered away. Ducking the next strike, she kicked out hard, aiming for the man's bad left knee. As Cian crumbled, she threaded her fingers through his balding wisps and drove her knee into his face. Rage drove her on, but anger made her attacks obvious and sloppy. He blocked her strike, pushing her off-balance and she spun away.

She was vaguely aware of other battles happening in the dining room, but they were men. And friggin' giants to boot. They'd be fine. This was her fight. This beatdown had been years in the making and she was going to enjoy this. With each punch she landed, she somehow gained strength. Her arms weren't tiring and her feet moved gracefully across the cracked tiles.

A tiny part of her brain warned this would come to no good, but her body was high on this new sensation. And it was addictive as fuck.

THIRTY-FOUR

As soon as Danika dashed after the specter of her uncle, Éamon leveled his gaze at the smug frog in the corner. "Do you get off on letting everyone else do the heavy lifting?"

Claude shrugged one shoulder and grinned. Éamon managed half a step before the kitchen was flooded with Rogues. Six more poured out of the living room. *Shit.*

Swearing loudly, he rushed to where Anton lay on a bed of broken wood. He dropped his body into a dangerous crouch and drove his shoulder into Boris' ribs. Like a charging bull, he tossed the smaller man into the air and smiled pleased at the loud crashes accompanying the asshole's landing. He extended his hand, wrapping his fingers around Anton's forearm and yanked him to his feet.

"Gonna need a bit of assistance on this one, boyo."

In his fleeting grip, he fired a healing jolt to give the big guy enough energy to defend their new foes. Anton hissed as he regained his land legs.

"Shit. Next time, give me a little warning when you're gonna plug my ass into a light socket." He grimaced and reached inside his coat. Éamon screwed up his face.

"Wait, you're telling me you didn't even fight armed?" He smacked his injured friend on the back of his head as he fished out his own weapon. "No wonder you've got another breathing hole."

Anton grumbled, flipping him off weakly. He pulled the short staff apart and with a flick of his wrist, the twin stubs transformed into a pair of curved blades. Éamon tsked his friend and snapped out his signature weapon. Nine feet of polished wood extended outward from his palm, a broad, thick, and razor-sharp scalpel-like spear tip appearing as well as a wicked looking back hook. In all his years of fighting, he still enjoyed the feel of a bladed staff, not to mention the extra length came in handy on more than one occasion.

Waves of concern for Danika flooded the room and Éamon bumped his shoulder, shaking his head. "Keep your head in this game. You're no good to her dead."

Once again in fighting mode, he moved to stand behind Anton. Back to back gave them more control of the situation. But the wrathful miasma filtering in from farther in the apartment revealed a terrifying truth.

"Anton! Stop Boris now!" He popped his shoulders back, shoving his friend away. These new combatants were nothing more than decoys, distractions to pull their focus from the true prize: Danika's soul. If they didn't play this just right, so much more would be lost. As he eyed the cannon fodder, he reached out for Anton's fiery spirit-mate. <Danika, don't give in to your hatred. Help is on the way.>

He could only pray his message got through. If she succumbed to her darker side, not only would that seal her soul into Rogue's hands for all eternity, but Anton would be destroyed. Literally. For a Guardian to have his mate turn, especially when the Claiming Ritual had yet to be completed, his life would be forfeit and he would be banished to the unending nothingness of the In-Between.

Fuck this shit.

Éamon curled his lip at the encroaching Rogues. "Boys, I am in no mood today. If you leave now, I can kill you on another day. The choice is yours." A couple of them faltered a step, pausing as they exchanged confused glances. He brandished his lethal staff, spinning the nine feet of steel above his head. All eyes focused on the helicoptering weapon, exposing half a dozen throats and Éamon grinned. Redirecting the momentum, he gripped the shaft and lowered the sharp blade with a flowing arc. He twisted his wrist, changing hands and halted the graceful spirally swing, tucking the long butt against his body. Six heads bounced and rolled about the room, truncated bodies following suit soon after.

Éamon lifted his gaze. The comical gape of Claude's jaw was priceless, but he didn't have time to gloat. "You have to admit. I did warn them." He stood tall and stalked toward the Rogue lieutenant. "You call up another batch and I swear I will lay them next to them." He tossed a haphazard gesture toward the carnage surrounding him. Stepping carefully over the sooty black oozing from the piles of bodies, he closed the distance. Initial shock had faded and Claude wore a mask of respectful anger.

"You can't kill me." The confident and smug sneer was like nails on a chalkboard.

The bastard was right. Killing a Rogue leader would mean the local bad guys would be without direction. And assholes running rampant in the streets meant destruction at a biblical level for the humans living in the area. He gnashed his teeth, sickened by the ridiculous rules governing this eon's old experiment gone awry. As the leader of the Guardians, Éamon should have enough power to wipe the floor with sniveling underlings like Claude. Should and did. But these were not his underlings. That glorious job belonged to his brother. And while Cabal was a self-indulgent little shit, he never outright broke the rules set up for this hellish game. All Éamon could do was pray his parents would finally grow weary of toying with the boundaries of human nature and release him from his cursed life.

Until then, he would continue to fight for free will and the good that dwelled in the hearts of all humanity.

But it didn't mean he had to be a nice guy all the time.

He grinned wickedly. "Yeah, but it's amazing what someone can live through."

Something solid, but breakable, smashed into the side of his head, knocking him off his feet. As he staggered for balance, blood blurring his vision, he searched for Claude without success. Only fading laughter lingered in the empty space. Growling at his own careless-ness, he rubbed the back of his hand against his eyes and picked the ceramic shards out of his hair.

"Puss."

Sounds of a scuffle to his left caught his attention and he shifted his gaze. Danika battled with the corpse of her uncle, unaware of the horrific manipulations. Their bout moved from the hall and returned into the kitchen, giving Éamon a front row seat to both life and death matches. He swiveled his head back to Anton and Boris, the two exchanging vicious and heavy blows. How the hell was the man still holding the illusion even in the heat of combat?

"Anton!" He shouted over the din of breaking furniture. "Dani-ka's lost in Boris' spell. You have to stop him."

And soon.

He spun around as Danika crawled to her feet and stood before a scene designed to push her the final distance. Her uncle loomed over the body of another man and judging from her reaction, the man was her father.

Rules or not, free will meant knowing all the facts and seeing with a clear head. He rushed to her, stepping between her and the puppet show.

Only Anton could end this nightmare. *<Anton! Hurry. Your mate needs you.>*

DANIKA SAILED ACROSS THE ROOM, the vicious uppercut from her uncle snapping her head back, and the ground vanished beneath her. Somehow, the man grew stronger with each of her attacks and now, he was invincible. The wall stopped her momentum and fear of further repercussions encouraged her to scramble back to her feet. She blinked rapidly, dismissing the pinpricks of light and veil of crimson until she could focus.

Cian smiled smugly, reaching down to drag her father's body before her. A blade dripping with crimson fire appeared out of thin air as he hovered above him. "He fought less than that fucking child. Not surprised, really. He always was the weak one." Horror rose in her gut listening to the raspy gurgles of the man who never gave up on her.

"Baby? Pumpkin, is that you? Please, help me." Her father reached a trembling arm toward her as his life poured out in a steady stream.

"NO!" She screamed out and tried to claw her way to the grinning villain, the orchestrator of the shitstorm that had become her life. The only thing stopping her was Éamon's powerful push against her shoulders. Her feet slipped in the gore coating the tiles but she refused to alter her course. Her gaze jerked up.

His mouth moved frantically but nothing broke through the all-encompassing silence. He gestured wildly, his hand stabbing to a direction off to her left before latching onto her arms again.

Pulled by a weak magnet, her gaze swung toward his indicated corner of the room. There, locked in combat, was Anton. Her Anton. The man who taught her she was worth a damn. The man who gave her heart a reason to beat. Her shoulders shook and she shifted her gaze back to Éamon. Although she couldn't understand his words, his face spoke for him. Compassionate pleading crinkled his one still open peacock blue orb. Blood lined the face of the warrior, but concern for his friend radiated through his pain.

"Come on, you little cunt." Cian's evil voice cut straight to her broken soul. Her body trembled as she was helpless to resist the urge to follow the hateful impulses raging in her veins. The sweet call to vengeance made her palms itch, made her eager to snap the fucker's thick neck once and for all. "Or does all the blood and death make you horny? Does it? Maybe you want me to bend you over the table and give you a good fucking."

"Danika? Help me." Again, she heard her father's weakening plead. The fingers gripping her arms tightened and yanked her away from the fucked-up family tableau. Éamon gestured wildly about the room, his mouth comically going through the motions of talking but without the payoff. His eyes locked with hers and he tapped his temple. He wanted her to think?

Think. Why can't I hear anything but those two voices?

Anton and Boris stumbled and crashed around the kitchen, knocking into everything nailed and not nailed down. Pictures fell off the walls and shattered in eerie silence. What the hell was going on?

"You're kidding me?" Her uncle scoffed behind her and she swiveled around to face him. "You're gonna let your father die? What a waste. You. Are. A. Fucking. Waste." He punctuated each word with stab after stab of the gore covered knife into her father.

Shaking like a leaf in a tornado, she threw her head back and wailed.

THIRTY-FIVE

"Borysko!"

Back on his feet and with a renewed purpose, Anton roared out. His one-time friend climbed out of the shattered cabinet slowly, wiping at the blood on his chin. Once again vertical, he sneered as a thick broadsword materialized in his hands.

"Come, *tovarysh*." Boris spat the word out along with a mouthful of crimson spittle. "I have been waiting for this moment for centuries."

Anton brought his crossed blades to guard and maintained distance. "Do you truly hate me that much?"

Boris swung widely and Anton easily blocked the sloppy attack. "Yes! I've hated you since long before I gained these powers." He spun around, slamming his elbow into the meat of Anton's shoulder. "You never wanted to fight. You thought peace was best for our country."

"It was!" Anton slashed high and low with his blades, meeting flesh with the sweeping backstroke. Boris winced, slapping his hand against the slender cut across his midsection. "You only craved destruction for the sheer joy of it. We were protectors of our people."

Boris bared his blood-stained teeth in a hideous grin. "Joy? Yes. You never understood the addictive power of seeing your enemy at your feet. I only followed you because you could sniff out a fight like a bloodhound."

Anton froze at the hateful words. In his mind, he quickly flipped through memories long buried under centuries of neglect. With new eyes, he studied the man now standing before him. All the arguments and the violent outbursts nearly a millennium past were viewed under a different light. Where he once saw a dutiful warrior, he now gazed into the face of a masochistic sociopath. How could he have been so blind?

Pain lanced from his shoulder to his soul, and he returned to the present. Betrayed to his core, he shoved away his former second and swept his blades across his exposed back. Boris threw his head back and screamed out, countering with a jabbing elbow. Anton raised his arms up, taking the brunt of the attack on his forearms. The jolt sent spasms into his hand and he lost the grip on his blades. As they tumbled uselessly onto the ground, Anton shifted tactics and tackled Boris. Driving his knee up repeatedly against Boris' chest until he finally heard the satisfying clatter of steel against tile.

He dug deep, finding strength and power, and he hoisted the man off his feet. The sudden shift in weight threw him off-balance but he twisted enough to allow Boris to take the brunt of the fall. They landed in a tangle of limbs and Anton slammed his head back. A sickening crunch met his ears and he scrambled to his knees.

He barely registered Éamon's voice above the ringing in his head. His vicious blow made a mess of Boris' face, blood and bone smeared across his pasty cheeks. He was too concerned with the damage he had wrought to catch Boris' double fisted strike until it smashed into his jaw, the man's entwined fingers catching a glancing blow with the force of a baseball bat. He collapsed onto his injured shoulder and gasped in sudden agony.

<Anton! Hurry. Your mate needs you.>

Anton struggled to focus beyond his opponent, but the frantic desperation in his mentor's call snapped his gaze up. His fierce warrior was teetering on the very edge of sanity, and it was his once friend who was destroying her from inside her mind.

In a moment of clarity, Anton made the only choice possible. He flopped onto his back, retrieving one of his fallen blades. With one swift stroke, he rolled to his knees and howled, driving the sharp point through Boris' heart. Pale blue eyes flared wide in shock. Anton thought he spied his friend in the final seconds, but it was too late. His decision had been made.

"I'm sorry, *zemylak*." Releasing the sword, he gripped the sides of Boris' face and yanked his head around. One loud, sick snap later and the body beneath him stilled, holding its final form another second before melting into the worn linoleum.

He sucked in a painful breath as the room around him flared to life. Danika's unmistakable voice threw him into action, her soul-crushing agony nearly shattering his heart. He lurched to his feet and stumbled to her. With gentle desperation, he tried to spin her away from the morbid scene before her, but she was solidly locked, confined within her own terror. He wrapped his arms around her shoulders and pulled her back against his chest.

"It's over, Danika. I've got you." To his astonishment, the coiled tension seeped out of her body. He pressed his lips against the crown of her head as she mumbled something. Leaning in close, he rested his cheek against hers.

"He killed him. He killed him, and I didn't stop him. I couldn't. I..."

He shifted his gaze down the hall. Two bodies lay in an untidy heap, their usefulness as pawns in this deadly game spent.

"Shh." He stroked his hand in calming trails along her arm. "There was nothing you could have done, *koxána*. Both men were dead even before I arrived. I am so sorry." He hated breaking the tragic news so harshly, but neither could he bear her self-torment. She paused and reached up to touch his arm. Again, he attempted to shift her in his embrace. She held on tight, her fingers digging into his forearm, as her tears began to fall. He rested his cheek against her soft hair, flooding her mind with acceptance and love. Her head tucked under his chin and he closed his eyes, savoring the powerful gift of her budding trust.

Anton tried not to think of all the lives ruined by Boris and his sick machinations. His old friend had long been lost to him, and only the knowledge that his spiritmate was alive, and still his, buoyed his fractured heart. From that moment on, he would spend every breath focused on the female curled in his arms. A gentle touch on his shoulder reminded him of his current surroundings. Dragging his eyelids up, he stared at Éamon. Without his timely warning, things might have turned out much differently.

<*I don't think I can ever say thank you enough, my friend.*>

Éamon smiled, dipping his chin. <*It was the very least I could do. I was wrong about her, Anton. She is pretty amazing.*>

Anton narrowed his eyes and chuckled weakly, pulling Danika possessively closer to him. Éamon tossed his head back and laughed in earnest, patting him on his uninjured shoulder. "You don't have to be barking at me, boyo. I know where her heart lies."

He relaxed his tight hold, but she did not. Her sobs had receded, yet her fingers retained their death grip onto his leather sleeve. He swallowed hard, dreading to break the momentary calm, but more than ready to leave their nightmarish surroundings. "Danika?"

She sniffed, refusing to move from the shadow of his body. And he was perfectly fine with that. When they were safely away, he would ask about the horrors she faced. But that would be much later. For right now, they had a bevy of bodies to tend to, and time was of the essence. Unsure how much of their combat had been cloaked from the other apartments' inhabitants, a decision about what to do for the fallen needed to be made and soon. A stuttered inhale and she inched out of his embrace.

"Yeah." She sighed the word. "Honestly, I'm just...numb. What do you guys normally do?"

Anton succeeded in turning her to face him and placed his

knuckles under her chin, drawing her gaze up. True to her statement, her brown eyes lacked their spark. He leaned down and brushed his lips against hers. A scant heartbeat passed before she returned his tender kiss. His soul soared, grateful for each of her timid steps toward him.

"We can give your father a proper burial if you'd like. But—"

She shook her head, her mouth a stern line. "Nah. I think that would raise a whole hassle of questions." With a serious sigh, she glanced around the wreckage. "He'd been a walking corpse for a long time, and this shit hole can burn in hell as far as I care."

"Is that truly what you'd like?" Éamon chimed in, glancing up from gathering the discarded weaponry scattered among the wooden debris. "It would be simple enough to trigger a gas leak and the fire would hide most of the damage."

She looked over her shoulder, one eyebrow shooting skyward at the decapitated Rogues. "Really? You think a fire is gonna explain the 'some assembly required' guys over there?"

Anton chuckled at her gallows humor and pulled her back against his chest, shielding her eyes before Éamon turned on the fireworks. A couple sparks and sizzles split the silence and plumes of thick black waves wafted up in slender pillars.

"Actually, we have a different clean-up method for our enemy." He choked through his explanation, fanning his hand before him to disburse the acrid fumes. "Gah. Don't any of those guys ever bathe?"

Danika coughed, batting at the vanishing smoke. "I'd say I've smelled worse, but I think I'd be lying."

He chuckled as he steered her away from the burning carnage. "Please tell me it wasn't coming from the grill at the Kozy Kitchen."

She groaned and dropped her head, climbing her gaze up to meet his eyes. Soot smudged her cheeks, and he carefully wiped away the smoky trail with the pad of his thumb. A delicate blush appeared as one corner of her kissable mouth titled up. "Damn. That's one hell of a neat trick. Looks like I've got a lot to learn."

A proud smile touched Anton's lips and he trailed his hands

along her bare arms. "All in good time, *koxána.*" He frowned, studying her current attire, his tank undershirt caressing her ample breasts. "Are those my boxers?"

She squirmed out of his embrace as Éamon's warm laugh filled the room. "She's a right smart one there, boyo. Still have no idea what she sees in you."

"I had to do something," she added, tugging at the button-down tied around her waist. "You're friggin' twelve feet tall and if you think for a minute I'm gonna go into combat with my ass hanging out, you've got another thing coming, buddy."

He blinked deliberately. "Combat? You mean, this thing was your idea?"

She shrugged a shoulder, a coy smile tilting her split lip upward. "Well, yeah. I wasn't about to sit by and...and..." She glanced away and his heart thundered in fear.

"And?" He encouraged her. His brave and fierce warrior. "*Koxána?*"

Seconds ticked by as Éamon busied himself with preparations for the torching. Finally, she lifted her gaze. Her deep chocolate eyes shone in the glistening light of unshed tears. Cuts and bruises blossomed on her jaw and tore her lush bottom lip, but she stood tall and proud.

"I...I love you, Anton. I couldn't just sit and—"

He silenced her with an all-consuming kiss, the heat branding his soul as she spoke the words he had only ever imagined. She covered his hands as he cupped her face. He carefully avoided the fresh wounds in his exuberance and he wished he wasn't too battered to heal her in this tender moment.

Damp tears trailed over his knuckles and he broke the seal of their lips. "*Ja tebe ljublju, koxána.*" Pressing his forehead against her, he swallowed hard, forcing down his soaring heart. "I love you, too."

She laughed weakly. "And since you're gonna be stuck with me for a long time, you're gonna have to teach me some of that stuff, too."

She tilted her head toward Éamon. "With him around, I'm sure you already know all the colorful language I got."

Smiling in spite of the pain, he scooped her into his arms, cradling her against his chest. "I will teach you anything you desire, my fierce warrior."

Éamon stood close and placed a hand on his shoulder. "All right, we're set on this end." He shifted his gaze to the bundle held close to his heart. "Is there anything here you need?"

Danika looked around, peering down halls and into corners. After a quick inspection, her face returned to his, locking her beautiful brown eyes with his. "Nope. I've got all I need."

Anton kissed her forehead, breathing in her heady scent. "C'mon, Éamon. Let's go home. I'm pretty sure there's a hungry kid wondering where we've all been for so long."

"Not to mention a couple hungry kids right here," Éamon joked and tapped his staff against the dingy linoleum. Anton gave one last look over his shoulder. With a tight hold on his spiritmate, he ignited the room before stepping inside the shadowy crack.

TO DISCOVER A DIVINE

Enter the world of Dantaran Galaxy, where even the outcasts can change the course of the universe.

The dunk into the pool was just what the doctor ordered, the temperature somehow perfect. Evainne hoped it would be cold enough to jolt her brain into some emotional state aside from pissed off, but she didn't relish the idea of a long swim in the arctic. The thing seemed almost intuitive, the water warming after one lap.

Why was she so angry? It wasn't as if she'd never been rejected before. She should be used to that, but she wanted so much to believe he was not like the asshats back home. *Guess it's a male thing, no matter what planet you're on.*

So lost in her own head, she didn't realize he was in the water until she heard him call her name. His voice brushed against her bare back, the single word trailing like fingertips along her skin. She closed her eyes, seeking strength in the darkness behind her lids.

"I don't know if I'm not mad at you anymore." She swallowed hard, listening carefully as he stepped closer, the wake of his approach lapping gently at the tops of her thighs.

"I do not wish you to be angered, but you must understand—"

That did it. She spun around to meet his apologetic stare, an unspoken sadness casting shadows in his tourmaline eyes.

"No, Kahlym. I don't have to understand anything. I have no friggin' clue about the rules here. I was never one to stand on ceremony on my own damn home planet and I'm not about to start now. I was an outcast, tossed out and alone, and I had to make my way without a whole lot of help. Hell, even the crazy homeless had people willing to step up and say, 'Yeah, that's my family.' All I trust is what I see from people's actions and what my gut tells me. And I just don't get you sometimes. One moment, you're all hot and bothered and the next, you shove me away, spouting all about how you're not worthy. I'm not some kind of princess or anything special, no matter what you might think. I just want..." She paused to take a breath and sort out her thoughts as they rocketed through her head.

That was when she realized he was naked.

Look for TO DISCOVER A DIVINE, RISE OF THE STRIA BOOK ONE on shelves Fall 2019!

AUTHOR'S NOTES

Thank you for allowing my stories into your life and I hope you stay along for the ride. Without readers like you, my characters would only live in my own imaginations.

Keep Believing in Magic!

NEVER MISS A NEW RELEASE

Be sure to sign up for my newsletters at www.TessaMcFionn.com to hear all the latest.

Connect with me!
www.TessaMcFionn.com
tessa@tessamcfionn.com
Twitter: @TessaMcFionn
Instagram: @tessam2112

ABOUT THE AUTHOR

Tessa McFionn is a very native Californian and has called Southern California home for most of her life, growing up in San Diego and attending college in Northern California and Orange County, only to return to San Diego to work as a teacher. Insatiably curious and imaginative, she loves to learn and discover, making her wicked knowledge of trivial facts an unwelcomed guest at many Trivial Pursuit boards.

Her love of the fantastical began at a young age while her mother read to her and her brother such classics as *The Hobbit* and *Rikki Tikki Tavi*. She continued this love, devouring Terry Brooks, J.R.R. Tolkien, Ray Bradbury, and Isaac Asimov as well as comic books galore. Romance entered the field in the guise of Anne Rice's *An Interview with a Vampire,* and during college, she discovered the works of Sherrilyn Kenyon and Christine Feehan, and the rest is history.

Her first novel, *Spirit Fall,* came to her as she looked over the edge of a very dark place. Since then, she's added three more tales to the world of the Guardian Warriors and *Spirit Bound,* Book Two in the series, was awarded the 2016 Write Touch award for Paranormal Romance from WisRWA. But she never lost her love for science fiction and began a space opera, The Rise of the Stria, in March 2018 with the release of *To Discover a Divine.* After the original publishing house went under, she has now decided to continue the series on her own.

When not writing, she can be found at the movies or at Disneyland with her husband, as well as family, friends or anyone who wants to play at the Happiest Place on Earth. She also finds her artistic soul fed through her passions for theatre, dance and music. A proud parent of far too many high school seniors and two still living house plants, she also enjoys hockey, reading and playing Words with Friends to keep her vocabulary sharp.

She has served as Treasurer, President-Elect, and President of the San Diego chapter of Romance Writers of America and loves spending time working with such amazingly intelligent and creative writers.

ALSO BY TESSA MCFIONN

Spirit Fall, The Guardians Book One

Spirit Bound, The Guardians Book Two

Spirit Song, The Guardians Book Three

www.ingramcontent.com/pod-product-compliance
Lightning Source LLC
Chambersburg PA
CBHW050245110726
47898CB00007B/2290